His
Disinclined
BRIDE

SEASONS
of
CHANGE

JENNIE GOUTET

CHAPTER ONE

October, 1810

A brisk gale swept through Royal York Crescent in Bristol, sending brown and yellow leaves scurrying down the street and through the wrought iron gates where they collected below at the windows and door of the servants' quarters. Phineas Stropford, the Viscount Hayworth, knocked at no. 17 and presented his card. It took only one glance for the butler to drop his quelling regard and open the door wide to admit Phineas.

"Mr. Stokes is expecting you, Lord Hayworth. I will make him aware of your arrival. Please step inside. May I take your hat and coat?"

Phineas divested himself of these and waited while the butler moved with quick steps to a room farther down in the corridor. Phineas wasn't nervous—he would not allow himself to be, despite the fact that he was here to set an irrevocable seal on his future. He brushed the creases out of his sleeves and glanced down. His cream pantaloons were impeccable, but there was a smear of mud on his Hessians. It annoyed him, but there was nothing he could do about it now. Besides, he supposed he did not need to impress Erasmus Stokes.

The butler returned within minutes. "Mr. Stokes will see you. Will you please follow me?" He led Phineas to his master's study, and Stokes stood as soon as he entered.

"Come in, my lord." Stokes bowed then advanced to meet Phineas, who took the room in at a glance.

There was an imposing desk at one end where Stokes had been sitting, and a Sheraton table beyond it that boasted an intricate model of a sailing frigate. Two bergère armchairs, brocaded in green and gold threads with mahogany armrests, were comfortably placed before the fire, and a large painting that Phineas guessed to be by Joseph Turner sat above the mantel, depicting a sloop lost on a stormy sea. He wondered whether Stokes's tastes were naturally elegant or whether he had furnished his home with the intention of impressing his guests.

"You are looking at the Turner, I see. It was not easy to get my hands on one, but I was determined. I will have nothing but the best." Stokes rubbed his hands as he chuckled, and Phineas had his answer. Stokes owned the art to impress.

Phineas turned and acknowledged Stokes's comment with an inclination of his head. The servant was waiting by the door, and Stokes barked out orders for him to bring brandy then gestured for Phineas to sit in one of the chairs facing the fire.

He did so, and Stokes took the other chair. "I will not hide the matter from you, my lord. I was highly gratified that you would condescend to consider my offer, once I'd learned you were in search of a wife." Stokes frowned suddenly and—much in the gauche manner Phineas expected of him—barrelled forward. "Not that you're doing me any favors, mind you. Kitty is no eyesore, and I've sweetened the cream pot to a degree you must admit is handsome. Why, when I told my associate what I was paying—"

"I should hope you are not bandying about your sister's name in such a public way. I assure you, I am not accustomed to having my own name spoken of so openly." Phineas dropped Stokes's gaze for fear his disgust over the nature of their dealings would become apparent.

"No. That is to say…" Stokes floundered. "I've told one or two of my closest associates, but I would not call it bandying anything about."

"I would be much obliged if you would keep the details of our negotiations private. You may use my name in your business dealings, as I am sure you have every right to do. My name is what you purchased, after all." Phineas paused. The whole of it was distasteful, but he would be frank this once. "However, I would like to stipulate that my private life—even when it is joined with your sister's—will not be open for scrutiny."

"Of course, my lord," Stokes replied hastily. He cleared his throat and frowned at the painting as an awkward silence settled between them.

When the door opened, Stokes leapt up and gestured for the butler to place the flat-bottomed crystal decanter on the table in front of them. Phineas studied the strange design, coming to the conclusion that it might be meant for a ship captain's use to keep the decanter from tipping over on the rolling seas.

Stokes picked up the glass of brandy his butler had poured for him. "When the French border was still open, I purchased enough of these bottles to fill a cellar. There are not many left, but I don't think you will find anything to complain of, my lord."

"No indeed," Phineas said, taking one sip then another. "It is rather good. I have nothing like it myself, although I believe my father has a few bottles." This seemed to please Stokes. He smoothed his mustache, hiding a smile in the process.

Although Phineas had received regular reports from his man of business, he had been trying to take Stokes's measure since he'd walked through the door. This first and final meeting would do much to determine Phineas's future happiness, after all. He concluded that Stokes was only happy if he could boast about possessing more than others—then curled his lip at the thought. *And I am no different.*

"You have had a chance to look over the contract, and since you are here, I assume everything is all right and tight." Stokes placed a jeweled hand on the armrest. "Kitty is not here, as I warned, but I'm sure you must have some questions for me. She's a good girl. You won't regret the arrangement."

Arrangement. It was such a clinical word for marriage, even when marriages were nearly always an arranged event. His father would have done the same thing for Phineas if he had allowed it, but he was not his father's puppet. Or, at least, after he married Miss Stokes, he would not be.

"I don't have any questions. None that come to mind," Phineas admitted.

"Good. Your mind is settled then. That is the kind of man I wish to do business with. I am such a man myself. My word is my bond. I'm a man that can be counted on." Stokes smoothed the cravat around his thick neck then tapped his hand on the armrest of his chair. "Kitty is in Bath, visiting our sister, but I have a miniature of her right here. You can take a look." Stokes made as if to rise, but Phineas put out a hand to stop him.

"That will not be necessary. My agent has done all that is required to ascertain that she is agreeable in form and figure. Nothing else is needed for me."

Stokes drew his brows together. "You do not wish to see her portrait? I'm not a man to take my investments sight unseen."

Phineas bunched his hand at his side, releasing his fingers when he realized he was letting his annoyance show. "As I mentioned, I have given the matter wholly into Carter's hands. You've met him, and you know him to be a capable man, I believe. We will let the matter rest."

"Very well, my lord." Stokes fingered the side of his brandy glass. "And the Society papers?"

"Carter will see that the announcement goes in, and he will make sure the banns are read. You have nothing further to do."

"Except show up at Bath Abbey on the eighth of November with your bride in hand."

Phineas gave a nod. He took another sip of brandy, more to be polite than from any real desire to drink. His stomach was roiling in an unpleasant way. He needed to bring this interview to an end. "If you have nothing else…" Phineas stood.

Stokes shot to his feet and bumped the table, nearly spilling Phineas's largely untouched brandy. Perhaps there was another reason for his ship's decanter. Phineas repressed an urge to smirk.

"There is one other matter, my lord," Stokes said, a bit of red creeping up the flesh above his neat cravat.

Phineas turned and raised an eyebrow. "Well? What is it?"

"I would like to call you Hayworth, and have you call me Stokes," he said in a rushed voice. "It won't look right to be calling my own brother-in-law 'my lord.'"

Phineas gave another nod. "Very well." Anything to get out of this stifling room and into the fresh air, though he wondered what devil's bargain he was tangling himself into.

"Well then"—another nervous chuckle followed—"we will meet in a month's time, and I will have your new bride waiting for you. I'm sure you can have no cause for complaint."

"Excellent." Phineas had to force the word out of his throat. He extended his hand and encountered Stokes's warm, fleshy hand in his own. Phineas could not leave soon enough, and as he stepped outside and walked down the stairs to where his father's undergroom was standing with the horses, he took in gulps of air.

"Ringham, let us go."

5

The undergroom handed him the reins and climbed up on the step behind the phaeton, and they were off.

Phineas had soon cleared Bristol, but it was some time before he could relax. This was only part of the battle—to abase himself and seek a wife for the sole purpose of building his fortune. Oh, perhaps for the purpose of securing an heir as well, but that did not bear thinking of yet. If he was going to be mercenary, he may as well put aside all chance of regret and accept the bargain for what it was. He trusted Carter to have done the work to make sure she was pleasant enough to look at. In any case, what was done was done.

Now Phineas had only to break the news to his parents, who were currently residing in their townhouse in Bath. He would need all the time the trip to Bath would require before he was ready for that meeting—to gather his resolve. Phineas couldn't wait until all this was over so he might settle into his new life with the bride he had chosen. She came with a fat enough purse to finally free him from the strings his father held. It went against the grain that choosing a wife came down to such grasping ways, but it was no less than the truth.

Phineas arrived at his parents' townhouse at half-past four, forcing himself to take even, steady breaths to calm his nerves before the butler opened the front door. "Where might I find my parents?" Phineas asked, avoiding Seamus's gaze. "I wish to speak with them." He removed his hat and gloves and handed them to the butler.

"Lord Midlington is in his study, but Lady Midlington is taking the waters in the Pump Room," Seamus replied, setting the hat and gloves on the table and helping Phineas to remove his coat.

This did not surprise Phineas, but it did put a chink in his plans to get through the unpleasantness of their upcoming conversation. He paused, and the butler waited for instructions, which Phineas did not give quickly enough.

"Shall I tell Lord Midlington you wish to see him?"

"No, there's no need to announce my presence to the earl. I will change out of my travel clothes and wait until Mother has returned," Phineas told Seamus. He took the stairs and went to the room that was reserved for him when he stayed in Bath. The one whose green paper-hangings curled at the edges, not having once been changed in his lifetime. Soon, he would have his own house in Bath and would not need to spend his time at his parents' like an indigent relative. *In fact*, he thought with satisfaction, *I shall not need to come to Bath at all.* He could keep to the estate his grandmother had bequeathed him in Castle Combe or purchase a residence in London.

When Phineas heard the sounds of his mother's arrival, he asked a footman to request that his parents honor him with their time. The footman returned presently with the news that they would receive him in the drawing room and that tea would be ordered. Everything communicated in the proper way, of course.

When he entered the drawing room, his parents sat across from each other in perfect silence. His mother was studying her hands on her lap, and his father was opening and shutting his snuffbox with rhythmic clicks.

"I assume you have something to announce," Lord Midlington said, looking up as Phineas entered. His mother began pouring tea from the pot that had been steeping, stirring in the sugar while his father continued. "I hope you have come with an explanation for the fields left to fallow, which I asked you to look into at Midlington."

Phineas shook his head and took a breath to begin, but his mother handed him a cup. He could only nod his thanks and take his seat on the settee, waiting for his father to finish.

"Although why you would need your mother here to tell me that, I don't profess to understand." His father reached his hand out for the tea she served him, eyes on Phineas.

He rarely saw his parents in the same room, but that was no surprise since he knew they each held the other in little affection. Phineas sipped the tea and set it on the saucer, every movement deliberate to hide his twinge of nerves. It would not do for that to show. A man of twenty-eight ought to know how to run his own life, after all. "I do have news, and it has nothing to do with the fields. I will look into that matter as promised, but perhaps not as soon as you would wish. There is work to be done on Giddenhall as well."

His father's face hardened. "And with what money do you plan to accomplish the work at Giddenhall? My boy, if you're going to inherit my estate one day, you will need to learn how it runs. When I tell you to look into a matter, it's with good reason, and I expect you to do it. There will be time enough to see to the affairs of Giddenhall, which is in a sad state of shambles."

Phineas studied the tea leaves in his cup that had escaped the strainer. The urge to lash out was strong—to inform his father that he would no longer be needing his monetary support, and therefore his father need not regard him as assistant to the steward. But Phineas had long decided he would be a better man than his father and would control his temper. When he looked up, he was nearly certain none of his emotions could be read in his expression. The handful of friends who claimed to know him had spoken of his glacial regard.

"I gave my word that I would consult the steward regarding that affair, and I will do so," Phineas responded with deliberate calm despite the pulse leaping in his throat. "But I will not have time to carry out a prolonged examination, for I am to be married."

His mother's teacup clattered on its saucer, and his father raised his heavy brows in surprise.

"I would have appreciated it if you had given me a signal that you planned to offer for Lady Jane before I had spoken to her father. You knew I had arranged to discuss terms with Lord Leighton as early as next week." Lord Midlington shifted in his seat and shot a rare look of complaisance at his son. "However, I am pleased that you have taken matters into your own hands. It won't do for a young man to be coerced to the altar. Our families will benefit from this connection, and you have shown yourself to be surprisingly obstinate in the past. I shall invite the Leightons over as soon as it may be arranged. And I will have Parkson send a letter to *The Gazette*."

Phineas had expected as much, and if his visit with Stokes had been unpalatable, this encounter was by far the more difficult. "Father, I believe you are laboring under a misapprehension. I have not offered for Lady Jane. I informed you it was not my intention to do so. I have contracted an alliance with Miss Katherine Stokes—"

"Miss Katherine Stokes—" His father stared open-mouthed at Phineas for several seconds as though stunned. "Who is she?"

Phineas continued as though he had not been cut off. "—and have already desired my man of business to put a note in the Society papers. I will see that the banns are read without delay so that we may be married in a month."

"Miss Stokes is not of the *ton*. Who is she?" his father asked again, his face taking on a purplish hue. "Is this a love match? You *foolish* boy. I told you nothing good comes of that."

Phineas darted a glance at his mother but read nothing in her expression. He knew those words could only hurt, for theirs had been a love match at the beginning. If anything were needed to strengthen his resolve to arrange a marriage of convenience, a look at his parents' "love match" was proof enough.

"No, Father. It is not a love match. I have never met the girl. Her brother, Erasmus Stokes, runs the largest shipping business in Bristol. Carter arranged this marriage for me, and the settlement money is not to be despised. It will give me what I need to fix up Giddenhall."

"What sort of girl is—" his mother began.

"What am I supposed to tell Lord Leighton now?" His father stood abruptly. "They will be expecting your offer to come for Lady Jane."

"Say nothing, Father. I told you I did not plan to offer for Lady Jane, and if the Leightons are harboring expectations, it is not from anything I have said. If I have looked elsewhere, it is quite my own choice."

"Would you choose to have your quarterly income withheld?" Lord Midlington shot back.

Phineas leaned forward to set his teacup on the table nearest him. "You may do so if you are inclined, but it will not be troublesome, for as I have said, Miss Stokes comes with a substantial settlement." Phineas was nearly ill from the conflict, but there was nothing for it but to see the interview through to completion.

However, his father did not seem ready to bring things to an end. "You are marrying a cit. Tainting your blood for money. You would've had both bloodline from the peerage and a comfortable alliance if you had just done what I'd said. You've always been obstinate, Phineas. I cannot understand you. But I will tell you that I am not pleased with this match. Very far from it."

Phineas allowed a small sigh to escape him. "I had not expected you would be, Father. But you must not be surprised if I do not marry to please you. I am a man now with definite ideas for how to live my life. And although it is not my intention to give offense, those ideas do not involve living under your thumb." He paused. The words had been perhaps too hastily spoken. He needed to rein in his temper. "I will bring my own estate into order and see that it is profitable before moving forward. If you wish me to continue to care for Midlington, I will gladly do so as it will one day be mine. But I will see to my own affairs as well. This decision of mine was not made in haste."

Lord Midlington turned, as if to leave, then paused and set his hands on the chair back. "If you'd had a stronger character—had shown a bit of heat, we might have rubbed along rather well. There is nothing I can do to disinherit you now—not that I wish to do so, for that would cause people to talk—but I will not hide from you my extreme displeasure. You will live to regret this mistake."

Phineas stood and bowed before Lord Midlington. "I am sorry to be such a disappointment to you, Father."

He remained standing until his father had left the room, then sat across from Lady Midlington, who had not moved. She sipped her tea calmly, the light from a nearby window playing on her blonde strands. She was still a handsome woman, despite having long since quit the first bloom of youth. Minutes ticked by, and her silence spoke volumes—it was often used as a weapon for her displeasure.

"Well, Mother, I imagine you will wish to ring a peal over my head, as well—particularly since Father did not give you a chance to do so." Phineas said this with a slight smile, but it took everything in him to keep to light banter, when all he wanted was to seek the solace of his room.

"When have I ever wrung a peal over your head?" she asked. While his mother rarely raised her voice, she could express her sentiments on a topic fluently without uttering a word. He'd hoped she had forgotten her question, but he was out of luck, for she asked again. "What sort of woman is she? Does she seem gently-bred?"

Lady Midlington extended her hand for Phineas's teacup, and he offered it for her to refill. He waited in silence as she stirred in more sugar and handed it back. "I haven't the faintest idea, Mother. We have not been presented."

She looked up in surprise. "You have not met your future bride?"

He shook his head. "We had not the chance. She was visiting her sister."

"Did you see a likeness?" his mother pressed. "What sort of looks does she have?"

Phineas exhaled. It seemed a little foolish now—this quirk of his not to lay eyes on even the portrait of his betrothed. "I did not wish to see a likeness. I did not ask for it. I do not know how she looks, but I believe I may trust Carter that she does not have a squint and is not missing her teeth."

Lady Midlington lifted her eyes upward then turned them to Phineas, her mouth forming a prim line. When Phineas did not rise to the bait of her unspoken accusations, she spelled it out for him in staccato speech. "A girl smelling of the shop, whose manners you have not had time to ascertain, whose face you have not laid eyes on. Phineas, I do not know what you were thinking. I am afraid this will all be a mistake."

"If it is a mistake," Phineas said, "it was mine to make." He drained his tea and settled back in his chair, mastering his impulse to flee. Better his mother put forth all her objections at once. Beyond a doubt, she would wish to revisit them over the course of the month—she never did engage Phineas in idle chatter without missing the opportunity to censure—but he suspected there would be less scolding later on if he did not thwart her chance for it now.

CHAPTER TWO

A ray of sun cut through the October chill and ushered Kitty into her brother's townhouse, the footman behind her struggling under the weight of her trunk. As soon as the sounds of her arrival filtered through the house, a clatter of feet resounded on the stairwell.

"Kitty, look at the bow and arrow I have whittled all by myself. I was able to have a strip of hickory wood to make the bow, which stretches mighty fine. And here"—Kitty's brother, Samuel, held out an arrow with feathers on one end and a triangular bit of metal attached to the other—"I tied this together and added grouse feathers. You shall see how it flies. Look!"

"I wish you would not, Samuel," Kitty warned. "You will only succeed in hitting Erasmus's favorite painting and bring down a sharp scold on your head. You may take me outside to the park later and show me how far the arrow will go."

"Kitty!" Edward and Helen, her nephew and niece, were hot on Samuel's heels—who they called cousin, although he was technically their uncle. Edward held out a bow he had made as well, whose cords dangled sadly. "I made one, too, but Samuel did not give me any of his wood, so I had to use whatever branch I could find when I went out with Jemima. Mine will not bend the same way."

Kitty turned to Samuel with a disapproving look. "What an infamous thing to do," she said. "I'm sure you did not share your wood with him because you knew Edward would make a better bow than you." She winked at her brother to take the sting out of her words, but Samuel, still young enough to need to win would not hear of it. "You shall see, Eddie. I will give you the same wood, and you will make another bow, and the arrow will not go as far as mine."

"Kitty—" The plaintive voice came from Helen, who was holding up a doll. "The dress you made for Theodosia has torn. I asked Mother to fix it, but she said she had no time and that you would do it when you came home."

Helen was near to tears, and Kitty knew that the sound would drive her brother out of his study in a black mood. She took the doll carefully. "Oh dear! Theodosia has had to wait ever so long to have her dress repaired. But I shall take care of it just as soon as I have put my things away and changed my gown. First, however, I would very much like a hug from each of you."

Samuel came reluctantly, which was only to be expected. Having obtained the ripe age of eight years the month prior, it would not be long before her brother would offer Kitty nothing more than a cursory bow. Edward and Helen wasted no time throwing their arms around Kitty, and it restored her heart. The visit to her newly married cousin, Mrs. Drusilla Mardley, had been a pleasant distraction. But once Kitty had been brought up to date on all her news, she began to miss the voices and youthful chatter that came with spending the days with her small niece, nephews, and brother.

Mary Stokes came down the stairs, holding William in her arms. "Oh, it is you, Kitty. Erasmus informed me you would be home today and that he wished to speak with you as soon as you arrived. I've had my hands full with the children, as you can see. So I will not be able to accompany you to your room."

"Never mind that," Kitty said, opening her arms for William. "May I?" Her sister-in-law handed William over, and Kitty tickled his belly until he laughed. She kissed the top of his head as she cuddled him in her arms, breathing in his baby smell. It had been a diverting trip, but a month was long and it was good to be home.

Kitty gave William back to his mother. "I can only imagine how you have been busy. I hope Samuel has not been causing you too much trouble without me here to lend a hand."

Mary was quick to suppress such hope. "I fear he will lead Edward astray. Why, he just had him learning to make *arrows*. Before I know it, Helen or William shall be shot straight through the heart."

"I hardly think Samuel will encourage Edward to use the children for target practice." Kitty stopped herself and sought a more conciliatory tone, glancing at Samuel, who peered up from under his blond curls with sullen eyes. "Surely not. They are both good boys—and creative, too."

"Perhaps my Edward is"—Mary primmed her lips and flicked her eyes in Samuel's direction—"but Samuel is getting more and more difficult to manage. I shall be glad when he goes off to Harrow." She rounded on Kitty. "And of course you would dismiss my worries about the boys. You have always encouraged them to wildness."

Kitty summoned a smile and paused a beat before responding. "Their high spirits are merely a sign of health and industry. It does them no harm, in my esteem."

Mary shifted William to her other hip and shooed the children away. "Edward, Helen, Samuel. Go find Nurse and tell her she must look after you." When they had run off, she shot Kitty a look of reproof. "I believe my Edward would be the perfect mix of gentleness and spiritedness if it were not for Samuel's influence."

The subject brought Kitty a familiar pang. Her father had died when Samuel was only a year, and his young wife had not been devoted enough to her new family—or her baby—to remain and take charge of him. At twelve, Kitty had hardly been the best person to look after baby Samuel, but Erasmus and Mary were settling in as newlyweds, and the role had fallen easily enough on her.

Kitty repressed a sigh. "Samuel will soon enough go off to school, as you said. And as my eldest brother's wife, it is you who have overseen the charge of raising him." She regretted the hasty words as soon as they flew out of her mouth. She had never been good at holding her tongue when her temper was aroused.

"I do not have as much influence on Samuel as you do. But on that, I shall say no more." Mary looked toward the study, frowning. "I believe Erasmus is ready to speak with you as soon as you may be available."

"Let him know that I will be down once I change. Albert, please have someone bring these to my room." Kitty indicated the boxes still remaining in the entrance and took leave of her sister-in-law with a cordial smile.

She walked to the stairs with measured steps, lifting her pink-striped percale skirt as she went up. She had hoped for a better welcome. The tension with her sister-in-law had been mounting since before her visit, but Kitty had thought that the distance would help Mary to appreciate her and the help she brought to the family. Kitty spent her days entertaining the children and assisting Mary and the nurse with whatever needed to be done. It was a small price to pay to have a comfortable place to live and to be part of the childrens' growing up—to see her half-brother have something akin to siblings his own age, even if he was technically their uncle.

Kitty had always hoped to fall in love, marry, and have children of her own, although she had never met anyone who inspired in her a desire for more than a passing acquaintance. She did not possess a dowry—a lack of foresight on her father's part which astonished her—but she could be certain that her brother would do well by her when the right man came. However, Kitty had not yet met him. In the meantime, she would devote her energy to being the best big sister and aunt she could and enjoy the uninhibited affection the children gave her.

In the quiet of her room, she washed her face and selected one of the gowns still in the wardrobe. The dresses in her trunk would need to have the wrinkles shaken out. She rang for a maid to help her into the fresh gown and restyle her hair. With that accomplished, Kitty went back down and knocked on the door to the study, entering when she heard her brother call out.

Erasmus looked up from his desk and got to his feet. He walked over and gave a perfunctory kiss on her cheek. "Well, Kitty? How is Drusilla? Is she faring better?"

Kitty smiled. "I believe her morning sickness is well on its way to being a thing of the past. She was already doing better by the time I arrived and did not so much need my assistance as my companionship. Andrew does not necessarily provide that service for her."

Erasmus gestured for Kitty to sit in one of the chairs near the fire, and he took the other one. "It is not the husband's job to provide companionship for his wife."

Kitty permitted herself a wry smile as she responded. "Job?—no. But in a marriage there can be friendship."

Erasmus leaned back in his chair and balanced the tips of his fingers together in his pontificating posture. "I'm sorry to inform you, but you're naive, Kitty. You don't yet know the way of the world, and I can assure you there is rarely friendship in marriage."

Kitty looked away. They would never agree on this point. "I see you've acquired the Sèvres vase you had your eye on. What else have you added to your collection?"

"Yes, and I had it for a very good price, too." Erasmus pointed to another shelf. "And those two smaller bowls as well." He had always been one who liked to possess, so it was befitting that he'd taken over the family business when their father had died. Erasmus had made a thriving company even more profitable by acquiring other smaller companies in complementary ventures and building a large fortune out of it.

Kitty took a deep breath. "Well, I believe you did not call me here to boast of your recent purchases, and you do not generally do so for family news. You had something to discuss?"

Her brother pulled at his cravat as if it were suddenly too tight. He didn't answer right away but drew his brows together and stared at his hands. What in the world had he to be uncomfortable about? Kitty could not imagine, and it unsettled her. She waited in silence.

"I have made arrangements for your future," Erasmus said in an abrupt start. Kitty stared at him unblinkingly, and he continued. "I have contracted a very good marriage alliance for you. Lord Hayworth—it's his courtesy title, Hayworth—but the man is heir to the Earl of Midlington. He has a large estate in Castle Combe near Bath. A most eligible match."

Her brother fell silent, and his look of discomfort turned to one of satisfaction. Kitty's indignation rose. "How dare you do such a thing? To not breathe so much as a word to me about something so … so *pertinent* to my future as a betrothal?" Kitty attempted to control her temper, but she knew she was betrayed by her flush. She turned away from her brother's growing obstinance, her own chin set. "I am sorry to disoblige you, but I will not marry him."

Erasmus shook his head. "Now, Kitty." His tone was coaxing, but she heard the threat all the same. Her brother did not like being crossed. "Don't say hasty words you will live to regret. The contract has already been signed. You *will* marry him."

Kitty turned in her chair and levelled her gaze on her brother. "What led you to believe I would ever agree to such a scheme? How foolish to have signed a contract that you will then have to break. It is not good business, and I am astonished you attempted it."

Now, Erasmus's ire had been fully roused. "Let me make one thing clear. You have been hanging on my sleeve ever since our father died. Nothing was left to you, and you have only Father to blame. But since you are wholly in my power, if I say you will get married, you will get married."

Kitty trembled from head to foot, and she leapt to her feet. Tears sprang from her eyes, and she wiped them away bitterly. She hated that she cried when she was angry. *Such* a weakness. "You have sold me, is what you have done," she ground out, trying to control the sob that sprang up from rage. "Why did you not allow me to stay here? I have been useful to your family."

Erasmus was not a successful businessman for nothing, and he must have known it would do no good to push his sister to desperate measures. He adopted his coaxing tone again. "Now, Kitty, you know you don't rub along well with Mary. She thinks you take too much interest in her affairs, and that you are too high-handed, meddling in the run of her household and how she raises her children."

"If you only knew how often I bite my tongue—"

"Let me finish. You know this isn't your permanent home, and it was never meant to be. Young women marry then join their husband's household." Erasmus's words caused more angry tears to stream down Kitty's face, and she dug her nails into her palm to control their flow. "You have already turned down one perfectly eligible offer, and instead of sending you off to be a governess or some such thing, I've arranged a marriage for you with a highly sought-after viscount. And believe me, I did my research. Hayworth doesn't gamble. He has no temper that anyone knows of, he doesn't drink. He's a decent looking fellow. You should be thanking me."

"Thanking you!" Kitty turned and looked down at him, still sitting in his chair. "You've stripped me of my freedom. I have served your family as little more than a slave, excepting the allowance you give me, and I did it out of *affection*, and I thought you held some small affection for me. This is how you repay me. I would rather be a governess." She turned to leave.

"Don't be a fool, Kitty." Erasmus's words stopped her short. "A governess's life would not suit you. And your remark about being a slave is doing it much too brown. You are not cut out to be a servant—you have too much of the Stokes blood in you. Here, you have a chance to have your own family, to run your own household. Think about this offer before you turn it down." Erasmus got to his feet. "You will come to see that it would be extremely foolish to do so."

Kitty moved toward the door without saying anything. There was a shard of truth in what he said, enough to make her pause. She could not trust herself to say anything else without once again breaking down in tears, and she had already shown enough weakness.

"Think about it, and see if I am not right."

She heard the words as she opened the door but did not deign to answer. Kitty thought it victory enough that she did not hurl his new Sèvres vase at him as she left.

THAT NIGHT, Kitty asked for soup in her room, claiming fatigue from a long journey. Mary and Erasmus would know it for a lie, but Mary would prefer it all the same. Kitty sat in the comfortable chair with the small embroidered footrest before the fire. It was a nice room—the same one she had grown up in—for even though Erasmus could have bought a larger residence, he must have possessed a degree of nostalgia. Kitty most certainly did, and she liked the calming influence her spacious and familiar room brought her.

She sighed. Erasmus's words had already needled their way into her reason. Her rage had died down to resignation. This was not her room—not really. Her brother had reminded her of that, and that nothing she possessed was her own. If she married, she would not be much better off. She would become her husband's possession instead of her brother's, and Lord Hayworth was an unknown entity. Kitty could not be certain if he would treat her with any sort of kindness, or if she would spend the rest of her life in a miserable battle of wills.

She would move away and no longer see her friends. Not that she *had* all that many friends or saw them with any sort of frequency—her niece and nephews and brother took up all her time. But she would be isolated on an estate, in a village unknown to her, and she would likely be expected to travel to London and meet a Society far above her touch. She would constantly feel herself at a disadvantage.

Kitty pulled up her bare feet on the chair and tucked them under her nightdress against the chill. She had taken down her hair for the night, and she tugged at the thick red braid that fell over her shoulder. The flames flickered in the chimney, and she stared at them without blinking until the heat forced her to close her eyes. She leaned her head back against the chair.

There was some truth in what Erasmus had said. Yes, he had arranged this marriage to suit himself because it would help his affairs to say he had family connections to a viscount. He was much like their father and thought about little other than what would puff up his consequence. That said, he would have looked into this Lord Hayworth thoroughly because he would not want to be caught short if the man proved to be an embarrassment. If she could not trust Erasmus to do well by her for her own sake, she could trust him to do well by her for his.

If Kitty decided to be a governess, she would have an employer to whom she would be beholden. If she married Lord Hayworth, she would be mistress of the estate. Her future husband might ignore her, or even despise her, but he would not easily be rid of her like unwanted chattel, much as her brother had just done.

She had wished to marry for love, but she already knew she would not turn down her brother's proposal. No! Not proposal. His high-handed, selfish, coerced arrangement that he had contracted with a man entirely unknown to her and without consulting her. She would accept it and start a new life because, really—what choice did she have, after all?

CHAPTER THREE

The wedding was held in the second week of November, and Kitty awoke at an early hour, her throat dry at the thought of the day's events. Though she had spent the last four days in Erasmus's rented house on Laura Place in Bath, the looming change in her circumstances still felt more like a dream than reality. It did not help that she had yet to meet her betrothed, who had sent his regrets for being kept away by pressing matters and would only arrive in Bath in time for the ceremony. Sounds of the maid filling the bath in the adjoining room reached her ears, and Kitty sat up in bed.

"I will bring your chocolate, miss," the maid said, popping her head into the bedroom. Kitty nodded her assent.

In the end, the service had not been necessary. It was not possible to swallow more than one mouthful of the thick chocolate, and by the time Kitty stood by the bathtub and trailed her hands through the warm scented water, she was already sick with apprehension. For the past weeks, Erasmus had been bursting with satisfaction at the match he had arranged. Lord Hayworth was still connected to the parish in Bath through the Earl of Midlington, and Kitty and Lord Hayworth would be married at Bath Abbey, a fact which gratified Erasmus. He was sure to bring it up in conversation with his fellow merchants at the slightest opportunity.

She slipped into the hot water and allowed the maid to comb her thick hair, while she attempted to relax. Kitty had been given a glimpse of her betrothed from a miniature formally presented to her with the viscount's compliments by his man of business. It was the only visit Mr. Carter had made to Royal York Crescent after Kitty learned of her fate. Lord Hayworth appeared not to be a bad-looking man—certainly not handsome enough for the gesture to have sprung from vanity. Kitty had to admit the gift of his miniature was thoughtful, but the portrait would not show her what his character was like. And that, after all, was what really mattered in the long view.

In silence, the maid lifted Kitty's hair while she dried herself with a towel and began to dress. The maid then tied Kitty's stays and had her sit to finish her coiffure. Fanny would be remaining in Erasmus's employ, leaving Kitty no maid to accompany her to her new household, but Mary assured her she would have her own household of servants to command.

Kitty watched Fanny in the reflection as the maid papered Kitty's hair into curls in the front and formed four coils of hair in the back, which she interlaced and pinned up. She set ringlets that fell on either side of Kitty's face and finished the coiffure by tucking a string of white pearls and green silk flowers into the chignon, circling the pearls and flowers around her head to form a dainty crown in front.

It did not matter that Kitty did not wish to marry; she would not allow herself to look less than her best and perhaps give her betrothed's family and its elevated circles cause to despise her. She'd had a new dress sewn of her own choosing. Done in an ivory silk brocade with Saxon green trim, the simple skirt fell from the tight bodice and high waist, and the small embroidered puffed sleeves off the shoulders had light muslin fabric extending to her wrists to ward against the autumn chill. Her cloak was of the latest fashion, and she would wear it until they arrived at the Abbey.

She descended the unfamiliar staircase with reluctant steps to an echoing corridor at the bottom. The absence of a mother to advise her, or a loving father to give her away was a loss she felt acutely. Erasmus could not fill such a role in any kind of satisfactory way. She did not have a very great recollection of her mother, and her father could never have been described as loving. Still, it was times like this that she wished ... Kitty rested her hand on the bannister post, her thoughts taking a gloomy turn that she hastened to shrug off. She stood in the corridor, listening to sounds from different parts of the house, unsure of what to do. Samuel appeared from the door leading to the small library.

"Kitty!" His eyes lit up. "I was hoping to see you. I wanted to go to your room, but Mary said you could not be bothered. She said you needed to dress for your wedding."

Of course Mary had not come to see how Kitty was faring. "Mary was right," she replied. "But I am happy to talk to you now. What did you wish to see me about?"

Samuel examined her appearance. His brow creased, and he didn't speak for a moment, so Kitty sat on the small bench in the corridor and patted the seat next to her. Samuel sat and swung his foot back-and-forth underneath the bench, and she clasped her hands on her lap, waiting for him to speak.

"Kitty, must you go?" he asked at last.

She looked straight ahead and swallowed the lump in her throat. "Yes, I must. But I shall miss you very much."

Samuel began tapping his heel on the leg of the bench. "It's just ... Mary doesn't like me very much. I know she doesn't. And Erasmus is not interested in me. You're the only person who cares about me, and now you're leaving."

Kitty gulped and took a deep breath. She did not want tears

to drop and stain her silk dress. This was so unfair, and she hated that having no choice in her own future meant that her little brother had no choice in his. Erasmus had been firm on this point. Lord Hayworth had made arrangements for a wife and would have no wish for a troublesome boy to hang about. *Besides*, he had said, *Mary does a fine job of raising him as one of her own.*

Kitty put one arm around Samuel. "It is most unfair. I would like very much to remain with you, but I cannot. And you are going to Harrow next year." She adopted a bracing tone. "I know you will make friends there and have a great many adventures."

"But it is a whole nine months away. And I don't know anyone at Harrow. What if they laugh at me there?" Samuel turned a freckled face up to her. He was missing two of his teeth. "What if they mock me because I don't come from the same kind of family?"

Kitty squeezed Samuel closer. "No one will laugh at you, Sam. Do not worry about that. You have been raised well just as they were—Erasmus saw to that. And those boys will be as nervous as you are." She lifted her eyes and stared at the wooden rails of the bannister, breathing in. Having a viscount for a brother-in-law would change everything. Samuel would be related to a lord.

Sounds of Erasmus and Mary raising their voices in argument from the drawing room, and the children exiting the rooms upstairs with their nurse, interrupted Kitty's speech, so she gave Samuel a kiss on his cheek and hugged him tightly. "Promise me you will be good—and gracious to your cousins. They do look up to you after all."

Mary came into the corridor with a look of irritation. Erasmus followed behind and stopped short when he saw Kitty. "Good. Very good. You look a picture, and I'm sure Lord Hayworth will be very pleased. Doesn't she look fine, Mary?"

Mary glanced at her before bending down to tuck the small cloak around baby William more securely. "Very fine, I am sure. Jemima, hurry and help Edward and Helen into their cloaks, or we shall be late."

The walk to Bath Abbey was short, which was why Erasmus had chosen the location. The few minutes were not ample time to prepare Kitty for what was before her, and the dread only increased as their group neared its destination. At the church, Kitty followed Erasmus numbly through the wooden doors into the immense building with its stone arches and echoing walls. They walked down the long aisle of the nave with just their footsteps to break the silence, and it was only when they reached the front, and her brother moved to the side, that Kitty saw for the first time her future husband.

Lord Hayworth was flanked by his parents, if their age and features were an accurate indication. There was another younger gentleman who was likely in place to serve as witness. Nobody else was in attendance, but why should there be anyone? Why should there be a large wedding party when he was marrying such a common creature as herself?

Kitty avoided the gaze of her betrothed as she followed her brother to the pews where he and Mary would be sitting. She allowed him to help her off with her winter cloak and turned at last to glance at her future husband. Erasmus nudged her to go stand at his side; she obeyed but could not summon a smile. For a brief moment, she looked at Lord Hayworth soberly then turned to face the vicar, her hands clasped tightly in front of her.

PHINEAS SAW his soon-to-be wife for the first time when Stokes stepped to the side, and one look was enough to strike him straight through the gut. He swallowed convulsively as if that could clear the heartbeat he could suddenly hear in his ears. His palms started to sweat in his gloves as his eyes followed her to the pew. She had looked regal enough when she walked in, shrouded in a brown cloak—her coloring harmonious with the wood pews and pulpit of the vast church, and her hair catching the light that shone through the stained glass windows and left pretty-colored patterns on the stone floor. But when she removed her cloak and faced him arrayed in an ivory and green dress, her skin radiant, her brown eyes warm, and her hair a mix of red and gold, Phineas's breath left him. He had expected to make do with whatever wife this agreement brought him. He had not expected to contract an alliance with a woman who would be the envy of every man in the *ton*. She was incomparable. Miss Stokes met his gaze, her look shrouding any feelings, and her eyes flitted away. She did not smile.

If she had been a member of the *ton*, she would not have looked twice his way, his title notwithstanding—of that he was sure. He supposed he was not dashing enough to tempt the women on the hunt for a matrimonial prize. An arranged marriage of his own choosing removed all the disagreeable parts of courting, for it assured he would not suffer rejection. However, Phineas had never in his life been more nervous than he was now. He was about to make an irrevocable change to his situation and his comfort. He would be sharing his life and concerns with someone else now, and her happiness would be his responsibility. He thought the arrangement would benefit them both, but how could he convey all this to his future wife?

The vicar motioned them forward. "Who is to be married today?"

With a glance at Stokes, Phineas turned to the vicar. "Phineas Stropford, the Viscount Hayworth, heir to the Earl of Midlington."

Stokes nudged his sister a step closer, and she stood at

Phineas's side with Stokes at her left. "My sister, Miss Katherine Stokes," he said.

The vicar continued. "Do you have the certificate of banns from the curate of your parish, Mr. Stokes?" When the vicar had received the certificate from Stokes and examined it, he turned to Phineas. "Lord Hayworth, do you consent to this marriage?"

Phineas did not dare look at his betrothed. He could hear his parents shifting behind him, sensing their displeasure from where he stood. "I do."

"And you, Miss Katherine Stokes, do you consent to this marriage of your full volition?"

She was silent long enough that Phineas glanced at her, tendrils of alarm creeping up his spine. What if one look at him was enough for her to say no? What if Phineas was made to look a fool in front of his parents and cousin who served as witness? What if he was back to having to obey his father's beck and call to pull Midlington estate into order? It did not bear thinking of. Miss Stokes glanced at her brother—tight-lipped and unfriendly. Had she really wanted to marry Phineas? He had no more time than for the thought to flit through his mind before she answered.

"I do."

The vicar gave a somber nod and clasped his hands together. "Dearly beloved friends, we are gathered together here in the sight of God, and in the face of his congregation, to join together this man and this woman, in holy matrimony, which is an honourable state, instituted of God in Paradise, in the time of man's innocence, signifying unto us the mystical union that is betwixt Christ and his Church..."

The vicar read their brief ceremony, ending with the exchange of their vows, whose solemnity brought unexpected tears to Phineas's eyes that he quickly blinked away.

"Wilt thou have this woman to thy wedded wife, to live together after God's ordinance in the holy estate of Matrimony?

Wilt thou love her, comfort her, honour, and keep her, in sickness, and in health? And forsaking all other, keep only to her, so long as you both shall live?"

Phineas cleared his throat. He would let Katherine—Kitty—know the depth of his promise to her. He answered in a ringing voice. "I will."

His betrothed listened to her charge and answered, "I will," in little more than a whisper. She had a gentle, pretty voice—one Phineas could happily wake up to each day. But he could discern no joy in her vow, no relief or acceptance in her tone, only resignation.

"Who giveth this woman to be married unto this man?" When Stokes answered, the vicar leaned over and whispered into Miss Stokes's ear. Her eyes trained downward, and she tugged at her gloves until they came off. Phineas jumped to life and pulled off his gloves, handing them to his cousin. The vicar took the hand that hung limply at her side and set it on Phineas's. His heart started pounding again at their first touch.

The vicar instructed Phineas to repeat the vows, which he did, attempting to catch Kitty's gaze. "I, Phineas Stropford, take Miss Katherine Stokes to my wedded wife, to have and to hold, from this day forward, for better, for worse, for richer, for poorer, in sickness, and in health, to love and to cherish, til death us depart, according to God's holy ordinance, and thereto I plight thee my troth."

Kitty repeated the same vows in a quiet voice with only one or two fleeting glances in his direction. The vicar said, "Now, we will have the rings."

Phineas turned to his cousin, Bartholomew, who had agreed to be his witness for the sake of family, although they were not particularly close. Phineas had often wondered if it was because Bartholomew was jealous of his title and inheritance, or if it was simply a matter of not having spent enough time together. Or, perhaps, Phineas was not so very interesting after all.

"I have the rings." Bartholomew extended the small box and the marriage fee that had been given him for safekeeping. Phineas handed the money and rings to the vicar, who set the marriage fee on the table and took the Holy Book in his hands. He gave Kitty the larger gold ring and Phineas the smaller and instructed them to lay their hands holding the rings on the Bible, which they did.

The man of God then instructed Phineas to place the ring on Kitty's fourth finger. The moment had come. Phineas took her hand in his, feeling its softness as he slipped the ring on her slender finger. The vicar then instructed Phineas to repeat after him once again.

Phineas did not remember ever having heard a wedding vow spoken before. Or if he had, he did not remember it. There was something so intimate, so raw to the declaration he was to publicly state. "With this ring, I thee wed." He gulped as the vicar said the next portion and desperately hoped his voice would not crack. "With my body, I thee worship. And with all my worldly goods, I thee endow. In the name of the Father, and of the Son, and of the Holy Ghost. Amen."

When it was Kitty's turn, she took his hand in hers and slid the ring onto his finger. She quickly pulled her hand away, and the vicar had to remind her to join hands again as she said her vows. They were then pronounced man and wife.

Phineas was married now. He glanced at his wife, but she stared at the oldest of the children standing next to Stokes, a tight smile on her face. There was no cheering, just his father clearing his throat, and the little girl who had come with Stokes asking her mother if Aunt Kitty was married now. Her mother, unsmiling, replied that she was.

They started the recession toward the back of the church, and Phineas was relieved that the formal ceremony was behind them. Life would begin now, and he would be able to start making the necessary changes to his estate without having to request the funds from his father, who was sure to reject his request or give the money to him upon terms.

He and Kitty would have a chance to become acquainted at last. He darted another glance at his wife, but she steadfastly refused to meet his gaze. How would he broach the subject of the wedding night if she would not even look at him?

Knowing his parents' aversion to the match, and their reluctance to attend the ceremony, Phineas had decided to forego a celebratory wedding breakfast. His parents did not demure. They had only attended the wedding ceremony to avoid the risk of scandal and talk among Society. They could not let it be known they had opposed the match. But to invite those merchants into their home to share a meal was beyond their capacity to act. Phineas had sidestepped the issue by having a note sent to Laura Place as soon as the Stokes had arrived in Bath, saying the newlyweds would be leaving directly after the ceremony.

It was time to walk the short distance to the inn, where the carriage was waiting to take the couple to Giddenhall to start their new lives. Phineas had not expected to be so nervous following the ceremony. He thought that in having arranged the marriage on his own terms he would be filled with a sense of authority—by the rightness of it all. He would know how to act around his own wife, who would be glad enough to have married above her station to be somewhat accommodating. But Miss Stokes—no ... Lady Hayworth—was reserved to the point of hostility.

Phineas gestured toward the doors of the church. "It is this way." He wasn't sure if he had uttered it loud enough for her to hear, but she followed his lead toward the light-filled exit that spoke freedom from the constraints of ceremony and kin.

CHAPTER FOUR

The wedding was over. With her hand tucked lightly in her new husband's arm, Kitty followed the procession out of the church. The chirping conversation of her niece and nephew trailed Kitty, but her eyes were focused on Erasmus ahead of them who was hurrying to catch up to the earl. He came abreast Lord and Lady Midlington in front of the heavy wooden doors.

"Good morning, my lord, my lady." Erasmus bowed low and pasted on a broad smile. "At last we are acquainted. It's a glorious day, is it not? For your son and my sister?"

Lord Midlington turned slightly but did not face Erasmus fully. "Indeed."

To Kitty's shame, Erasmus would not be snubbed. "It is unfortunate your family's affairs did not allow for a wedding breakfast. I would have been happy to provide food for as many people as you cared to invite. Money would have been no object with me to provide a breakfast worth talking about in the Society papers."

Lord Midlington exchanged glances with his tight-lipped wife, allowing a short silence to ensue. "I am afraid it was unavoidable." He tilted his head. "Good day." Kitty's heart sank.

This was to be her family? She did not dare to look at her new husband for fear she might see the same ironic curl on his lips.

They exited into a blinding sun, and it was only when the cold hit her that Kitty realized she had left behind her cloak and gloves. She turned to retrieve them, but Mary was behind her with the forgotten articles, cutting off Kitty's chance for a brief reprieve in the quiet church. Mary handed them to Kitty, her look more sour than celebratory. There had never been any affection between them, but Kitty could not understand why Mary was unable to muster a spark of enthusiasm for her own sister-in-law's wedding, particularly as it would remove Kitty from a house where she was made to feel an encumbrance.

Kitty murmured her thanks, wrapping her brown, blended-wool cloak around her and pulling on her gloves. The early November air bit at her neck and ears, which were exposed. Her bonnet was more decorative than warm, and she was missing the larger poke which would have shielded her somewhat from the stares.

A motley crowd crossed the square in front of the Abbey, and some glanced their way before bending their heads together. Kitty had yet to look at her husband fully. However, from what she could ascertain from her discreet glimpses, he was a head taller than her, and his form was not displeasing. He wore sober colors for the wedding—a dark gray coat with a silver waistcoat and light gray pantaloons. His light brown hair reached his collar, and he had short whiskers that followed the line of his cheekbones.

Their party had by now all exited the church and stood in silence. It seemed as if everyone was waiting for Lord Hayworth to speak, and he turned slightly, glancing at his parents then at Kitty. Was he *now* going to introduce his parents to her after they'd wed? Why had he not done so before? It seemed the most ridiculous thing.

Apparently, it appeared so to Lord Hayworth, as well,

because he cleared his throat and swept his gaze generically over the crowd. "I thank you all for attending our wedding. Mother, Father. Bartholomew," he added, nodding to the gentleman standing next to his parents. Turning to Erasmus, he said, "My thanks." Lord Hayworth looked at a loss for what else to say and gave a general bow to everyone gathered. "Well, we had best be going. My servants are expecting us this afternoon at Giddenhall."

Not a man for words. Kitty gave Mary a dutiful kiss, but she could not bring herself to give one to Erasmus. She hugged Samuel, Edward, and Helen. Struggling against the lump of emotion rising in her throat, she reached out her hands for William, and Mary handed him over for a last kiss. Despite all the tension she had with Mary, her sister-in-law had never begrudged Kitty an affectionate relationship with her nephews and niece. That was something to be grateful for, at least. Kitty cuddled William, rocked him with her lips pressed to his head, then handed him back without a word. It was not too soon. She was about to break down in tears on the spot.

Kitty turned to Lord Hayworth, but she was unable to hold his gaze. It was the strangest thing. She was married to him now, and all she wanted was to hurry in the other direction. It was not that she found him repulsive. In fact, there was some-thing about the form of his lips and nose that made her think it might not be unpleasant to kiss him, although such a thought made Kitty want to *tsk* in irritation. *Did one's reason fly out of one's head upon marriage?*

She had never been one to desire a man's embrace. Kitty supposed she was one of those women who possessed no romantic inclinations. Besides, she could discern little warmth in Lord Hayworth's eyes, and his voice had been expressionless as he'd stated his vows. One could only surmise that here was a man who would not let anything stand in the way of what he wanted, since he was willing to contract a marriage with someone he'd not met even once. It meant he would not likely take her needs and wishes into account at all. The thought left her cold.

Lord Hayworth held out his arm, and Kitty put her hand on it, the pressure as light as she dared. "Farewell," he said, vaguely addressing the party, and led her away from the church.

Bereft of the comfort of familiar faces, Kitty found herself at a loss. What could she find to talk about with a man she did not know? It was astonishing how short the ceremony had been, and now there would be no wedding breakfast afterward to celebrate. It all seemed cold and contractual rather than a union of minds and hearts. It was apparent her brother had known there would be no celebration, but he'd not said anything to Kitty. She had thought there would be a chance to spend a last bit of time with her family before she went to a strange home.

They had not walked far when Lord Hayworth shifted in his stride to catch a glimpse of her face. "I have arranged for us to eat something at the inn near Pulteney Bridge where my carriage is waiting. But I should not like to set out too late." There was nothing more, and Kitty was disheartened by the civil tone of his voice. It seemed their marriage was to be one of formality.

"I am not particularly hungry," she replied. "I would just like a moment to refresh myself and have something to drink, and we may set off as soon as you like."

"I believe your brother had your trunk delivered to my carriage earlier. The inn is just ahead"—he indicated a wooden two-story building with small square-paned windows—"and I've hired the private parlor for you to use while I check that your trunk has arrived. What would you like to drink?"

Kitty did not care overmuch, although she had not even been able to drink her customary chocolate that morning. "A glass of lemonade, if you please."

Lord Hayworth installed her in the private parlor and left,

presumably to check on the coach. She used the necessary, drank her lemonade, and felt a tiny bit better when the sweet citrus drink moistened her lips and brought life back to her.

There was a knock. Kitty looked up as Lord Hayworth paused on the threshold, appearing as though he were waiting for her permission to enter. She set her lemonade on the table, and he came and took a seat across from her. "Your trunk is installed on the carriage. The innkeeper will bring me a tankard of ale, and then we may set off." Kitty nodded.

Silence reigned as Lord Hayworth waited for his ale, drank it—quickly, she thought—then indicated they would be leaving. He handed some coins to the innkeeper on their way out and assisted her into the coach, got in himself, then tapped the roof for the coach to set forward. It was an older vehicle, less well-sprung than she was used to, but Kitty was grateful to be in motion. Anything rather than sitting in awkward silence with a stranger she was now tied to for life.

They had ridden a quarter of an hour when Lord Hayworth broke the silence. "I hope you will like Giddenhall."

He had taken off his tall beaver hat, revealing the light curls that had just started to thin on the very back of his head, which strangely did not lessen his appeal but made him seem more human. Kitty averted her eyes. "I'm sure there will be nothing to dislike."

There was again silence, and Lord Hayworth fiddled with the brim of his hat. "I do not know if you are accustomed…" His words trailed away, and she wondered what he had been about to say. He opened his mouth again to speak. "In public, you may call me Hayworth, and I will call you my lady. In private, you may address me as Phineas." He glanced at her quickly then dropped his gaze to his hat. "And what shall I call you?"

There was a beat or two, with only the sound of the horses' hooves and carriage wheels on the ground to fill their ears, before she answered.

"Kitty."

It was vulnerable—giving a complete stranger free use of her Christian name. And now she was to call him Phineas. Yet it was a step forward. Perhaps her new husband was uncomfortable with their situation, as well, and they would eventually come to some sort of an understanding. Perhaps one day they would even laugh about this unpromising beginning.

More silence ensued, and Kitty was in no mood to break it as she studied the texture of her gloves or the bottle green squabs on the rear-facing seat. Her new life loomed before her —the wedding night loomed before her. And if Kitty were being honest with herself, she was absolutely terrified.

"We are not acquainted," Phineas observed after a long stretch with no conversation. He was taking great pains to make her acquaintance—a rather remarkable effort for a husband, she thought. "Perhaps I should have arranged for us to meet before the wedding." He stared ahead instead of at her. "However, I fully expect this arrangement to be mutually agreeable. With the funds that come from your settlement, I will be able to make a comfortable home for us. I will not be dependent on my father's estate to bring Giddenhall in order. This marriage has brought us a freedom by which we both can only benefit."

Both benefit? All charitable thoughts toward her new husband fled, and a surge of irritation welled up in Kitty's breast. She was unable to hide entirely the hiss that escaped her lips, as she swatted at her skirt, as if to smooth it. She had never been able to rein in her temper with much success.

He looked at her now in surprise. "You do not seem pleased with this arrangement. And yet, might I remind you, you have married above your station. You will be a woman of conse-quence and will be well provided for. Your brother did not give me the impression that your alternative was particularly tempting."

Kitty turned to him, her eyebrow raised. He thought to

inform her that she should be honored by his condescension? A derisory laugh escaped her. "Who gave you to believe I required a husband with a title? Erasmus has benefitted from the match, not me. You have bought your freedom with my brother's offer, but in doing so, you have stolen mine." She turned to face forward again, gripping her hands together on her lap.

"You will have just as much freedom as Lady Hayworth as you had as Miss Stokes, if not more." There was confusion in his voice. "I have no intention of restraining your movements. I do not understand—you ought to be grateful for the offer, even if it was not of your instigation."

Kitty's mouth fell open. "Grateful? To be sold by my own brother, to be pushed out of the only home I have known, to be thrown under the protection of someone I've never met and be expected to serve his every whim." Her chest heaved as she remembered Samuel's plaintive words that morning. "Grateful? I was perfectly grateful where I was before, I thank you." To her horror, tears began to leak out of her eyes.

Phineas shifted. He had been facing her slightly, turned toward her, as if to facilitate their conversation. But now, he sat forward, and she sensed his tension—one brought about by her hasty words. She began to regret her outburst. More time went by, with both of them facing the opposite direction, and at last she heard his gruff voice. "You had best dry your eyes. You will not want the servants to see you've been crying when we arrive at Giddenhall."

Kitty tried to check her tears as she reached into her reticule in search of a handkerchief. She did not find one there and wondered how she could have been so scatter-brained. Kitty sniffed discreetly and tried to swipe at her tears with her gloved hand. After two swipes, Phineas reached into his coat pocket and pulled out his own handkerchief and handed it to her without a word. She hesitated, then ever-so-slowly took hold of it.

She used the handkerchief to wipe her tears, blowing her nose in a way that was too robust to be dainty. "I will see that this is washed and returned to you," she said in a muffled voice.

The carriage rumbled ahead to their destination, and neither spoke. Kitty's thoughts wandered in the ensuing silence. Although she was relieved that there had been no amorous gestures—that had been one of her fears—she did not know how to reconcile the estrangement that had sprung up between them. It would be impossible to go from this silent war to any sort of real marital relationship. Unless husbands could so easily flip that switch. She had to admit to herself that she did not know.

The tears had calmed Kitty, as had venting her spleen—it also embarrassed her. Yes, she had let him know she was not a willing party to this union, but now how to bring about a truce? Her heart was just open enough to the idea of being wooed. They were married, after all, and must bridge that gap at some point. If Phineas planned an assault on her heart, there was enough of a breech that he would be able to enter. If he attempted it, she would be his wife of her own desire and not because her brother had forced it upon her. She sought a way to open the conversation. "It appears we are slowing. Are we drawing near to your estate?"

Phineas looked startled that she had finally spoken, and he peeked through the window curtain, then nodded. "We will turn at the next lane, and that will lead us to my property."

My property, he had said. Kitty should not have been surprised. Even if this were a love match, it would still have been his property. It did not matter that her brother likely had needed to negotiate a large settlement to acquire a peer for a brother-in-law. It appeared to Kitty that Phineas considered her to have brought little of substance to the arrangement—or at least only what was her due. That thought cut all desire for further conversation and, apart from discreet glances Phineas gave her as if to assess how she felt, they reached Giddenhall in silence.

Kitty hoped her anxiety over meeting an entire household of servants did not show. It was not that she was unaccustomed to hired help. With her brother as wealthy as he was, they had any number of servants. But Kitty did not know the first thing about running a large estate. She did not even know whom to ask. How much oversight did the housekeeper require? How informal should she be with the servants? At Erasmus's house, she was rather informal. There was not such a huge distinction between them, after all. It was only wealth, not blood, that separated them.

The footman opened the door to the carriage, and Phineas descended first and held out his hand for Kitty to alight. The manor was built of reddish stone and had nine windows on each floor of the façade, some of which were double. The front of the house could be accessed by a double staircase that trailed down from each side of the door. Standing at the foot of one staircase was a row of servants, waiting to receive the viscount and his new wife.

"May I present your new mistress, Lady Hayworth," Phineas announced as the servants stood at stiff attention. He led Kitty in front of each servant and performed the introductions, asking for the names of some, who appeared to be new. The only one Kitty retained was Mrs. Morley, the housekeeper, and Bexley, who was the butler. She would need to spend more time with Mrs. Morley than anyone else. There were seventeen servants in all, and Kitty could barely summon a smile. She just nodded at each of them in what she knew to be an overly stiff manner.

"This is Craddock, the groom. He is another recent addition, but I am told he has a knack for choosing horseflesh. Carter said he comes recommended." Phineas had reached the end of the introductions, and Kitty locked gazes with the groom, who appeared to be about her age. He had removed his hat, and with his cropped blond hair, distinguished brow and square chin, Kitty had to own that the man standing before her was particularly handsome. It gave her a feeling of disquiet. He'd given a short bow, but there was a glimmer in his eyes when he raised them that she found overly familiar, and it unnerved her.

Kitty did not want a handsome stranger coming into the circumference of her heart. She had one stranger there to deal with already. Kitty was married and must learn to be won over by her own husband—never mind that his appearance was only slightly above average, and his disposition a bit on the cold side. *He* was the one fate had handed her. She gave the groom a small nod and put her hand in her husband's arm so he could lead her up the stairs. Best she show right away where her loyalties lay.

CHAPTER FIVE

Having presented Lady Hayworth to the servants, Phineas was unsure what to do next. There was something delicate about having just been wed but not *married* in the true sense, and it was not like he could rush them off to his room to remedy that. They were several hours into their married life, and he still did not know how to approach his wife. As they entered the house, he addressed Mrs. Morley. "I am sure Lady Hayworth will wish to refresh herself after the journey. Tomorrow, you may show her around the manor and acquaint her with where things are kept."

"Very well, my lord." The housekeeper appeared to be efficient, if a bit stiff in her interactions with him. She had replaced his grandmother's housekeeper, who had gone on to retirement, and he had only met Mrs. Morley a handful of times on his brief visits to the estate. He assumed she would soften a bit, now that they had taken up residence at Giddenhall.

Kitty was darting glances in the rooms visible from the entryway, and he wondered whether the house pleased her. "We normally dine at six, but I gave instructions to hold the dinner back one hour so we would not be rushed. I believe Mrs. Morley has found a maid for you?" He turned to the housekeeper with a questioning gaze, and she nodded.

"Bexley's niece, Anne Sterling, is coming from the village. I sent someone to fetch her as soon as you arrived."

"It would have been better had she been here to greet her mistress upon arrival as I had requested." Phineas turned to Kitty. "My lady, you must decide if Sterling suits you for your maid. You may make any changes to the arrangement you wish."

Mrs. Morley had reddened at the mild rebuke but did not reply. Kitty's only response was a short nod. He began to wonder if he and his wife would ever have anything to talk about.

"I will show you to your room, then," Phineas said. "I believe the footmen have already brought your trunk there or will do so shortly." He lifted his arm for Kitty to take and wished she would grasp it with something heavier than the featherlike touch she'd given each time. It was as though she could not bear to touch even his arm.

Kitty lifted her skirt as they went up the stairs, and he caught a glimpse of a dainty ankle. It was no surprise since the rest of her seemed equally as fragile—well, fragile until she'd begun stripping him with her words. They walked up the wooden stairs and turned left down the corridor that held only two rooms. He brought her to the farthest one and opened the door, their silence seeming to take a more weighted meaning when they were alone in front of her bedroom.

He cleared his throat. "This is your room." Kitty dropped his arm and entered it, and he stood at the threshold. "I believe Mrs. Morley will send the maid without delay. My room is just next door, and I will be there if you need anything."

"Thank you." She turned and gave him a fleeting smile then shut the door, finalizing the barrier between them with the soft *click*. Phineas walked the short distance to his own bedroom—

the one he was in the habit of sleeping in whenever he stayed here, although it had not been as often as he would've liked. The estate could not sustain prolonged stays without the money his marriage had brought into it, and indeed over half the servants that greeted them were newly hired from the money Kitty's settlement had brought in. There was that, and there were his father's expectations and frequent demands for Phineas regarding Midlington Estate.

His bedroom was still threadbare. Now that he had a small fortune, he would spend some effort on fixing it up—but he had hoped his new wife would give her counsel on the matter, as they would surely spend some of their time here. Phineas walked over and picked up the razor that sat on the small shaving table, running his finger over the thin shell that covered the handle. Fortunately, he was skilled at shaving himself since the valet that had seen to his affairs until today was employed by Phineas's father and had refused to leave Bath.

The quiet of Phineas's room was in stark relief to the loud thoughts that resonated in his head. He hoped Kitty and he could be man and wife in earnest, but he did not know how to close the distance between them. He was a gentleman and would not claim a prize by thievery, which was essentially what she had accused him of. He would only claim a prize he had won fairly. And although he'd found her far more appealing than he had initially bargained for—to the point where he'd begun to hope for more than just a civil contract—he was far from having won her heart. In fact, he did not even know where to begin.

Rustling movements sounded in the adjoining room, and quiet footsteps. He walked over to the door that connected their rooms and listened, but the noise stopped, as if she were listening too. Feeling sheepish, Phineas went back to his wardrobe and selected a coat to change into for dinner. He fumbled with the cravat but managed to tie it at last and, at seven o'clock precisely, he knocked on his wife's door. He had not dared to use the adjoining door for the purpose, which was too intimate. Kitty opened the door for him, wearing exactly what she had worn in the carriage, never mind that the dress must have gathered dirt from their journey.

Phineas puzzled his brows. Was Kitty trying to make a statement? Did she wish to let him know she did not consider him worthy enough to impress? Perhaps she did not know the ways of Society—that one was expected to change one's dress before dinner. The idea daunted him. How much would he have to teach Kitty so she might fit into his world? The disparity in their cultural education was not an element Phineas had thought to consider when contemplating a marriage for mercenary purposes. The fact that he found her so desirable was only a stroke of pure luck—especially after having had a glimpse of her brother.

In the end, Phineas was unsure how to broach the subject, so he extended his arm once again. And once again, she slipped her hand into the crook of his elbow before taking three steps and pulling away.

"If you don't mind, I am accustomed to walking on my own when we are indoors."

Phineas felt heat creep up the back of his neck. What a bumbling fool he was! Would he ever be at ease with this woman? He had only been trying to find a way to close the distance, but now that she had fled from his touch, his efforts seemed worse than feeble—they seemed an essay in ridicule.

Phineas and Kitty ate their dinner in relative silence, on opposite ends of the table, with only commonplace remarks and the clink of silverware to break the silence. When their dessert had been served, Phineas knew he had to surmount the barrier that separated them, and that he could only do so by opening a conversation that held more than just commonplaces. Kitty was capable of it. She had shown him so on their carriage ride, even if that had ended in tears.

However, once the footman left, Phineas was at a loss. How did one begin a conversation that led to intimate knowledge of another person? He was not a man of words, and as he was more likely to cultivate male friendships over female—an easier feat in his eyes since it did not require any degree of intimacy— he remained stupidly silent.

Kitty nibbled on an orange meringue and raised her eyes to his. The light in them was not exactly warm and inviting, but to his relief, it was no longer hostile—or tearful. She spoke first, sparing him the indecision of what to say. "Where did you attend school?"

"I was at Harrow, then Cambridge."

She looked down and dipped her meringue in the glass of ratafia, and the graceful way she slipped it between her lips entranced him. He almost missed her next words. "I know next to nothing about your family. You have no siblings, I presume?"

Phineas sipped at the port that had been brought to him. He'd given orders that he would take his port at the same time as dessert since he had no intention of loitering at the table while his wife sat alone in the drawing room. "None. My parents are not overly fond of one another." This disclosure he let slip with a little grimace.

Kitty seemed to understand his meaning at once, and she did not pursue the thread of conversation but picked at another biscuit, although she did not eat it. Phineas's muscles were tense as he struggled for a way to set his wife at ease. He hadn't thought this through—hadn't realized how hard it would be to go from the actual ceremony to everyday life as a married man. For him, it had been nothing but a business arrangement from which he certainly did not expect love, knowing what a fleeting and elusive notion that was.

However, there was something so flesh-and-blood about Kitty that drew him to her. Her tears had touched him, for he knew they did not flow from artifice but rather from a heart that beat warmly. Each fresh glance at her unexpected beauty filled him with desire. He *had* to find a way to uncover who his wife truly was. The silence had gone on long enough, and it was up to him to break it.

"The children I saw at your … at our wedding ceremony, I imagine they are your brother's offspring?"

A fleeting smile crossed Kitty's face. "Three of them are. Edward is seven, Helen is five, and William is one. However, the oldest boy you saw—Samuel—he is my half-brother. He's eight."

Phineas's eyes widened. He had not realized she'd had another sibling—not that it would have mattered. He just assumed the only blood relation left to her was her older brother. "I presume it was your father who married again?"

Kitty nodded and rubbed her fingers on her napkin. "My father married a woman much younger, who was barely out of the schoolroom herself. Samuel was only a year old when my father died. Erasmus and Mary were newly married, and when Samuel's mother proved unfit to care for the baby, they took him in."

"How old were you?" As soon as the question left his mouth, Phineas did the math. If Kitty was now twenty, she would have been twelve when her father died.

As if to confirm his guess, she answered. "Twelve. And since my own mother died when I was three, I had spent nine years without a female figure in the house, apart from my governess, who essentially raised me."

Phineas lifted his brows at the revelation. So, she'd had a governess. Of course. It would make sense. The refinement in her voice and manner was an unexpected surprise and could only have been brought about with proper training. "Did your governess stay on to help raise Samuel?"

"No. To my dismay, for I was very fond of my governess.

Erasmus dismissed her when he married. It was thought that Mary could achieve the rest of my training, but she was disinclined to do so, I believe." Phineas detected a flash of something —irritation, or perhaps irony—in her features.

Their brief conversation was certainly revealing, and Phineas had a better idea of her upbringing, even from the things she left unsaid. Kitty had not expressed any of the bitterness she would have every right to feel. "It was your father, I believe, who began the shipping business?"

Kitty absently crumbled the meringue biscuit into powdered dust on her plate. "No, it was my grandfather, although neither he nor my father can claim to have truly built the business. No one has had as much success—or passion—as Erasmus has had to transform the company into something this thriving. It is to him we owe our fortune."

Phineas had finished his port, and when Kitty was not more forthcoming, he coaxed more from her. "I imagine Samuel and his cousin must be great friends, for they are of the same age." Phineas could almost be envious of them. He had grown up alone, and although he had Bartholomew as his cousin, and some distant female cousins, with whom he was rarely in contact, he and Bartholomew had never been particularly close. He blamed it on his father's brother, who seemed to think that fate had aligned itself against him by giving the inheritance to Phineas's father.

However, Kitty dispelled the ideal he'd conjured in his mind by shaking her head. "Samuel and Edward…"

She paused and took a trembling breath, and Phineas's gaze shot to her face in surprise. He had not thought to bring up a delicate subject when he'd spoken of her little brother, but only to express his interest. He waited for her to continue.

"They are not as close as one might hope. I believe there exists a great deal of competition between them, urged on by Edward's mother. Unfortunately, Erasmus considers domestic affairs beneath his notice, so he does not take a hand in Samuel's upbringing as perhaps he ought."

"Will your brother attend school?" Phineas asked. It was a ready solution to an unhappy home. Going away to school would remove him from the clutches of a complicated family environment.

"He has a place at Harrow next year, so yes, he will go." There were two spots of color on her cheeks, and Phineas stared at her in concern. He had not intended to stir the deep emotions he now saw rising. "But I very much worry about him. We are quite close, my brother and I. And although I dearly love my nephews and niece, they have their own mother to look out for their interests. Samuel has no one but me. And—" She broke off with a sharp breath, as—to Phineas's dismay—the tears started to leak out of her eyes again.

He got up from the head of the table, walked around it and went to sit next to her, pulling his handkerchief out of his coat. "I beg you will not distress yourself. I had merely meant to make conversation." He handed the handkerchief to Kitty, and she used it to wipe her eyes.

"It is simply ... if I had only myself to sacrifice in marriage to appease Erasmus, I could abide by the decision." She paused as she fought to gain control over her tears. *Sacrifice?* The word goaded Phineas, both striking him as unjust while also touching a nerve and filling him with guilt.

"However," she went on, "in this case, my brother has been sacrificed as well, for there is absolutely no one to look out for him. This morning, before we walked to the church, he confessed his fear and uncertainty about being left behind, and he is not one given to hysterics. It was painful to witness." She met Phineas's gaze briefly. "I am very sorry to treat you to such a waterworks, which I am sure must be distasteful to you. It is just that this change is more difficult than I had anticipated."

"It is of no matter," Phineas replied—words he knew were

vastly inadequate, but he could do no more. He could not offer to host her brother with relations so tense and new between him and Kitty. He needed to bring this dinner to a close, for all that had been accomplished was to remind him of his errors in conducting the engagement. There seemed little chance for recovery, at least not for tonight. "Shall we ... retire?"

He glanced at her, certain his nervousness was obvious, fearing he appeared ridiculous. If she noticed, it could not have eclipsed her own, which was evident. She swallowed and stood. "It appears I now have a second handkerchief to render you, which I will do as soon as it is washed."

Phineas knew better than to offer his arm, and he opened the door, allowing her to precede him into the corridor. There was a footman at the base of the stairs, but he stepped back into the shadows. They climbed the steps and Phineas, who had been searching for a topic to dispel the awkwardness, grasped at the first that came to mind. "I have been thinking to raise the matter with you, Kitty. As a general rule in Society, we change our dress for dinner. I thought you should like to know it to spare you future embarrassment, although I am sure there is much you must learn about our ways, and it need not be rushed."

His wife stopped suddenly at his side, and he paused to look at her, suddenly uncertain of the wisdom of his words. Her eyes blazed with indignation.

"I assure you, I do not need lessons on etiquette or how to dress for dinner. My governess was a baron's daughter, and though her family had fallen on hard times, she taught me everything I needed to know." Kitty's lips went into a straight line. "But I found it very difficult to change my gown when I had neither my trunk delivered to me in the two hours I waited, nor a maid to assist me into it. I beg your pardon for having offended your sensibilities." She continued up the stairs and, after a moment, thunderstruck, Phineas hurried after her.

"I had no idea your maid had not appeared. I understood she

was to arrive at any moment. I will send someone to learn what happened. And your trunk as well? I am all astonishment, and I will do what I can to find out what the problem is. I assure you, I meant no offense." Phineas's words were conciliatory, but his irritation rose. He had not bargained on such a prickly wife for a spouse—and he so mild-mannered, himself!

"I am sure you did not mean to offend." Kitty continued to her room at a brisk pace, her voice low, but no less passionate. "It is only that you think me so beneath you and ill-equipped to live in your world that you need instruct me. I can scarcely wonder at your having agreed to the match at all. Well—until I remember what figure you were given to take me."

They had reached the door to her room when her final words were spoken, and Phineas felt the blow of them in his chest. He faced her. "Stop. You have gone too far. I will accept the blame that I did not take the time to court you and turned the marriage into a business transaction—even if that is nothing out of the ordinary, you must own—but I did not sacrifice you, or purchase you, and I have no intention of treating you with anything less than respect."

She stared at the doorknob instead of at him, and the silence following his words was deafening. "I apologize."

Phineas softened. If she could apologize, there was hope for them. He set his fingers lightly on her arm. "I, too, apologize for having offended you." After a moment he added, "And for not attempting a meeting before our marriage."

She dipped her head in acknowledgment and at last met his gaze. He saw a depth of feeling in those eyes that spoke of passion and sensitivity and spirit that was everything he could desire. But there was reserve there. Through his own misman-agement and thoughtless words, she was inaccessible to him. It would be a betrayal to that passion to force himself on her without her consent. It would only make a bad situation worse.

"I will ring for a servant and get to the bottom of this."

She nodded, hesitating with her hand on the doorknob. At last, she opened it to enter her room, and his gaze rested on her figure. The embroidered green leaves and vines that covered the sleeves of her gown wove across the back to where tiny pearl buttons closed the bodice. Kitty turned and appeared startled to see him still standing there, and Phineas recollected himself. He bowed and turned.

In his own room, Phineas rang the bell vigorously, and within minutes the servant arrived—the same one who had been hovering near the stairwell. "What is your name?" he asked him.

"Marcus, my lord," the man answered.

"Do you know why my wife did not have a maid to attend to her before dinner? Why her trunk was not delivered to her room?"

The footman bowed his head. "Miss Sterling arrived while you were eating dinner, my lord. There'd been some turn-up with the coach and—wishing to arrive as soon as possible— she'd set out on foot. But it took much longer than expected."

Phineas relaxed his shoulders, relieved that there was a logical reason for the maid's delay, and that it wasn't mutiny from his servants for having brought home a wife who was not gently born. "And her trunk?"

Marcus gestured behind Phineas. "My lord, begging your pardon. Her trunk is there next to yours."

Phineas spun around and saw for the first time the trunk that did not belong to him. He had not noticed it in all his pacing before dinner. He sighed and shook his head. "Carry this to my lady's room. She is expecting it there."

Marcus did his bidding, and when the door to the corridor was shut, Phineas sat in the armchair near the fire. He could hear voices in the next room, as his wife gave instructions to the footman and thanked him. He heard the maid knock softly, and again the gentle voice of his wife as they spoke. He imagined that the maid was removing her hair pins and brushing Kitty's thick red hair.

Phineas looked to the small table at his right. Someone had left a decanter of brandy there. He unstopped it and poured himself a small glass. It was going to be a long night.

CHAPTER SIX

Lord Hayworth had made Kitty angry enough that she forgot to be nervous. It was only now that she looked at the clock and saw that it was still early, and that he had not proposed they go to the drawing room for tea or to play a game of cards as they might have done at her brother's house. Now that she was alone in her room and her trunk had been delivered, she supposed she knew *why* and what sort of activity would take place instead—it was their wedding night after all. But she wondered what to expect for all the nights thereafter. Would there be tea and companionship? Games? Conversation … fights? Would there be children?

Kitty's words had been hasty, and Phineas had objected to them, but he did not appear to be unreasonable. He'd even apologized, which gave her hope. She almost thought he would give her some inkling as to what to expect that night, as he bowed and promised to look into the absence of her trunk and the new maid. In the end, he had simply turned and walked the length of the corridor to his room. Perhaps he needed time to do whatever it was men did to get ready for the night. Or perhaps he was giving her the time she needed. She glanced at the trunk, uncertain.

There was another knock on the door, and her heart leapt with nerves. He had come back. When she opened the door, it was only the maid who had at last arrived.

"My lady, I beg your pardon for my tardiness. There was a wheel broke, and I had to walk. If you wish, I'll help you out of your dress."

"Yes, thank you." Kitty allowed the maid to unbutton her dress and assist her into a new night shift. This one, Kitty had chosen with care, despite how little she had relished preparing for her upcoming wedding. The shift was made of thick white cotton and delicate lace, and was both warm and pretty.

"Shall I brush out your hair?"

"No, I will do it myself. Thank you—" Kitty paused, realizing she did not remember her maid's name.

"Sterling, my lady."

"Thank you, Sterling. That will be all." Kitty did not wish for her maid to still be in the room when her husband made his appearance. It was awkward enough as it was, and she had no need for an audience.

When Sterling left, Kitty's fingers trembled as she pulled the pins from her hair, along with the decorative string of pearls and green silk flowers that had been hidden underneath her wedding bonnet. The added touch had been visible only to Phineas in the end, since there had been no wedding breakfast in Bath. He had not made any comment about her appearance— or, really, any comments at all. Now, her hair fell down to the middle of her back in thick waves. She peered into the looking glass and was met with large eyes that looked fearful to her.

I must simply get through this. It is no more and no less than what women have been doing since the beginning of time.

Kitty heard movement from the other side of the adjoining door, and she went and sat on the side of the bed, her hands clutched on her knees. No, this would not do. She shot up again and crossed the room to sit on the chair near the fireplace, still waiting. In her husband's room, there were footsteps crossing back and forth, and eventually these sounds died down. She thought she heard the rustle of covers … was that the sound of him lying down? Kitty clutched her arms around her middle and leaned forward. Why would he be getting into the bed in his room?

Her brow puzzled, Kitty went over to her own bed, which suddenly seemed rather large and cold. She climbed under the covers and bunched them around her, sitting cross-legged as she waited, listening … The cold draft on Kitty's back soon had her curling up in a ball under the covers. Surely Phineas would come? She must have misunderstood or misread the sounds of him lying on the bed. Perhaps he would come to her in the middle of the night—or shortly before morning.

The exhaustion of the day, the strangeness of being yoked to someone she did not know, the emotions of their conversation, the long travel and painful dinner she had undergone finally overcame Kitty. Sleep was calling to her with such force, she did not have time to feel desolate. Her bare head was cold, so she scurried over to her trunk and retrieved a sleeping cap and pulled it over her hair then got back into bed. She likely looked a fright, but Phineas had only himself to blame since he had not come when she was ready for him. With the blankets tucked securely around her, her head now warm, Kitty began to relax and think that perhaps everything would be all right. Apparently, she was to be a viscountess to the outside world, and a spinster in her own home. But there was not so much to complain about, after all. It would not be so very different from her life before.

Still, the ache inside became pronounced as she reflected on the stark reality. She was friendless.

A DIM LIGHT creeping through the curtains woke Kitty the next morning. And if she awoke feeling much more cheerful than the night before, she was just as confused. Her husband had not come in the end. A momentary sense of well-being settled over Kitty as she stretched her bare toes in the warmth of the sheets, before an unpleasant thought assailed her. Did Phineas truly marry her just for her fortune? Did he have a mistress elsewhere to meet all his other needs? Kitty turned and buried her face in the pillow.

It could only be because she was not a lady. He must have married her solely for the money, because no daughter of a peer would receive such an insult on her wedding night. And yet, Kitty was supposed to accept this sham marriage as her lot in life. On one hand, the realization brought some relief. She would not be bothered by a physical relationship but could enjoy running a household, if Phineas fulfilled his promise to let her do as she wished. On the other hand, gone was the hope of something good coming from the match. Gone was the hope of children. Kitty bit her lip. Perhaps there was still hope of that at some point, but he hadn't come to her on their wedding night, had he? What else could it mean?

The match had been arranged in a cold and calculated manner between two men, each to achieve his own end.

Kitty rose from bed and rummaged in her trunk for a morning dress. Her new maid would need to come and put her things away so she could find them easily. She glanced around the room, found the bell, and rang it. Within a short time, Sterling appeared.

"Is my husband in the breakfast room?"

"I believe he is, my lady. I saw him go from the library to the breakfast room as I was coming up."

Kitty did not want to miss him. Being so thoroughly out of

her element, she had no choice but to take her cues from Phineas as to how she should spend her day and what role she was to have here. Kitty's heart beat in her throat, however. There was something else she needed to ask him, as well, for she could not bear having to continue to guess on the matter. She needed to know what kind of marriage they were to have.

"Assist me quickly into this gown. I should not like Lord Hayworth to finish his breakfast before I have made my appearance."

The maid smiled to herself, obviously misinterpreting the words to mean that theirs was a love-match. Kitty would allow Sterling to think that. It would be less painful than the truth, which was sure to come out soon enough. Servants had an uncanny ability of knowing exactly what went on in the house, and what was worse—speculation was always rife.

In short order, Sterling assisted her into a rifle green walking dress with puffed sleeves near the shoulder and a patterned empire sash with tiny burgundy flowers. Kitty knew it was one of her better dresses. She sat, and Sterling pulled Kitty's thick hair into a simple, attractive chignon, curling tendrils of hair near her temple with an iron rod the maid had placed in the fire. It was imperative that Kitty look her best. Phineas might reject her intimacy, but he would know what he was missing.

"I will unpack your trunk while you are at breakfast, my lady," Sterling said, arranging the brush and pins on the dressing table.

Kitty made her way downstairs on embroidered, satin-slippered feet, with much trepidation in her heart. She opened the breakfast room where Phineas sat with his plate nearly empty in front of him. He looked up, and—was that admiration she saw in his eyes? *Oh, I hope it is.* Her husband quickly got to his feet and bowed.

"Good morning, my lady." He waited for her to go to the sideboard to fill her plate.

"Good morning, my lord." She curtsied then chose a soft roll and spooned jam and butter on her plate, sitting as the footman walked forward to fill her cup with coffee. Phineas sat as well, his eyes not leaving hers. Kitty was so aware of the awkwardness that attended their situation, she knew her face must reflect it. She could not bear to look at the footman, who had gone back to stand near the wall, his expression closed. She wondered if everyone knew she had slept alone that night.

Phineas addressed the servant. "That will be all. If we need something, I will ring for it."

The footman bowed and took his leave, and Kitty was alone with her husband. The breakfast room was cheerful, with a serge linen rug underneath the table, and several tall windows overlooking the lawn, which held hints of green and brown on the shrubbery and frozen grass.

Kitty attempted to eat her breakfast, darting glances at Phineas, who seemed equally as conscious of her presence as she was of his.

"I trust that you slept —"

"My lord, I should like to —"

Phineas smiled, which made him seem more approachable than the stern look he had given her last night—or the smug look in the carriage. "Please, what is it you wish to say? Also, may I remind you to call me Phineas when there are no servants nearby, if you are amenable to the idea."

Kitty nodded and sent him a fleeting smile. She did not know how she dared to bring up the matter that was closest to her heart. It was so vulnerable, and the idea of voicing it seemed shocking to her. She stalled for time. "Growing up, did you eat breakfast with your parents?"

Phineas looked surprised at her question. He had clearly

expected her to say something else, but her true question would only surprise him more if he knew.

"Not generally." He looked down briefly, as he cut the last of his ham then glanced back at her. "My parents kept to their own habits and did not often dine together. My father was an early riser, and my mother a late one. So it was pure chance if we met for breakfast."

"Are you an early riser of nature?" she asked.

"That depends," Phineas answered. "I generally have much to keep me occupied. But I will not deny that there are days when the greatest pleasure imaginable is to spend a longer time in bed and not have to rush out of it." He looked at her with such a significant expression, Kitty blushed—shocked.

Had he infused that sentence with the particular meaning she thought he did? Had she read that correctly? With one corner of his mouth lifted in the smallest way, as if hiding some private source of amusement, he bent his eyes to his plate and kept them there. If he had indeed found something to amuse him, Kitty was not sure she could share in the joke.

Phineas had finished his breakfast, and Kitty knew she had to speak before he left to do whatever it was he did. It was her chance to set their marriage on the right foot, and she was not one to hold back from expressing what she thought. There was just enough openness in his answers—just enough in his expression to give her hope that they might be able to converse more freely with time.

Kitty glanced at the door, hoping there were no servants hovering nearby. No, she could not do this sitting so far from him. They were a respectable distance apart, on the opposite ends of the table, as was fitting for a lord and lady of an estate, she supposed. Seated thus, she could not raise her voice to ask the question that was burning inside of her. However, she would not give up her opportunity to begin their marriage in the way she wished for it to continue.

"Phineas, may I come and sit at your side to ask you a question?"

He looked up, startled, and she thought she saw an eager light come to his eyes, a hint of color in his cheeks, a tiny lift to the corners of his mouth. But he remained motionless. The expression was so subtle, she was not sure if she had imagined it.

"You may."

Kitty stood, leaving her half-drunk coffee and unfinished roll on her plate, and she walked around the table and took the chair at his side. They were now close enough that if they both turned, their knees would touch. She shifted in her seat to look at him, and he put his napkin down, his arm outstretched on the table. There was something in his eyes that sparked in her breast the hope of connection. He waited for her to speak, and she took a convulsive breath before saying the words.

"Why did you not come to me last night?" Kitty met his gaze, but embarrassment, nerves, and fear kept her from holding it. Head lowered, she waited for his answer—a victim of the misery and hope that battled within.

Phineas was silent at first, and when he spoke, his voice held no trace of the smile she thought she had seen. "You said you were forced into this marriage. I blame myself for not attempting to see you before we were married to ascertain how you might feel. I am not a man to claim a prize I did not earn squarely, and I will not force myself upon you. I will not come to your bed unless you invite me to it."

Kitty's eyes grew round in surprise, and she could not hold back the words that sprang to her lips. "But Phineas—you must have an heir. Surely your purpose in marrying was not just for money, but also to secure an heir for the estate."

With the hand that was extended on the table, her husband reached for his napkin and twisted the cloth into a ball. "Truthfully, I did not think that far ahead when I made arrangements to marry. The idea of having an heir was not my foremost objective in seeking a wife."

A sense of dread crept into Kitty's heart, even though it was no less than she had suspected. Her gaze crept back up to his face, and she feared the answer to her next question. "And what was your foremost objective?"

Phineas appeared to see nothing wrong with his reasoning, for he shot her a cool glance and replied without hesitation. "To save my estate from ruin and free myself from the control of my father."

Kitty looked down again. The implication of his words brought a sense of doom. Whatever she had read in his open gaze upon entering the breakfast room was now but a fleeting hope. This marriage would not bring her happiness or love. It would not even bring her companionship. She inhaled, fighting against the despair until she could seek the privacy of her room.

"However"—her husband's voice coaxed her gaze back up with its tenderness—"as little as I thought about securing an heir when making the arrangement, that is an objective with me now."

Kitty's heart started to beat wildly, and she furrowed her brow. "I see..." She did not know how to express all the questions that were whirling around her head or beating in her heart. If he now wished for an heir, what could she expect from him? An heir required certain ... arrangements. Yet he had decided not to impose himself upon her. In her confusion, Kitty could only repeat herself. "So why did you not come last night? If having an heir is now one of your objectives?"

"I meant what I said," Phineas replied with the ghost of a smile. He glanced at her hands clasped on her lap, then up again at her face, and there was something rueful in his expression. "I will come when you ask me to."

Heat flooded Kitty's face as she turned forward in her chair and studied the stitching on the edge of the white tablecloth. He expected *her* to invite him? How could he think she could do something so brazen? It was utterly impossible. "I could *never* do such a thing," she whispered.

Phineas shrugged, and the gesture appeared forlorn even from the corner of her eye. He dropped the napkin he had been fiddling with on his plate and sat up. "Then I suppose my cousin will inherit."

CHAPTER SEVEN

P hineas paced the library in an attempt to cool down and apply himself to rational thought. His wife had been a vision when she walked into the breakfast room, and Phineas had had to set down his coffee cup before he dropped it on the tablecloth. If he had found her lovely in her wedding dress, there was something more bewitching about her stunning green dress against her red hair, and the domestic picture it presented as she served herself breakfast. His one thought was to walk around the table, take her in his arms and kiss her senseless. Of course, the footman had been there. And then, of course, this sort of thing was just not *done*.

It was nevertheless a form of torture. Phineas still could not accustom himself to the fact that he was married to such an exquisite creature. She was nothing like what his parents had hinted at over the course of his lifetime—that to marry outside the gentry was to court those *smelling of the shop*. Kitty had come and sat at Phineas's side as though she wanted to be near him, her floral scent tantalizing his senses. Then she had asked *the question*, prompting Phineas to blurt out the noble resolution he had crafted last night after their disastrous dinner. That he would wait upon her invitation.

Phineas was beginning to think he was a fool of no small proportion.

How had he gone and committed himself to not approaching her until he had received permission to do so? How was he supposed to woo her if he was waiting for her to make the first move? No gesture on his part would appear innocent. It had seemed like a good idea last night when he was still hot under the collar from their quarrel. It was only upon seeing her reaction in the cold light of day that he realized what a hopeless thing he was asking of her. She could not extend such a bold invitation to someone she barely knew, never mind that they were joined before God and King. No gently bred woman could do such a thing.

Phineas strode over to his reading chair and picked up the book he had been laboring through for the past month and placed it back on the shelf with a vicious shove. Life was too short to read Machiavelli for pleasure. There was only one thing for him to do. Phineas sat in his chair and dropped his chin in his hand. He would have to win Kitty's heart so she could speak those words, or he'd have to die of frustration. Hopefully, he could succeed in wooing her without laying himself open to ridicule by being excessively vulnerable.

At the end of the morning, Kitty and Mrs. Morley came up the stairwell leading from the kitchen, with Kitty inquiring about the variety of dried herbs found at Giddenhall, and Mrs. Morley answering her. This second domestic scene of their first morning as man and wife delighted his senses. Kitty looked up and met his eyes. He saw hesitation there, but he did not see fear or indifference. That was already a step in the right direction. He moved to join them.

"My lady, if you are finished with Mrs. Morley, shall we visit the grounds? Or perhaps you would care to have some tea first?"

Kitty shook her head. "My breakfast was satisfying. However, let me go and fetch my cloak, for the air is rather sharp. I felt it creep in from the windows in the larder."

"Very well, then. I will fetch my own which is in the study, and then we will be comfortable." He smiled, and Kitty returned it before moving to the staircase. She was really a delight to behold with her delicate chin and her hair as elegant as a crown. Her voice was well-modulated and hinted at a fine upbringing. Phineas was beginning to realize he had not given her enough credit for her education.

He was in the corridor when his wife joined him. The footman held open the door for them, and they walked outside and down the circular stairwell to the gravel path at the bottom. Phineas chewed his lip before glancing at Kitty and held out his arm. "You said you are not accustomed to walking on anyone's arm indoors, but would you take my arm for our walk?"

There was a pause where he nervously held his breath, but in the end she did take his arm as they began to walk. A silence fell between them that Phineas was anxious to fill but did not know how to begin.

This was the first step in their courtship—for he could look at it as nothing other than that. If he was going to win her, he would have to court her. When Phineas had arranged this marriage, courtship was something he had hoped to evade. After all, he had studiously avoided the notion in all the Seasons he'd been in London. There were enough lures cast his way to flatter him, but he was not one of those highly sought after beaux, despite his title. The thought of having to woo a woman with artificial words and gestures was repugnant to him. And the thought of expressing words that came straight from his heart—that could be rejected or laughed over in private company—was equally impossible. He now found himself in the unique and unenviable position of being forced into the very situation from which he'd fled.

They rounded the corner of the estate, and Phineas lifted his arm to encompass the scene before them. "The meadow slopes downward to a stream that runs along the bottom of the hill. The woods you see on the other side of the meadow extend for some miles. All this is part of Giddenhall Estate, which was bequeathed to me by my maternal grandmother. I have been in the habit of assisting my father to run Midlington, and the estate attached to my courtesy title, Hayworth. But it is this estate which holds my interest, for it is all my own."

He cocked his head at her. "If you'd like—either today or at another point—we may go for a ride, and I will show you the tenants that support the estate." He pointed beyond the meadow. "There. East of here. I hope I will not be bringing up a sore subject when I tell you that your settlement will allow me to make significant improvements on the tenants' houses, and I imagine they will greet our presence with pleasure once they learn of it."

Kitty smiled and shook her head. "I believe in this instance, the money is better served in your hands than in my brother's. He does not have tenants to look after, only workers. However, I suspect he is not overly concerned with their well-being."

She looked up at him, and the direct gaze stopped his breath. "I will not complain of the arrangement you made with my brother. I was angry, and you received the force of it yesterday. However, I understand the world which we inhabit. A man must live upon something, and a calculating businessman such as my brother will not lose an opportunity to marry off a sister if it will benefit his dealings. I am merely the pawn in such a game."

She moved forward again, and a twinge of discomfort pinched at Phineas. It had never once occurred to him what it must feel like to have so little control over one's own destiny.

True, his father liked to keep a tight rein on him, but one day he would inherit and would be Earl with no one to give him orders. Phineas had to try to set her mind at ease. "You will not be a pawn in my household. You will have a rightful place."

She gave a brief smile and met his look fleetingly. Phineas was not sure how well she believed him, but he would be stupid to think he could fix everything with a few well-placed words on the second day of their marriage. "Would you care to ride today? To visit the tenants? The steward has set plans in motion to begin the improvements, but it would be a pleasure to announce the news to the tenants directly."

Kitty pulled her hand out of his arm with a troubled look. "I am sorry, my lord—Phineas—but I cannot ride."

"Are you fearful of horses?" Phineas did not know of anyone who could not ride, women included. It was essential for someone living on an estate, even if merely to travel from one part of the land to the other. Perhaps for a merchant family there was no reason to become a proficient rider? He had much to learn about marriage with someone from a different social circle than his own.

"I suppose I am a bit fearful of horses, but it is more that I never had an opportunity to learn." Kitty put her hand back in his arm, and they moved forward in the direction of the stables. "When my father was still alive, he was more concerned with his business and making sure Erasmus was taught. When it came to me, he did not think riding as important as sewing samplers." She shot Phineas a wry look. "I do not know what is so important about sewing samplers, but I assure you I possess every talent you might need in that area."

Phineas smiled at that. He liked to hear teasing in her voice, as it promised a hint of friendship. It also hinted at intelligence. Stupid people could not make jokes.

"I see. Well, perhaps we can visit the stables and choose a mare for you, one who is gentle. My groom, Craddock, has been recently employed by the estate, so I cannot speak for his capability as a teacher. But if he is anything like my father's groom, he will know how to give you lessons." Phineas paused in his steps and looked at her. "If you'd like to learn, that is."

"I believe I should like to," she answered, allowing him to lead her forward again. "If it is something you frequently do, then I should care to learn more about it. After all, we come from such different worlds, whatever pastimes we may enjoy together should surely be promoted."

Phineas hoped she was not being ironic when she spoke about their different worlds, throwing the unwisdom of his comments the night before back in his face. He ignored his suspicion and latched on to her words in sincerity. "Very true. It can only prove beneficial to discover interests we may share. Let us go then."

They entered the stable together to find Craddock feeding one of the horses and rubbing his mane, as he crooned to him. He looked up as Phineas and Kitty blocked the light streaming into the stable, casting a shadow across his face.

Craddock pulled his cap off his head and bowed. "Good afternoon, my lord. My lady." He flicked a glance at Kitty before meeting Phineas's gaze. Spreading his legs apart in a comfortable stance, he waited for instruction.

Phineas pulled his mouth down in irritation. Perhaps the groom simply needed to accustom himself to the way the estate worked, but there was a familiarity to him Phineas could not like. He was accustomed to servants showing more respect. However, it had not been an easy matter to fill the household with the necessary servants on short notice, and the groom deserved a proper trial period.

"Lady Hayworth will need to learn to ride a horse, and I am assuming that is something you can do? Is there a sidesaddle to be had?"

The groom returned his gaze to Kitty and rested it there

before giving a short nod. "I have experience teaching ladies to ride. There is a sidesaddle, my lord, but it is old. The girth will hold, but I don't believe my lady will find it stylish."

His wife remained silent so Phineas responded. "I will see that we order a new saddle for her. Why don't you lead us to a horse suitable for a lady. I was thinking either Fancy or Fawn."

Craddock assessed Kitty and gestured forward. "Right this way, my lady. Fancy has an odd kick to her gallop, though she's generally well-behaved, and Fawn is on the docile side. You might like beginning with Fawn."

They had reached Fancy's stall, and Kitty pulled her glove off and reached her hand up to let the horse sniff at her palm. At least she had the instinct not to present her fingers for biting. She rubbed the horse's nose, and the mare bumped against her hand playfully. Craddock then led them over to Fawn where Kitty did the same thing. The mare eyed her with large brown eyes and stood patiently while Kitty rubbed her tan neck.

"She's a Welsh Cob with a gentle nature," Phineas said, watching his wife. The mare did not move as Kitty stroked the black mane, but the horse's large eyes followed Kitty's movements.

"I think you might be right. Fawn and I have taken a liking to each other. And it might be wise to start with a horse who *doesn't* have an odd kick to the gallop." She turned and smiled at Phineas, and he couldn't help but respond. The effect her smile had on him left him dazed.

Craddock was also staring at Kitty, and Phineas cleared his throat to gain the man's attention. "When can you begin?"

The groom looked down at his boot, then up again at Phineas and Kitty. "I don't mind. Whenever my lady has time, I can make myself available. I'll ask one of the stable hands to exercise the horses if need be."

Phineas sent his wife a questioning look, and she nodded. "I believe mornings are best. I will come just after breakfast. Around ten o'clock."

"Yes, my lady." Craddock bowed, before turning to enter Fawn's stall.

Phineas led Kitty outside, and as they reached the sunlight, their breath coming out in puffs in the brisk air, he stopped short, struck by a thought. "Do you have a riding habit?"

Kitty ducked her head shyly, a mannerism he could not but find charming after the myriad emotions she had shown him in the last twenty-four hours, of which hostility and aloofness were the most prevalent.

"As a matter of fact, I do," she replied. "A riding habit was one of the dresses I had made up in case I should need it. To own the truth, I assumed I would need to learn to ride at some point, for not everything is within walking distance the way it is in Bristol. I was unsure if there were places I would need to go that were not accessible by carriage."

"So you thought to cover all eventualities," he said.

When Kitty nodded, Phineas smiled and held out his arm to bring her to the grounds on the west side of the estate. "A heartening quality to have in a wife, I find."

CHAPTER EIGHT

Visiting the grounds with Phineas had been an amiable experience, much to Kitty's surprise. In any case, there had been nothing in their conversation that brought her to tears. *A positive development indeed,* she thought wryly. He seemed to have been choosing his topics carefully with an aim to discover what interested her—a fact that touched her, since no male relation of hers had ever done the same.

The remainder of the day had followed along the same lines as their wedding day. They went their separate ways in the afternoon then met for dinner at six, where the conversation was stilted before the servants and flowed more freely over dessert when they were alone. And still—no tears.

Finally, the walk to her bedroom door, where he'd bid her goodnight in a civil manner then went to his own door. She heard the floorboards creak with her husband's footsteps in his room, and again the rustling of sheets. She saw the light disappear from under the crack in their adjoining door when he must have blown out the candle. Somehow, Kitty thought he still might visit, and when he did not, was strangely restless in her own sheets while waiting for sleep to come.

The next morning, Kitty sprang out of bed, wishing to look her best for breakfast. She rang for Sterling to assist her into her riding habit and style her hair, which the maid did with efficiency. Her maid was not chatty, but she performed her work well. Phineas was coming out of the breakfast room, and he stilled as she approached, his eyes resting on her. She fixed her gaze on his hand, still holding the door and gave a shy smile.

"Good morning." Phineas bowed and let the door fall closed, his expression soft. "I see you are ready for your riding lesson. I fear I will not be able to join you this morning, which is undoubtedly my loss, for I would have liked that very much. I am to meet Mr. Ameson, my steward, and he is expecting me at the tenants' houses in a half-hour."

"I see." Kitty offered him another smile to cover the twinge of disappointment that sprang up. She opened her mouth to ask when he might be available, before stopping herself short. Such a thing smacked of desperation. "Well, I shall not keep you then."

He held her gaze a moment longer before reaching across her to open the door. The footman in the breakfast room sprang forward to perform the office, and Phineas turned to go.

"Oh, my lady—" Kitty turned and lifted her eyes to meet his, and he said, "It did not occur to me until this morning, but you might very well receive visits today. I imagine some of the local families will wish to call on you. I am told the Duttons hold influence in the town, and Mrs. Dutton will likely make the first gesture. Others of the gentry will certainly come as well, once they know we have taken up residence. I should have thought to give you some instructions, but you might learn the names from Mrs. Morley. Otherwise, we may talk more about it tonight."

Kitty nodded her agreement, and her husband left. The intimacy of meeting for dinner calmed her. It showed they belonged to one another, and this new life was hers. She entered the breakfast room where she ate in silence and noticed for the first time that the room smelled faintly of paint. It must have been refurbished before her arrival.

THE AIR WAS brisk and cloudy with a faint scent of chimney smoke. Leaves skittered across the path before being swept up by the wind. Kitty was beginning to view her circumstances with more cheer, considering her new husband did not appear to be a tyrant, and—if she was being perfectly honest with herself—was pleasing to look at. His expression was habitually grave with a permanent crease between his brows, and his lips firm, but when he smiled his eyes seemed to dance. Kitty laughed at the fanciful thought.

In the stables, Craddock was tightening the saddle girth on Fawn. "Good morning, my lady." He met her gaze squarely when he smiled and did not remove his cap or bow before her, which she imagined he might do for someone who was born to the peerage. It was the same forwardness he had treated her to when she'd first arrived at the estate and the servants were presented. She maintained an indifferent expression rather than smile back. She could not fool herself about her origins, but she could not like being shown disrespect.

"Good morning, Craddock. I see you have Fawn ready for me. How shall we begin our lessons?"

Craddock pulled the bridle over the mare's head and slipped the bit in the horse's mouth. "I thought we might go to the fenced-in paddock. I'll teach you to mount and will lead the horse as she walks around the circle, so you might get the feel for each other. When you are accustomed to riding at a walk, we may then attempt a trot, and go farther than the pasture with me on a horse next to you, if that pleases you."

Kitty was secretly relieved she would not have to begin

cantering out into the open fields on her first day. "I find that to be an agreeable plan."

She followed Craddock as he led the horse to the stable opening. He gestured to the mounting block. "Take my hand, my lady, and I will assist you into the saddle. Put your foot here on this stirrup, and I will give you a hand up. Slide your other leg next to the horse and bring it up to where the hook is. Wrap your leg around the hook … That's it. Now seat yourself comfortably."

Kitty had been on a pony a small number of times when she was a child, so some movements did come back to her. However, she couldn't get over the feeling that the horse was an unpredictable creature that could bolt at any moment, throwing her to her death.

"Here, hold the reins. Don't be afraid. I won't let go." Craddock held the bridle and pulled the horse forward a few steps.

Erasmus should oversee Sam's riding while their brother was still young. He was preoccupied with his business affairs, and she knew Sam could not be receiving regular lessons when he was still trailing Nurse everywhere with his younger cousins. It was one thing for Kitty not to have learned to ride; it was quite another thing for a young boy about to set out for Harrow. He would stick out and perhaps be teased mercilessly. She would write to Erasmus to make sure he saw to it.

As Fawn began to move forward, Craddock loosened his hold and walked at her side, and her heart rate picked up a notch. "Why is the horse bending so far forward? It feels like I'm about to fall." Kitty did not like showing her fear so readily, especially to someone who was practically a stranger, but she could not help herself.

"Fawn is only getting accustomed to her rider," he said, taking hold of the bridle again and pulling the horse's head up. "She's leaning down because it's easier, and you have not yet shown her who's mistress." He flashed Kitty a grin and started leading the horse in a slow circle around the fenced-in pasture. The horse began to move at a smooth gait that lulled Kitty into feeling more secure. They walked for some way in silence.

"How did you find yourself married to Lord Hayworth?" Craddock's blunt question pulled Kitty out of her thoughts. She looked down to give him a piece of her mind for his impertinence, but the words vanished when she saw his friendly look. It was with a twinge of discomfort, springing from guilt, that she noticed how handsome his features were when formed into such an easy smile. Perhaps he had not meant impertinence. It was certainly an overture of friendship of which she was sorely in need.

Kitty looked ahead, away from his mesmerizing eyes. "It was an arranged match between my brother and Lord Hayworth."

"*Hm.*" The groom put so much significance in the sound, she could not help but look at him for an explanation. "I did not think it could be a love match," he added.

Kitty should depress such pretension, and she most certainly would. But right now she had to know why he would say such a thing. What was it about Phineas and her that led to speculation, and was he the only servant speculating? "Why would you think such a thing?" she asked.

"You seem very careful with one another, I suppose." Before Kitty could tell him that it was none of his business, he went on quickly. "And lest you think me overly impertinent for a groom, I would like to tell you that you and I have friends in common."

"Do we?" She looked at him in astonishment. "Pray tell, whom?"

Craddock's lips curved upwards, a dimple appearing in his cheek. "The Boultons. I believe they are your neighbors in Bristol? Maria Boulton is my cousin, and she wrote to inform me that her neighbor would be marrying Lord Hayworth."

"Oh, what a wonderfully small world it is," Kitty exclaimed. It warmed her to have someone in her new life who was

familiar with her old. Perhaps that was also why his speech was not so different from hers. "Did you ever visit them in Bristol? We might've crossed paths—not that I ever went out all that much, apart from walking with my niece and nephews," she amended. Her breath clouded in the cold, but the exercise kept her warm and she did not feel it.

"I did visit two or three times, but my own interests and employment kept me away. I should have liked to have made your acquaintance"—he looked up and met her gaze—"under different circumstances."

Kitty furrowed her brows slightly. She wasn't entirely sure of his meaning, and whether he had not spoken in a way that approached impropriety. Surely he was not referring to meeting her when she was yet unmarried. In any case, since she *was* married and the matter was very much settled, it did not bear thinking of.

"Well," she hemmed, "I find it a relief to have someone connected to my family here in my new home." She smiled at him briefly, determined to keep things on a friendly level. After all, she might very well have mistaken a deeper meaning when he'd only wished to be neighborly.

"I have a plan to set up my own stables and buy and sell horses. I've made the right connections and am just working here until everything is settled." Craddock clucked for the mare to follow him as he turned around the pasture. "This is only a temporary employment."

"I see," Kitty replied, unsure of how to respond.

Craddock took her around the circle a few more times, asking questions about Bristol and her family and sharing about his cousin until she began to feel at ease. The saddle chafed at her legs, although she would not mention such a thing to anyone.

"I believe that is enough for today, my lady," Craddock said when they neared the stable, to her relief. They would not be doing another round. "And if I'm not mistaken, you have some chafing on your legs, and it will not do to let that worsen." She blushed at *his* mention and did not answer it.

"I thank you for my first lesson, and I'm looking forward to growing more proficient," Kitty said as he helped her down. "Then I might accompany my husband to visit the tenants." She turned to face the groom and caught a stiff turn of his lips.

"You will learn quickly, I am sure—most particularly with my help." His full smile was back in place, pulling deep dimples into his cheeks. He took off his hat and bowed before her, but somehow instead of showing respect, the gesture seemed playful, almost flippant.

Kitty gave a nod before turning away. She could not help but fear that the courteous gesture was nothing more than flirtation; and that was a dangerous game she had no interest in playing.

CHAPTER NINE

P hineas dismounted and handed the reins to Craddock, who took them without a word and led the stallion to his stall. The sun was beginning to set, and its dimming rays still lit the stable enough to set in relief the profile of the horses who peeked their noses out of the stalls. Phineas strode past them to go wash up before meeting Kitty for dinner. Upon crossing Fawn's stall, he turned back.

"How did the riding lesson go? Was Lady Hayworth at ease?" he called out to Craddock, who had exited the stall, holding the saddle.

"We did not go far, my lord. Just around the far pasture, and I walked at the horse's head to make sure Fawn would not bolt. Though I didn't think she would."

The groom reentered the stall to unhook the horse's bridle, and it gave Phineas the irritating sensation of having been dismissed by a mere servant. It did not sit well after his trying day of attempting to bring his tenants' houses to more livable conditions. Rather than utter hasty words that would come out too sharply, he left the stable and headed toward the estate. He would need to inquire after Craddock's employment details before deciding whether to keep him on.

Phineas did not have long to dress before dinner, and his desire to see Kitty quickened his steps. Today's discovery was distressing, and Phineas had a feeling he could confide in his wife and that her opinion on the matter would be valuable. He wasn't entirely sure why he thought that since they had not engaged in many conversations—and the ones they held were often fraught with emotion—but their discussions were authentic, and that was not something he had looked for in a wife.

Phineas did not cross paths with Kitty until he tapped at her room to take her down to dinner. When she opened the door to him, he found her ravishing in her simplicity. Would he never tire of looking at her? It needed one glance at the fine quality of her clothes to know that her brother was well-off. But Kitty's taste in selecting the colors which would best suit her complexion and the cuts he guessed to be the latest mode—though he was no expert in such matters—was a gift all her own. The combined effect of her fine gown, slender figure, and artful chignon was stunning. And when one of her curls fell out of the chignon and framed her face, Phineas had to hold himself back from reaching up to tuck it behind her ear.

Everything was off to a good start in this marriage, all things considered. Although he could not call it love—they hardly knew each other for that—he was particularly attracted to his wife, and that was something above and beyond what he had bargained for. Only one small problem needed to be settled before arriving at perfection. He had no idea how his wife felt about him.

"Shall we go to dinner?" he proposed, the corner of his mouth lifting along with his spirits as he rested his eyes upon her.

Her answering smile seemed more open than she had yet

bestowed upon him. Perhaps she had missed him today. He held out hope that Kitty was coming to be attached to him.

In the dining room, they sat in their usual places at the head and foot of the table. After a moment's consideration, Phineas got up from his seat and walked over to the right of where his wife sat at the foot of the table. The footman rushed over to bring the place settings. Phineas no longer wished to submit to the formality of dinner while waiting for their more informal stance at dessert. The dinner seemed insufferably long that way.

When they had eaten, and the dessert had been set down before the servants left, he offered her the plate of ratafia cakes. "How was your riding lesson today? I asked Craddock when I came in, but he did not give me a very detailed reply."

Kitty narrowed her eyes as she considered the cakes. Her hand brushed his as she selected one, and with the jolt that came from her touch, Phineas nearly dropped the plate. Had that been intentional?

"It was not as terrifying as I expected," she answered with a comical glint to her eye. Phineas laughed, as he thought she'd intended for him to do, but his mind was still on how soft her hands were. "Craddock walked at the horse's head, and I was not made to gallop on my first day."

"I should hope he would not make you do such a thing," Phineas replied. Surely her touch had been accidental. He would not read anything into it. "Do you have plans to ride again tomorrow?"

"We did not discuss it, as a matter of fact. But I plan to present myself at ten o'clock tomorrow morning and assume he will be expecting me. If he is not, it is of no matter. I will occupy myself in some other way."

"I will wish to ride with you, but perhaps that must wait until you are able to venture forth with a little more assurance." Phineas sipped his drink. "As for now, unfortunately, the repairs at the section of tenant houses will keep me fully occupied. I did not find the improvements there I had hoped for—at least not the progress I had been expecting."

Kitty looked at him in concern, and her eyes sparkled in the candlelight, warm and beguiling. Her reddish auburn hair gleamed in the soft glow. "Has anything happened today particularly? Or are you speaking of a more general problem?"

It was not in Phineas's nature to unburden himself to others. Not even at school with his closest friends did he reveal much of himself. And he certainly had never confided anything to his parents. The idea was laughable, since he was likely to receive either a rebuke or a lesson. But there was something so sincere in her expression, so inviting, he could not but respond.

"Mr. Ameson, my steward, had not carried out my instructions. He has not begun any of the repairs I ordered for him to make. True, there has not been much time to have done so after having received my letter. When I obtained the money from your dowry, however"—Phineas paused, suddenly conscious that this might be a delicate topic for Kitty. She showed nothing but interest, so he went on—"I gave explicit instructions to begin at least re-thatching the roofs as soon as possible because the cold will settle upon us quickly. I want the tenants to be warm enough and well cared for. Besides having concern for their basic human conditions, I am aware that they will work faithfully for the estate if they are content."

Kitty toyed with her spoon and tucked her lip between her teeth, a gesture he found endearing—and kissable. "Yes, your tenants need to be well taken care of. Do they have the food they will need for this winter? You said the estate had not been running very well." As she spoke, she turned Phineas's way and now her knee brushed his under the table. Phineas gulped. She moved again, releasing the contact, and he was sure her movements had no ulterior meaning behind them—not when her expression had not changed.

"I have not even got that far with Mr. Ameson," he said,

attempting to focus on their conversation and not where this *tête à tête* might lead if only she would give the signal. "To own the truth, I don't know precisely where things stand. Although I inherited this estate three years ago, I have not had the money to bring it into order. In addition, my father has been exigent about how much time I spend at his estate, which I will one day inherit. I do understand his motivation."

Phineas studied his hand holding the stem of the wine glass. "However, if I know my father, he will last for many, many more years, and I don't wish to be forever at his beck and call. I must have my own estate to look after, and I want to bring this one to self-sufficiency, so I can eventually pass it on to my…" He paused and looked at Kitty, prey to the longing and ridiculousness of what he was about to utter—"heir."

It seemed that Kitty's color rose, although it was difficult to discern between the candlelight and the glow of the orange flames flickering in the fireplace. She held his gaze for a moment, longer than she usually did, and his heart thudded in his chest. She looked away.

"I think it noble that you wish to improve upon the estate. It is a shame to let any estate go to ruin if there is a means to bring it about. Although I could not like the manner in which my fate was decided by anyone other than me—" She penetrated him with a speaking look that bordered on reproving, although he no longer felt the anger directed at him. He had even begun to agree with her. Phineas did not like his father dictating his every move. How could he expect his wife to feel any differently?

She went on. "If my settlement is my sale price, I prefer it to go to the functioning of an estate, making it solvent and taking care of the tenants in a way that gives them their dignity. After all, the dowry might just as easily have gone to gambling and drink if my brother had chosen less well for a husband. Any heir to an earldom would have done."

"That is high praise," Phineas said drily. She laughed, pulling a chuckle out of him. Her laughter was musical and light, and he stopped to watch the amusement play on her face until she grew conscious of his regard.

She breathed in and picked up the cake between her fingers but did not take a bite. "What will you do with Mr. Ameson? Had you been led to believe he was more serious in his affairs?"

"Truly, I reposed entirely too much confidence in him." Phineas frowned. "I suppose I did not have much choice in the matter, given how little time I had to oversee the estate and how little money I had to invest in it. However, now that I am able to provide the amount necessary to set the repairs in order, I can only see his tardiness as negligence. I have not yet told him, but he will have to be replaced. I suppose I shall have to go to Bath and speak with my father's man of business to help me find someone trustworthy since my own man is on leave."

There was a moment's silence before Kitty said, "Will you be leaving shortly?"

Phineas thought he detected disappointment, and it heartened him. "I truly should not delay the trip, but I believe I can stay only one night and come back the next day. That is, unless my father requires my assistance on some matter. I cannot know until I arrive." He furrowed his brows and inhaled. "I would invite you to come, but I fear I cannot entertain you there as I would like, and to travel again so soon after you have arrived here…"

"It is of no matter," she replied quickly. "I should like to continue to learn the run of things here. And yours is not a task that can be put off. Of course you must help your father if he has need of you." Kitty brushed her fingers and set her napkin on the uneaten cake. She had a habit of crumbling her sweets rather than eating them. "I will be perfectly content here."

Phineas nodded, relieved. The truth was, he was not ready for Kitty to become further acquainted with his parents until their own marriage was on a firmer footing. He was not sure what kind of welcome his wife would receive in his father's house, and their marital bonds needed to be firm.

It was growing late, and Phineas was reluctant to bring their conversation to a close, especially when he had known what it was to touch her bare hand and her knee. She had not spoken the words to release him from his promise, and he thought he knew what to expect. The suggestion to retire would simply mean the end of their time together for the evening. Still, he held out a glimmer of hope. Were they not coming to an understanding? Did they not have an ease in conversing that was not a gift shared by every couple? The candles were burning low, and still he could not say the words to end their meal.

"Did you receive any visitors this afternoon?" he asked.

Kitty's cheeks tinged pink. "None." She darted her eyes up at him and gave the ghost of a smile.

Phineas frowned. "How unusual. I would have thought the local families would have visited by now."

True, he did not have much experience with calling customs —it was usually his mother who handled such things, and he had never paid much attention. But he and Kitty had been in residence a couple of days, and the leading families would not have delayed in making his wife's acquaintance. Perhaps they did not know she was here? They hardly even knew Phineas because he was so rarely at Giddenhall, although that would change now.

"It would have been better for the families to come and leave their calling cards if you're not able to receive them than to risk offense by not coming. It is very strange they did not do so."

"Perhaps they are not pleased with your choice of a wife," Kitty replied and gave him another significant glance. He began to appreciate the way she could voice opinions with the expression in her eyes. "After all, I do not know who should be visiting me, but I imagine it is the gentry and not the merchants."

He looked at her and gave a slow shake of his head. "It would not be the merchants."

She raised her eyebrows and smiled faintly. "I fear we may have our answer. Do *you* know the neighbors?"

"I do not—not very well." Phineas glanced at Kitty from under his brows. She held his gaze, and he drank in the sight of her unadorned beauty. He wanted to take her to every house in the village himself just to make sure they recognized her quality. "Well, I suppose we shall wait and see. We have time before the Christmas holidays, and that is generally a season when people begin to be more charitable and welcoming." In any case, nothing could be done tonight.

The inevitable moment had come. "Shall we retire?"

She gave a nod, and the brisk manner in which she rose to her feet erased all cause to hope. They walked up the stairs in near silence, and Phineas brought her to her door. They stood outside of it, and he waited for her to say something, his heart rate picking up slightly. He was standing close enough to her to pick up a soft, unmistakably feminine scent and see the curve of her lips in the dim light. His feet were rooted to the spot.

A soft smile touched those lips. "I enjoyed talking with you over dinner." She turned to open her door and looked back at him.

"I also enjoyed it." Phineas stared at her an instant longer, noticing her hesitation. *Would she invite him in?* When her smile began to falter, Phineas saw that he had misread her intent. He bowed and turned toward his room, overcome with a sense of foolishness for having hoped. But he reflected on their conversation over dinner. It had been … comfortable. She seemed to care about what occupied his thoughts, and they had even laughed together. Try as he might, he could not imagine his parents having been able to do such a thing, even in the first blush of love.

CHAPTER TEN

Two days later, Kitty managed to catch Phineas at breakfast before he left by calling for Sterling an hour earlier than usual. If her aim was to spend time with him because it brought her pleasure, she kept that to herself, employing the excuse of desiring to speak with him on diverse topics, such as where he intended to find a new steward, what to do if none of the neighbors came to visit, and how much of the linens it was within her power to replace. Mrs. Morley had maintained a reserve with Kitty whenever they spoke, but she did disclose that the linens were near worn through, and that there were only two sets suitable for guests.

"I give you full run of the household," Phineas had said, flashing her a smile as he slathered butter on his roll. "You shall bring me your receipts, of course, to make sure we don't run into dun territory. But I believe you will do just as you ought." This he said with something so akin to a wink, her heart was insensibly lifted. It appeared they had found peace for the present, despite their different means for coming into the marriage, and that they would henceforth be friends. It was a glimpse at domestic felicity to which she had not dared aspire.

When the carriage was brought to the front, Kitty followed Phineas outside. He began to walk toward it but stopped after a few steps. Kitty lifted her eyes to his when he turned back, stood before her, and clasped her hand in his. He turned her hand to expose her wrist and pressed a kiss on her bare skin. When he raised his head and studied her face, she saw his eyes were more hazel than brown.

"Unless my father insists I prolong my stay, I will bid you *au revoir* for one day." Phineas bowed, his lips stretched in a smile. "Until tomorrow."

"Until tomorrow," Kitty repeated, her heart thumping as he climbed in the carriage and the driver pulled forward. Phineas had treated her with unaccustomed tenderness—affection she had never known, even in her childhood home—and her heart continued to beat painfully when the carriage was no longer in sight.

Kitty could not stand in the drive like a mooncalf wearing her sentiments for all the servants to see. It was time to demonstrate she was capable of running this household. Her husband's show of confidence in her at breakfast was an encouraging start, for he planned to let her run things the way she liked. And Kitty did indeed enjoy running a household. She would most particularly enjoy running a nursery. The notion brought a sharp pain of longing, and she quickened her steps into the house.

She distracted herself from Phineas's absence and the thought that she might face yet another day that brought no visitors, by seeking out Mrs. Morley and asking to examine the two tea services.

Mrs. Morley set down the quill she had been using to label preserves. "Of course, my lady. Right away." She glanced at the stack of unlabelled jars, as if affronted by the delay, and walked with a stately gait into the narrow hallway that branched off into the kitchen and led to the upstairs. When Kitty did not follow, the housekeeper paused and turned. "The tea service is kept in the chinoiserie cabinet in the breakfast room."

"Of course." Kitty started forward instantly, somewhat chastized. At home, their tea service was kept in the kitchen for easy washing.

The Spode blue and gold tea service was elegant and in perfect order, except for a slight wearing on the rims of certain cups and a tiny crack in the handle of the cream pot. She examined the Sèvres tea set, which was an interesting deep pink color with gold accents, and this one did not appear to show any wear.

"The Spode is generally used for lesser company," Mrs. Morley said, as she carefully lifted the tall cup from Kitty's hand. "The Sèvres is newer and has a more complete set. The dowager favoured the Spode, however, and rarely used the other."

"Have you inventoried the pieces?" Kitty asked, and received a look of reproof in return.

"Of course, my lady. You will find the list of items here." Mrs. Morley unlocked the narrow drawer in the cabinet and handed Kitty the paper. Kitty began to compare the Sèvres service with the list, but the weight of the housekeeper's stare became uncomfortable, and she replaced the inventory in the drawer.

"I will look this over at another time and will get the key from you when I am ready for it."

Mrs. Morley locked the cabinet and clasped her hands in front of her apron, waiting. Kitty was tempted to cower under the housekeeper's cold demeanor, but she was the mistress after all. "Since I've seen the silver and the linens, let us now go over the napery."

Mrs. Morley gave a cool nod and turned without a word to lead her to the linen cupboard. She opened it and turned to the portion dedicated to tablecloths and napkins. "These are all in good order, save this set here, which is growing threadbare. It is used for the grandest dinners and will need to be replaced."

Kitty touched the perfectly pressed and folded table linens on the shelf above, which appeared to be similar in quality. "Can we not use these in its place? We have bed linens to purchase and that must receive our first attention."

"My lady," Mrs. Morley answered, in a voice that bordered on disapproval. "You have perhaps not noticed that those are embroidered with green foliage on the corners. That is our Christmas napery."

"So it is," Kitty said, quietly, her brows drawn together. "But surely that does not prevent us from using them until something suitable may be bought."

A growing suspicion that her housekeeper was not overly pleased with the viscount's choice of a wife was born upon Kitty when Mrs. Morley stated with as much grandiloquence as a daughter of the peerage, "Most ladies know by instinct which napkins are to be used for the Christmas dinner, and that the cutlery showing the arms should be placed face down. But I suppose you are not to be blamed if you do not know these things."

Kitty pressed her lips together. Never before had she met with such insolence from a servant, but she did not think her husband's full confidence in her extended to firing faithful servants whose employment at the estate predated her. "Mrs. Morley," she answered evenly, "I was educated in the same manner as a gentleman's daughter. It is only that I did not know the customs of this estate."

It did not take long for Kitty to excuse herself from their inventory and pick up a load of sheets she thought could be saved with a little darning. There was no shame in doing such a domestic chore herself, and it was something she rather liked.

The concentration required would do much to soothe the ire that had built throughout the conversation with her housekeeper.

A knock resounded through the hall, and Kitty looked up, her heart thumping. At last, there was a visitor—and one who would hopefully provide her introduction into village society. Kitty heard the butler's footsteps as he went to answer the door. She folded the sheet she had been darning and tucked it out of sight with the other sheets behind the servant's door in the corner. Suddenly gripped by nerves, Kitty sat and gave a quick glance around the room to make sure everything was in order. If the neighbors had meant to let her know she was not welcome, she would not give them anything further to gossip about by having a mismanaged home.

Bexley entered the drawing room, carrying a card. He handed it to her, and Kitty read the name, gratified to see the name Phineas had mentioned. Mrs. Dutton and her daughter, Miss Lucretia Dutton. "Send them in. I am at home to visitors."

Minutes later, Mrs. Dutton and her daughter were ushered in, and Kitty rose to her feet to greet them. They smiled and curtsied as they assessed one another, and Kitty signaled to the departing butler to have tea sent.

Mrs. Dutton was a short woman with a heavy bust and small waist. Her daughter took after her, but the effect was less pronounced, and she had sweet blonde curls to her mother's severe black hair tied under her bonnet.

"We did not want to delay in coming to seek your acquaintance," Mrs. Dutton said, "but we've been frightfully busy. I imagine you have had little time to spare with your other visits?" Her raised eyebrows and penetrating look seemed to show her hope to the contrary.

Kitty briefly considered the idea of lying but thought the better of it. In such a small village, word was sure to get out that she'd had no visitors. "I am afraid there has been no one to see me as of yet. You are my first guests, and I'm very glad to make your acquaintance. Do sit down."

Mrs. Dutton's eyes widened as she sat on the embroidered silk couch. "You don't say? Not a one? Sometimes Society, even in a small village such as this one, can be quite vicious."

Kitty studied her, speculating, and thought she had taken this woman's measure. Mrs. Dutton was here to collect gossip for the rest of the village and leave behind any barbs she possibly could for Kitty to painfully pluck from her heart when the visit had concluded. She decided not to be so weak. "Do you know why I am being snubbed?"

Mrs. Dutton faltered, as she had clearly not expected such directness. It took her a moment before she was able to formulate her reply. "I am afraid I have no idea. Certainly nothing that would stop us from coming, as you can see for yourself." Kitty did not remind her that it had taken her a week before she'd finally made her visit.

The younger Miss Dutton seemed to be at pains to soften her mother's words. "Where do you come from, my lady?"

Kitty bestowed a smile upon her that was more natural than the one Mrs. Dutton had inspired. "I am from Bristol, where my brother runs a shipping company. This is how he and Lord Hayworth met."

"Very interesting, to be sure," Mrs. Dutton said, seizing the reins of the conversation. "We were certain the story of your betrothal must be vastly interesting for Lord Hayworth to have favored you over all the eligible maidens who could be found closer to home. Once we saw workmen coming into the estate, we realized, of course, his wife must be someone of substance."

Kitty leveled a gaze at Mrs. Dutton. She was being measured once again—and this time by someone who should have no say in Kitty's worth—sized up like some piece of merchandise that one decided to purchase or reject. Either Kitty would fit into the community or she would not, but she refused to give that power to anyone.

"Yes, it must seem that way from the outside, but ours was a love match." Kitty swallowed nervously, astonished that such a lie flew out of her mouth, and almost blushing to think what her husband would say if he heard it.

Mrs. Dutton opened her eyes wide and exclaimed, "Why, how marvelous. Not one of us would have guessed it. And how did you two meet?"

Kitty's mind was not very nimble, but she managed to conjure a most basic scenario. "It was at a private gathering of friends of my brother. Lord Hayworth was invited, and we were seated next to one another at the table. We found it very easy to converse, and our courtship started then."

"That is a lovely way to begin a marriage," Miss Dutton said with a soft smile. But she seemed to possess little power next to her wolf of a mother.

"How very astonishing," Mrs. Dutton exclaimed, the sound of gloating evident in her tone. "I am particular friends with Lady Leighton in Bath, who grew up on the estate nearest to mine. She said that Lord Hayworth's parents were simply amazed that such a match had taken place and without their consent. They were sure Lord Hayworth had intentions for … someone else."

Kitty directed her regard to Mrs. Dutton, her hands clenched tightly on her lap. "A man does not generally marry to suit his parents, I believe. Whatever hopes they may have had for him, he is a grown man, of age, and able to make the decision for himself—as is evidenced by his marriage to me."

Every smile became more fixed. The door opened, and the butler brought the tea tray in, and Kitty stood to open the tea cabinet for the leaves and sugar. However, Mrs. Dutton stood as well, giving Kitty no time to extend an invitation. "Well, we shall not overstay our welcome. In Society, I believe a short stay is preferable to a long one. Is your husband at home now? Mr. Dutton had some matter on which he wished to speak with him. Perhaps I may give my respects."

Kitty turned from the cabinet and clasped her hands. "No, Lord Hayworth had business in Bath, and he is gone these two days."

"Gone so soon in the marriage? That must be very hard on you," Mrs. Dutton said with spurious sympathy. "I will tell my husband to come at the end of the week, so that he is sure to catch him."

"I am sure my husband will be delighted to welcome him. He expressed surprise that so few people from the village had come by to felicitate him on his marriage. He will be eager to see more of his neighbors as soon as the visits may be arranged." She met Mrs. Dutton's stare with an even one of her own. She would not back down before such a woman.

The three women curtsied, and when the guests turned to leave, Miss Dutton sent Kitty a soft, apologetic smile that promised, if not peace, then at least not outright war. When they left, Kitty could not sit back down. Her mind was in a turmoil. She was not accustomed to being treated to such condescension. Her brother was a respected member in Bristol society and even the Prince Regent had requested an audience with him once about a naval matter, although it had not been as long as Erasmus would have liked and had not been repeated. Everyone had always looked up to the Stokes family for their connections.

Surely her husband could not have guessed she'd have to endure such treatment, or he would not have left her to face them alone. Although there had been no very great affection in her home, Kitty had not been raised to think so little of herself.

She stared at the closed door and listened to the sounds of the Duttons taking their leave. She supposed if they made no friends here, it did not matter so very much. In any case, Midlington would eventually be their home. However, since she did not expect much better treatment there, the thought did little to elevate her spirits.

She had forgotten to speak to Craddock about her lesson, and she was just about to do that when the butler brought the mail in. There was a letter for her, which she took with eager hands. She had never felt more out of her element than she did today between Mrs. Morley's treatment and that of Mrs. Dutton's.

"Thank you, Bexley." Kitty sat and slid open the seal on the letter. The direction was in Mary's hand, and Kitty thought it decent of her to write. She had wondered if Mary would be able to find time to return her letter.

Kitty scanned the missive, which was filled with news about her niece and nephews. At the end, some small space had been allotted to her younger brother, and she drank the words in eagerly, realizing just how much she had missed Samuel.

Mary has allowed me a very little room in her letter, it said, *and said I must use my best penmanship. I wanted to ask if I might come visit you? I believe I will not be a trouble. And I am not to leave for school for some months yet. Answer me quickly please. Yours, Samuel.*

Kitty set the letter on her lap. With Erasmus's warning, she had set aside any hopes of having Samuel come, but now that she and Phineas had begun spending time together... Dare she ask her husband? If he said no, her disappointment would probably put more distance between them, and she thought they had been growing friendly—familiar, even. However, there was only one way she could know, and that was to ask. She resolved to do so when he returned from Bath.

She picked the letter up to read it again, taking comfort in the few words that Mary wrote, and most particularly the plea from Samuel. Time passed in her musing, and she forgot all about her lesson until the shadows grew long and the silence overwhelmed her. Kitty sat up with a start. *Oh dear.* She hoped Craddock would pardon her forgetfulness. Her lesson would have to be for another day.

CHAPTER ELEVEN

Phineas let his thoughts wander with the sway of the carriage. When Kitty stood on the driveway at their parting, she had tightened her hand in his; and when he'd turned her hand to kiss the inside of her wrist, her skin was as soft as silk. Their eyes met, and he saw in hers the same pull of attraction that he felt. It had taken one look in those eyes for him to want to pull her into his arms, never mind the servants.

He scarcely noticed the ride to Bath and thought about nothing but Kitty—her expressions, her voice, her figure, her laugh … His desire for his wife might have felt like an obsession were it not for the fact that she *was* his wife. There was no second-guessing about whether she would have him—no threat of pain. Phineas had already won her, and he needed only conquer the last stronghold before she was his. If only it did not seem quite so insurmountable.

What would their children look like? Would they have her serious gaze? If they did, they would be the sweetest things. Perhaps his son would have his tousled hair with that tendency to stick up in odd directions, but surely one day some woman would love him anyway despite that? Phineas laughed at himself for such a ridiculous notion—worrying about whether his future sons would find love. In any case, there was much to give him hope for his own marriage.

He did not stop at his parents' home before going directly to Mr. Parkson, his father's man of business. His own man, Carter, had gone on leave to care for his ailing parents and was unavailable. Fortunately, Phineas knew Parkson well, having frequently consulted him on Midlington affairs his father had left in his care. It was a simple matter, Parkson assured him, to find a steward willing to relocate to Giddenhall, and one who could be relied upon. Phineas could leave the matter in his hands, and Parkson would send the new steward to present himself the following week. That accomplished, Phineas set out for his parents' townhouse.

"Good afternoon, my lord. It is a pleasure to see you." Seamus took his hat, cane and gloves. "Might I felicitate you on your marriage? It appears to agree with you. You look very well."

"Thank you for your kind wishes. As you say, I am doing well." Phineas smiled, adding, "Are my parents at home?"

"Your mother is in the drawing room, I believe, and your father is in his study. Shall I inform them both that you are here?"

"Please do. Have someone bring my portmanteau to my room, and have Wilson come take care of my coats and boots. I have not yet engaged a valet at Giddenhall, and I must confess the absence is beginning to show." Phineas waited in the entry hall until the butler returned with the news that his father was busy for the moment. However, his mother would be happy to see him in the drawing room.

When he entered, his mother was already on her feet, and she stepped forward. "Has your … wife accompanied you here?"

"No, Mother. I would not have brought her without first

sending you word. I simply came on a matter of business and would like to stay the night if it will not inconvenience you."

His mother exhaled and resumed her seat. "I suppose it is good that you have come without her. Then we may talk freely. Please sit. I have asked Seamus to bring us some tea."

Phineas gave a tight smile. "We could have spoken freely in front of my wife as well."

"Of course. It is only that she is so newly attached to the family. She does not know our customs, and I believe it will be more comfortable this way."

Phineas crossed one leg over the other and leaned back in his chair. He could not resist the temptation to talk about Kitty. "Do you not find her lovely? She has a genteel air about her."

His mother's gaze flitted to the window, her expression masked. "It is true, she did not smell of the shop, as I must say her brother certainly did. Honestly, Phineas. I do not see how you could have offered for her without having seen even a portrait. One look at her brother ought to have scared you."

Phineas experienced an odd mix of anger and the desire to laugh. His mother's sentiment had only echoed his own. Marrying Kitty sight unseen, a penance Phineas imposed upon himself—although Carter had thoroughly investigated the match—was one he could not explain. However, he did not like any aspersions cast on his wife.

"I had my own purposes for wishing to marry her, and looks did not come into the equation. I trusted Carter's investigation into the matter. As it turns out, I was more than pleasantly surprised, for I was willing to settle for much less." That last sentence slipped out without his intending it, and he regretted it instantly.

His mother shook her head. "Now, this is what I do not understand. Why would you think about settling for less? We had planned a very good match for you—one whose face you have beheld, and whose family you have known. Her dowry was not to be despised, although it was likely not as much as what you've earned by marrying Miss Stokes."

Phineas frowned at his mother's stubbornness. "*Miss Stokes* is now Lady Hayworth. And if you must know, her settlement was thrice what I would have received from Lady Jane."

He was not able to continue before his mother gasped, and her hand flew to her mouth. "Three times? It is no small wonder that you did indeed offer for her."

Phineas tightened his lips and studied his clasped hands. "I did not mean to tout her portion. That is not the main reason I am satisfied in my marriage. Although, I must say that the settlement has helped tremendously to improve the affairs at Giddenhall." He sighed. "I will own that I did not wish to marry Lady Jane and be slave to the whims and wishes of our two fathers. I wanted something for myself, and that is why I arranged this marriage with Kitty's brother. However, my satisfaction is with my bride more so than her purse."

The tea tray arrived, and Phineas was spared hearing whatever his mother would have answered, which would not likely honor Kitty for her proper worth. He was not sure his mother was capable of such a thing, considering how highly she rated bloodlines. His father, who was of a much more mercenary nature, would undoubtedly know and appreciate what Phineas had accomplished. The advantageous settlement was the only excuse he could give his parents that they would understand. He could not tell them that, despite his low expectations of such a thing happening, the beginnings of friendship and romantic interest were blossoming with his wife.

His mother began preparing the tea when his father entered the room. She greeted Phineas's father with cordiality but no warmth. "Midlington, would you care for some tea?"

"Yes, I'll have a cup." He looked at his son, and Phineas got to his feet.

"Hello, Father. I am here until tomorrow. I needed to speak

with Parkson about getting a new steward, as Carter has gone to see his ailing father. He said he would send someone to me next week."

"Your visit is timely," his father replied, sitting. "I have several matters to discuss with you regarding those investments that are not going as well as can be hoped. We have to decide what to do. There are some things we must go over with Parkson as well. It should only take a couple of days to cover everything."

Phineas resumed his seat. "Father, I don't have a couple of days. My intention was to return to Giddenhall tomorrow." After glancing at his father's expression, he amended his plan. His father's reliance on him was not something he could change overnight. "I can stay one extra day, but not more than that."

"So I suppose Midlington is of no interest to you now?" His father managed to sound haughty and petulant at the same time. "I shall have to see to all the affairs myself."

"When things are put in order at Giddenhall, I will be very happy to focus my attention once again on Midlington. It is my intention to continue to oversee things there, so that I might learn the estate." Phineas leveled a glance at both his parents. "I only hope that my wife will be welcome as well."

Lord Midlington tugged at his coat sleeves and folded his arms. "To be frank, I am still irritated with you for this whole affair. If only you had done as I suggested, you would now be married to Lady Jane—a woman who would cause you no embarrassment. As it stands, I have already endured snide comments about the hasty marriage, and the manner in which you ran off afterward. There was not even a wedding breakfast to celebrate it."

Phineas cast his gaze through the windows on the far side of the room to hide his annoyance. "You said you could not stomach the idea of sitting down with the likes of Stokes and his family for a wedding breakfast. And now you tell me the *ton* gossips over the lack of a celebration. I am afraid we cannot have it both ways."

His mother, handing a cup of tea to her husband, added, "Did you know that Phineas has negotiated the obscene sum of seventy-thousand pounds for Kitty's settlement?"

His father dropped his spoon onto the saucer with a loud clatter. "Seventy-thousand? Why did you not think to tell me this before? You have done well in that, at least, although I still say that the bloodline will be clouded by having contracted outside the peerage."

"I am not the first man to have married for money." Phineas glanced at his father and decided to speak his mind. "And as I was telling Mother, I believe myself to be fortunate in my choice of a bride. There is nothing in Kitty's demeanor or speech to cause embarrassment. In fact, in many ways she is superior to some of the women who have been brought up in the *ton*. Her own governess was the daughter of a baron who had fallen on hard times."

"Which one?" his mother asked curiously.

Phineas stirred sugar into his tea, and he looked up. "I did not think to ask."

His mother raised an eyebrow and adjusted the teapot on the platter so it was in the center. "It may all be a hoax," she said, "to make her look more genteel than she truly is."

Phineas set his cup down abruptly. "If you cannot see for yourself that she has a very genteel manner, I shall not try to convince you. I only desire—if you are to receive her—that you will do so with a modicum of respect. She does not deserve your condemnation."

His father folded his hands. "When do you plan to bring her to Bath? I suppose we shall have to present her in some way to Society, so that everyone believes we were behind this match from the start."

Phineas almost could not contain his ire. His parents were so set on appearances. However, there was truth in what he said, and Phineas would not stop his father from doing something noble, even if it were for selfish reasons. "I believe that would be a good idea. Perhaps we should arrange to come to Bath in one month's time so you may present her. That will allow us to participate in some of the assemblies and be home in time for Christmas."

His mother furrowed her brows. "You intend to celebrate Christmas with her then? You have always celebrated Christmas with us."

Phineas did not particularly like their cold, stiff manner of celebrating Christmas. There was an exchange of gifts and stilted dinner conversation, but it was not the Christmas he had always longed for—the Christmas he hoped to celebrate for the first time with his new wife. They would create their own traditions. "I believe Christmas will be better spent at our home, since it is our first one together. We will have much to do at Giddenhall even outside the celebrations."

His father pulled out his pocket watch and glanced at it. "I don't have any more time to spend sitting here chatting. Now that you're seeing less to the affairs of Midlington, I have much more to do. However, you may bring Kitty, and we will host a ball in her honor. We must introduce her at the Pump Room and get subscriptions for the Upper and Lower assembly rooms. That will show everyone we are perfectly satisfied with this match, and it ought to stop tongues wagging. You will stay here, of course."

Phineas took a long drink of his tea as he figured out how to answer. Certainly they could stay at his parents' house. But it wouldn't have the intimacy he was hoping for, especially if they were to make progress in their own relationship. However, it would not do to set his parents at odds. "Very well."

His father left with a request for Phineas to come find him before dinner, and Phineas spent another half-hour talking with his mother. She spoke about such trivial subjects, he was able to think about Kitty without losing the thread of the conversation. Her hair and eyes floated before his vision, and his heart gave a lurch. He tried to remember her scent. He thought about the shape of her nose, her slender fingers. When his thoughts once again turned to pulling Kitty into an embrace, Phineas forced his mind to the matter at hand. This schoolboy crush he appeared to be experiencing at his ripe—and married—age was not productive.

After his mother had said everything she wished to say, studiously avoiding the subject of his wife, Phineas made his escape, claiming he had errands to run.

His initial reasoning for leaving the house was simply to breathe fresh air and walk off his frustration at being so newly married and *not* currently with his wife. When he came to his parents' home, it was as if he were still their boy to order about. As if he had not just taken this monumental step in his own life. He found the experience exasperating, to say the least.

He walked without purpose around Queen's Square then headed down Wood Street without a clear idea of where he was going. He had no desire to go to the Pump Room and bump into all the local quizzes who would surely have something to say about his marriage. On the other side of the street, a couple walked in the same direction. He didn't recognize them but could tell from their appearance that they were rather well-to-do. Perhaps they had not lived long enough in Bath to have formed acquaintances with local Society. The woman had her hand in the man's arm, and they leaned in close as she whispered something in his ear. The couple laughed, and Phineas saw a look of adoration on the woman's face as she studied her husband. Only a recently betrothed couple could demonstrate such affection.

The woman stopped and called out. "Nurse, take care. Matthew will get his breeches soiled, and we are to visit his grandmother this afternoon with no time to change beforehand."

Phineas peered ahead to where "nurse" was in charge of two young children. So … this couple had been married for some years now to have produced two children, the eldest of whom was breeched. Yet the husband and wife still looked upon each other with obvious affection. A desire to have such a marriage for himself swept over Phineas—one of such great longing he turned his face away. Their domestic scene was almost too intimate to look upon.

What could he do to win Kitty over? To show her that she mattered to him? Never mind that he had married her for practical purposes, he was fully in this union now and had no regrets—nor desire for another.

"Hayworth!"

A man approached, whom Phineas could not identify with the sun at his back until the man grew nearer. His face was lit in a broad smile.

"Robert Bromley." Phineas smiled in return. "It has been ages."

"Not since Cambridge. We've recently moved here so my wife could be near her ailing mother. I heard you are married now, as well. Allow me to shake your hand." Bromley reached out and clasped Phineas's hand, adding, "Is your wife here in Bath?"

Phineas smiled at the pleasure of hearing the words "your wife" and the novel experience of seeing someone happy for him. He shook his head. "She is at Giddenhall. I did not like it, but I needed to hire another steward, and the business could not wait."

"Well, fortunately Bath is not far. Do not forget to bring her some gift when you return to let her know you thought of her while here."

Phineas looked up, surprised. "Is that what I should do?" The words came out before he could think the better of it, and he groaned inwardly. What a way to show that he had absolutely no idea how to be a husband. Bromley must take him for a simpleton.

His friend merely laughed. "It's a good thing you've run into me. I've been married these two years now, and I have experience. Yes, most certainly bring her a gift. You will see that it makes her happy—and if your wife is anything like mine, it won't be the gift, it will be that you thought of her when you were away."

Well ... in for a penny, in for a pound. If Phineas was going to look doltish, he may as well get all the information he could while he was at it. "And what should I get her?"

"You poor fool." Bromley took the sting out of his words by grinning and clapping Phineas on the back. "You have a long road of learning ahead of you, but have no fear. You will get it eventually. Buy her something that lets her know you've thought of her. Something you think she will like. You must know a bit of her tastes by now."

Phineas managed a smile. He should know her tastes by now, but he wasn't so sure he did. When he remained silent, Bromley studied him more closely. "Well, you're headed in the right direction. The shops are that way. If you're looking for a modiste, my wife thinks Mrs. Laurent is the best. She's on Union Street. You could try Franklin Morris, who does portraits and landscapes. He has a gallery with some ready-made paintings a few shops farther on. Other than that, there are no less than three jewelery shops to choose from."

Phineas, armed with this crucial information gave a genuine smile. "I thank you. This should set me up nicely. I will be bringing Kitty to Bath in a couple of weeks. Perhaps we might meet up then if you and your wife are available."

"With pleasure," Bromley said and took his leave. Phineas had vaguely heard about Bromley's wedding when it had occurred, but since such a thing had not at all been in his own plans, Phineas had not paid it any mind. Now things were different.

He entered the first store, and when the modiste stepped forward with her assistant, both assessing him with eager smiles, he knew an impulse to run out. He stood his ground manfully. "I would like to buy something for my wife."

"Very good, sir. I am certain we may be of help. She did not come with you?"

"No, I thought to bring them as gifts for her." Phineas looked around, hoping something appropriate might leap out at him in the way of a gift.

"I see." The modiste gestured toward a table with bolts of fabric arranged, it seemed, according to thickness. "Are you looking for a morning dress or an evening gown? Does your wife ride?"

Phineas almost gasped. That was the very idea. "My wife does ride," he answered with confidence. "As a matter of fact, I should like to get her a few riding habits. Can you help?"

"When can you bring your wife in so that we may take her measurements?" The modiste looked at him expectantly.

This was a difficulty Phineas had not entertained. Of course she would need to be measured. "She is not currently in Bath. I would just like to buy her a few gifts, and when we come next month, I can bring her in to be measured."

The modiste bit her lip and looked down at the fabric, considering. "*Hmn.* I see. Although we are not in the habit of giving fabric to have the dresses made up elsewhere, I might make an exception in this case. The draper is on the other side of Bath, and it will put you to a great deal of trouble to go there." She smiled at him. "Your wife can come when she's in town and be measured for any gown she wishes. Here are the cloths suitable for riding, and if you tell me her complexion and what pleases you, I will give you suggestions."

Phineas explained about her red hair that had hints of brown and gold, and when he came to her pale skin and brown eyes, he stopped short. The modiste and her assistant appeared perfectly serious, but he could not help but feel they were laughing at him for his obvious calf love, especially when he let fall that he wanted one fabric in a color to match her hair, another her skin, another her eyes… Together they chose five different fabrics for riding, and Phineas pulled out his card and handed it to the modiste. "You may send the purchases and bills to this address."

She glanced at the card, and her eyebrows lifted just slightly. "We will do so right away, my lord. If it pleases you to purchase matching hats, you may bring these swatches of fabric to the milliner, who is across the road, a bit farther. Tell him I have sent you."

Phineas left the modiste with his swatches and walked with purpose to the milliner's shop where an assortment of caps and bonnets were displayed. When he showed the swatches of fabric and explained what he was looking for, the clerk quickly found fetching hats to match all the fabric. Phineas had no trouble imagining his wife wearing them. These were also sent to his father's residence.

Following the milliner was the art gallery where, to Phineas's astonishment, he discovered among the landscapes a painting of Bristol overlooking the wharf. It looked very like the street where Stokes lived. He bought it immediately, wanting Kitty to gaze upon the scene of her childhood, so she would not be lonely for it. The painting was large and unwieldy, and he ordered to have that sent to his father's home as well.

A sense of foolishness followed him as he left the gallery. His father would have something to say about all these packages that were arriving for Phineas. Still, he walked even farther to the jeweler. He would stop at this one last place. Inside, he looked over each set of jewels the clerk showed him and settled on the yellow and green sapphires, the green of which reminded him of Kitty's wedding dress. The chain of the necklace was gold, which would be pretty against her neck. And yellow was a color of autumn, which would suit her to perfection.

Phineas had them wrapped up, and he tucked them in his pocket before heading to his parents' home. It was growing late. He had spent all this time outdoors and in the shops, but he now walked with brisk steps against the cold. There was something good and right in showing his wife how much he valued her. He could not wait for her to know it.

CHAPTER TWELVE

Kitty's new life, as wife to a viscount in a strange estate, in a strange village, had not had a promising beginning. She had met with resistance from both her housekeeper and Mrs. Dutton, having expected it from neither. She well knew the loss of freedom she was likely to have as a wife negotiated for convenience rather than sought by love. What she did not expect was the lack of respect shown her—a thing she had never experienced in her small but esteemed former circle. How odd that the thing she feared the most—being married to a stranger —ended up being the thing she most cherished. And the thing she took for granted—respect and a degree of honor from the servants, at the very least, if not the local families—was withheld from her.

Kitty missed Phineas. She could only describe her mood as despondent when he didn't return the next day as she'd hoped. That was another odd sensation—feeling incomplete when someone wasn't there. Perhaps it was simply because he was the only person she could talk to as an equal, and his conversation had been surprisingly agreeable. He was not above showing himself interested in learning her views. This was something to which she was not accustomed, for neither her brother nor her father had ever shown the slightest interest in what she had to say. Between the sullen housekeeper and the veiled hostility of her guests, Kitty had no one that entered into her feelings. The loneliness she was used to. The animosity she was not.

It was time for her riding lesson with Craddock. So far, she had not missed a morning since her first lesson, except for the day when she had decided it might interfere with her husband's departure and her meeting with Mrs. Morley. Considering how things had gone with the housekeeper, she would have done better to have gone riding. In their lessons, she and Craddock had grown more familiar to a certain degree, and the groom had succeeded in making her laugh and forget for a minute that she was in a household where the housekeeper did not esteem her very much, and the local families were not overly desirous of meeting her.

Today, Craddock would be riding next to her on his own horse instead of walking and leading hers, and they would venture farther on the path that wound around the estate and through the woods that encircled it. They set out at a comfortable pace, and the conversation sprang up more easily between them when riding side by side.

"I have had news from my sister-in-law, which should not be astonishing, I own. But with Mary it is. She is not overly fond of me."

Craddock held a rope attached to Fawn's cavesson, and he gave a gentle tug when Fawn threatened to fall behind. "Mrs. Stokes, is it? I believe I have met her once. My cousin invited her to tea while I was there." Craddock shot Kitty a measuring glance. "She seems an unfriendly sort. Spoke about her children."

Kitty did not want to throw her own sister-in-law to the wolves, so she merely shrugged. "She is not so very bad. It is true she concerns herself with her own children and the affairs of her household, but I suppose that should not be surprising. However, her household interests did not extend to me. That is why I was all the more delighted to receive a letter from her with news of my niece and nephews, whom I miss dreadfully—and my brother was given space to write, as well."

"You mean Stokes? Mary's husband?" Craddock clarified.

She shook her head. The thought of Erasmus taking the time to write made her want to laugh. "No, my younger brother, Sam. He will be heading off to Harrow next autumn and has asked if he might come here to visit. I hope it might be arranged."

Craddock gestured to the left. "We will follow this path for it is smoother, and the horses are less likely to be spooked by a rabbit darting across the road or some such thing." She followed his lead, and the conversation turned to trite subjects as they rode on the path that eventually circled back toward the estate. She relaxed as she listened to his Bristolian accent, only slightly different from Somerset and Wiltshire. It sounded familiar and like home, and Kitty could almost fill in the gaps and add affection where there had been none just from its musical lilt.

She had forgotten their earlier topic of conversation until he said, "Do you think your husband would allow your brother to come and visit? You being so newly married?"

Kitty breathed in the brisk air and looked over to where the meadow stretched and sloped downward. There was a line of trees far in the distance. "I cannot know until I ask him," she replied. "I shall have to do so."

"So he does entertain your requests?" Craddock glanced sideways at Kitty, his gaze assessing. The thought flashed through her mind that perhaps this friendly conversation was not entirely proper between mistress and servant—discussing her husband's affairs with the groom, never mind that he was her neighbor's cousin.

"I have no reason to believe he would do otherwise," she

said, her gaze forward. She hoped he would sense the inappro-priateness without her needing to wound him by a snub.

"He is an unusual member of the peerage, then." Craddock trained his gaze ahead, his posture and voice easy, as if he were a peer himself, or a gentleman coming to court her, rather than a groom. "I had guessed yours was an arranged marriage that gave little promise for happiness. There is small chance of having an understanding like you might find with someone from your own set. Surely you must have turned down several offers?"

Kitty pressed her lips together. She would not speak about her offers. As it stood, there had been one, and as wholly ineli-gible in her mind as it had been unwelcome. However, this was not a subject to discuss, no matter how connected she was to the groom.

After some silence, Craddock looked up at the canopy of bare branches stretching over the road and sighed. "I suppose I must ask your forgiveness. I am being impertinent with my questions."

Kitty focused on the bobbing head of her horse before answering. His questions had crossed a line, but he had apolo-gized. He did seem to come to her in the guise of a friend, and she had so few of those now. "It is kind of you to concern your-self with me," she said at last. "However, I will say that I don't believe my husband to be an ogre."

"No, he is not that. He may not be distinguished looking, but he is not so repulsive as an ogre." Craddock laughed, and she was struck by the air of coldness underneath his handsome features.

Kitty furrowed her brows. She supposed in objective study, Craddock was by far the more handsome of the two with his even features, glinting regard and masculine jaw. But Phineas was distinguished looking. Perhaps his natural expression was one of brooding, but his smile lit his face and reached even his eyes. She would have to see that he smiled more often.

Not distinguished looking. The words continued to echo in the silence, grating like vinegar on a wound. Perhaps that was the measure used by a man such as Craddock, who had been blessed with more than the ordinary share of physical attraction. But her husband was certainly distinguished looking, at least in her eyes. She could not let the claim go unchecked.

"He is not repulsive, no," she replied with a small smile, causing Craddock to glance at her again. He reached over as they neared the stables and steered the reins, his gloved hands touching hers. She knew an impulse to pull away, but she did not want to make a scene. He was her instructor after all, and there was nothing so inappropriate in that.

Once inside the stables, Craddock slid off his horse and latched the reins around the peg on the stable door. "Here, allow me to assist you," he said.

Kitty sat without moving for a moment, unsure how she was to dismount. Her thighs were chafed and her legs were very sore. This was the farthest they had gone yet, and she was not used to this particular exercise. However, she could not remain sitting on the horse. With a deep breath, she lay her hand on the one he held out and slid to the ground. Her feet stinging with pins and needles and her knees weak, Kitty found her legs could not hold her, and she stumbled forward. Craddock caught her around her waist.

She was shocked into inaction at their nearness and her knees too feeble from riding for her to pull away. Craddock bent his head down and caught her gaze, his smile too intimate for what their situation could allow. She opened her mouth to speak and pushed off from his chest at the same time. Her attempt was far from effective.

"My lady." A familiar, albeit icy, voice reached Kitty, and she turned and saw her husband standing in the entrance of the stable.

Phineas! He must have breakfasted early and left Bath immediately afterward. The look in his eyes was hard and glittering, so wholly unlike anything Kitty had seen in him before. What must her husband think? Phineas doubted her innocence. How could he not when he came upon such a picture? His frowning gaze caused her own guilt to prick at her. Perhaps she was not quite so innocent, having allowed such familiarity to grow between her and Craddock. She tried to respond calmly.

"My lord, how glad I am to see you safely returned. Might I request your assistance? My ride has been longer than I'm accustomed, and I fear my legs will not hold me."

After an instant's pause, Phineas bowed and moved her way.

"Craddock," he said curtly, as he passed the groom. He held out his arm, and Kitty put her hand in it. Using her husband's arm for support, she left the stable on shaky legs that did not entirely have to do with having ridden for two hours.

They walked out of the stables into the bright sun. Their feet crunched over the frozen ground and Kitty's nose smarted from the cold air. It seemed it would not be long before there was snow, although it was early in the season for that. They were silent, and Kitty felt her husband's anger through his tense muscles and the brisk stride to which she had to hurry to keep up. She ought to say something, to defend herself, because she was certainly innocent. Phineas likely drew some conclusion over her proximity to Craddock, but he should give her the benefit of the doubt. Perhaps she was not a lady in the sense of having been born to the gentry, but she was certainly raised as one.

However, the silence could not continue. She had to say something. "Was your journey a successful one?"

"It was." She thought the clipped reply would be all he

offered her, but Phineas added, "I have a steward who will join me next week."

Her husband slowed his pace somewhat, perhaps at last realizing Kitty had trouble keeping up. She strove for a topic that could ease them into the natural conversation they'd had before he left. She missed it. "My riding lessons have gone well. I have progressed to riding outside the pasture."

"So I see." His voice had reverted to its harsh tone and was now tinged with awful irony.

A surge of irritation welled up in Kitty's breast. He was set on punishing her. Should not a gentleman have more trust in his wife? Still, she strove for reconciliation by keeping to more neutral topics. "I have gone over various housekeeping duties with Mrs. Morley and have made some small changes." She did not think it necessary to add that the housekeeper treated her with barely concealed disdain. They were nearing the manor now, and Kitty had the unreasonable fear that if they reached the house without understanding one another, all was lost.

"That is good," was the only answer he gave. All would be lost.

They climbed the stone steps, and before they reached the top, Phineas paused and looked at her. His eyes had lost some of their hardness, but they were still veiled and distant. "I have purchased a few necessities for you. I will see that the footman brings them to your room." He continued the rest of the way up the stairs, and the butler opened the door from within. "I have much to see to," he continued. "I will be in my study if you need anything." Once inside, he dropped his arm and slid away from her. Her own arm dropped to her side.

Kitty had been so looking forward to her husband's return, and this was not the welcome she'd hoped for. She did not know how to bridge the gap. It seemed like such a trivial, ridiculous thing to confess that nothing had happened with the groom. It would almost make her seem guilty to have to defend herself in this way. And she had needed Phineas's support, not his condemnation. No, begging his understanding was not something she could or would do.

The butler was looking at her strangely, and Kitty realized she was standing, lost in thought, in the semi-darkened hallway. She turned and went up the stairs. Perhaps if she rang a bell, someone would bring a tea tray to her room. Maybe there were at least one or two servants loyal enough to her to do her bidding.

A short while later, Sterling brought her a platter of tea, and there were cookies as well, and the two restored Kitty's comfort. Sterling was not warm, but she did not openly rebel against Kitty. No footman had arrived with any of the items Phineas had thought her in need of, and she had had time to wonder what they might be. A full wardrobe accompanied her, and Kitty could not imagine what he thought she lacked. Perhaps he had bought her books, thinking to educate her. Apparently, his opinion of her did not run overly high if he thought she was so ill bred as to engage in some dalliance the minute he left the estate. She set her cup and saucer down with force, and the porcelain clinked on the tray.

An hour later, Kitty heard a knock, and she opened the door. There was not one, but three footmen bringing in packages for her. Her eyes widened as she stepped aside to make way. "You may set those things on the table near the fireplace." The three footmen did as she bid and closed the door behind them when they left.

Kitty examined the packages. One of the objects was rather large and was wrapped in cloth. She pulled at the string, and it opened to reveal a square gilded frame that was the perfect size for where the wall was bare above the chest of drawers. The painting was heavy, but she was able to pick it up and lean it against the table and stand back to look at it. Her breath caught in her throat. It was a painting of Bristol, not far from where she lived at her brother's house—a portion of the wharf she sometimes walked with Sam and her niece and nephew. She blinked several times, prey to a mix of emotions that encompassed nostalgia and a strange vulnerability. Her husband had not purchased a necessity, but rather an exceptionally thoughtful gift. And he had thought of her when he was in Bath.

Now she eagerly went to the other packages. There was one that had several yards of cloth, made of a stiff fabric that she could only surmise was to be used for riding habits. It was too thick for anything else. She fingered the cloth and lifted one piece after the other. She knew each color would fit her perfectly, but it was astonishing that he should have had such foresight. And they were of an exquisite texture. A box contained a fetching hat that matched one of the yards of fabric perfectly, and the other boxes revealed various hats fulfilling the same purpose. They were all meant for riding.

Kitty was confused. *He had said necessities.* True, she eventually would have had other habits made up because she did not have enough for the amount of riding she was doing. But there was a great deal of thought that went into these gifts, and they showed he approved of her riding. So why had he treated her coldly when he interrupted her lesson, which—if she had correctly interpreted his gifts—was a thing he approved of? It was the scene with the groom he didn't like, but that was not her fault, and he should have known it. And Kitty did not know him well enough to broach the subject.

She sat on the upholstered armchair looking at the gifts strewn about her, touched beyond words that he had gone to all this trouble for her. Why had he called them nothing but necessities? Why had he not given them to her himself? He could have watched her open the gifts.

It was perhaps for the best. She would not have wanted him to witness her emotion upon seeing all these treasured items bestowed upon her. Erasmus had always given her free hand to purchase what she liked, but no one had ever purchased a gift for her, except occasionally on some birthdays. Not even all of them—some had been forgotten entirely.

Her gaze fell on a velvet box that had been partially hidden from the lid of one of the hat boxes. She seized it with eager hands and opened it, the hinges propping open with a sudden spring. Inside lay a breathtaking diamond necklace with yellow and green stones that she guessed might be sapphires—or maybe sapphires and emeralds. There were earrings to match, and the entire set was elegant and discreet—perhaps the loveliest piece of jewelry she had ever beheld.

Kitty stared at it for some minutes, then closed the lid and hugged the velvet box to her chest. *Necessities*. She shook her head.

CHAPTER THIRTEEN

Phineas paced back and forth in his study. It had been something akin to torture to walk calmly and sedately with Kitty on his arm after having seen her in the arms of that blasted groom, Craddock. What a fool Phineas had been. He had spent all of an afternoon in various shops collecting gifts for her that she would likely despise. He supposed he could have discarded them all, but he was not a wasteful man. It likely gave her a disgust of him to have worn his heart so blatantly on his sleeve. Who knew? Perhaps she would seek out Craddock, and they would laugh together at her hapless fool of a husband who all but admitted his feelings for his wife.

Initially, he had ordered the footman to bring the gifts into his study. His plan had been to invite her to join him there for some tea, because the room boasted comfortable chairs and a large fireplace. He'd requested the tea service brought and the fire stoked while he went to the stables to await his wife's return. His steps had quickened as he went out to greet her, his breath steaming the air, but he hardly felt the cold in his haste to see her again.

What he had *not* expected was to find his wife in the groom's arms.

Phineas pressed his knuckles to his teeth. If he were more of a man he should've hauled off and punched the clodpole before swiftly sending him packing. But Phineas had been too stunned to react, and his wife, other than showing a flash of consciousness, had pulled away and asked for his assistance. There was enough of a seed of doubt over what he was witnessing, and he was not one to make a scene. Their walk to the house, however, had only served to harden his heart. Perhaps he was not ready to haul off and punch a man without being certain of what he saw, but he would not let Kitty be privy to his inner turmoil. It took Phineas a full hour before he could summon the footman to bring the gifts and have them delivered to her room. No, he would not throw them away, but he would not be so foolish as to hope she would run into his arms over the few trinkets he had brought home.

There was no word until dinner, not that he expected anything. He wondered how the dinner would go. Would it be just as awkward as that first day? Would she say something about the gifts? Would she laugh at him? She was not likely to do so outright, but she surely snickered in private.

Phineas clenched his fists, his brow as tight as a coiled spring. Perhaps he was not being fair to his wife. There had been nothing in her behavior to lead him to believe she would play him false. And yet …

There was nothing to it. He would simply have to wait until dinner to judge for himself.

As was their custom before he left for Bath, Phineas knocked on Kitty's door precisely at six. She opened the door and raised her lovely eyes to his and smiled. The uncertainty to her smile sent a mix of pleasure and pain coursing through him. If nothing else, it showed she was not entirely conniving. She slipped her hand into Phineas's arm, and his pulse quickened at her touch. She had said she did not wish to hold his arm indoors.

Her presence at his side was as light as a breath. "Allow me to thank you for your thoughtful gifts. It has given me much pleasure to contemplate them."

Phineas's spirits rose. She'd spent time appreciating his gifts? Perhaps not all was lost. It took only a moment to dismiss such a notion. He could not mistake what he'd seen. "They were not too much trouble to procure. Of course if they do not suit, you may disregard them. Or give them to one of the servants. I am not much informed about ladies' fashions."

Kitty pulled away slightly, so she could look at him. "Give them away?" she repeated in surprise. "Even if they did not suit my complexion, I should not give them away because they were a gift from my husband."

Phineas was more cheerful upon hearing those words, even if the good humor was tempered with the weight of his distrust. He could not wipe the image of Craddock's arms around his wife. It made him want to wrap his hands around Craddock's throat. Even Phineas had not had the pleasure of putting his arms around his wife. The thought seared his mind. He wondered what Kitty would do if he hauled her off to the side just now and pulled her into an embrace. He quickened his steps to avoid falling into that particular blunder.

Kitty quickened her steps as well to keep up with him, though she darted a glance at his face. "I particularly appreciated the painting of Bristol. I do not know if you are aware of this but the wharf is very close to where my brother lived, and I often walked that way with my little brother."

They reached the dining room, and Phineas gestured her in. "No, but I had some idea that even if it was not a particular scene you are familiar with, an image of Bristol would have pleased you."

Kitty graced him with a smile. "It did please me very much," she said. "I must have one of the footmen hang it in my room. I have already decided where it should go."

Phineas was somewhat mollified, and the beast of jealousy began to subside. He found he was able to envision the idea of sitting down to dinner with her and even prying open his lips to make conversation.

The footman brought their dinner and they carried on their usual discussion of everything and nothing, including the state of the roads from Bath, and all the non-private information such as the new steward that would be joining them. When the footman brought the dessert, he retired from the room at last.

"Will you not join me as you did before, Phineas?" His wife gestured with her eyes at the empty chair near her, and Phineas hesitated before picking up his plate and moving to sit near her.

He tried to think of what he could say that would not address the issue that was at the foremost of his mind. "Did you have visitors in the two days I was gone?"

Kitty breathed in with a controlled expression, and a peculiar look flashed across her face. "Yes, I had Mrs. Dutton and her daughter come to visit."

"At last," he replied. "I hope they will provide you with companionship. Did they stay long or speak of any invitations?"

Kitty looked down at the blancmange on her plate. "They did not even stay the customary thirty minutes but left as soon as they could. The daughter seems to have a more conciliatory nature than her mother. They did not speak of any invitations, although perhaps we will receive something." If her expression could be believed, she was doubtful of that.

There was enough reserve in her voice to make him nearly certain the visit had not gone well. He wondered what one did about fostering good relationships in a village of which both he and his wife were newcomers to a degree.

"We shall see, I suppose," she added.

Silence reigned, with only the tiny clink of spoons as they

dipped into the blancmange. His wife was less talkative than she had been before, and his doubts came galloping back. Did she find him boring? He was sure most of the women with whom he had danced at balls had thought so, even if they managed to muster enthusiasm for his title.

At last Kitty lifted her eyes and said rather diffidently, "I received a letter from my sister-in-law. There was not much news, but at the end of the letter, she'd left a bit of space for my younger brother to write. He asked if he might come here for a spell." She pressed her lips together as if she wished to say more but did not dare.

Phineas sipped his port as he attempted to formulate an answer. He had no objection to having her little brother here in theory. He understood that Kitty would miss her family. But would this visit put an end to any potential honeymoon atmosphere between them? It might establish them as a couple that had a marriage in name only, and no affection. There would be no romantic interlude before settling down to raise a family of their own. The thought made Phineas sick at heart. After all, he wasn't sure now the relationship had ever had much hope in the first place. He'd left so soon after they were married, there had been no real union, he came back to find her in an intimate hold with one of the servants, and now she was asking for him to host her family.

It was only what he deserved for having arranged a marriage without seeking to find someone whose heart struck a common chord with his. "I had promised my parents we would visit before Christmas, but I can write to cry off," he said. "If you wish, you may make arrangements with the butler and housekeeper."

Kitty looked at him doubtfully, and Phineas knew his voice had a hard edge to it.

"We must certainly visit your parents as you have planned,"

she said, her eyes still on him. "When have you arranged for us to go?"

"In just under a month," Phineas said, darting a glance at her. His heart warred within, but he would grant her request. "If you wish, you may arrange to have Samuel for a short stay, and we will accompany him to Bath where we might restore him to your brother and his wife."

"If you are sure it will not bother you." There was a crease in Kitty's brow, and there was a part of him that wanted to smooth it away. He clamped down on that part.

"No, why should it?" he replied in a flat tone. "You have every right to expect your family to visit. You may make arrangements as soon as you wish."

When their dessert was finished, he walked her to her room as had been his custom. And when they stood at the door and faced each other, Phineas simply bowed and walked away. He did not even entertain the hope of an embrace.

KITTY'S BROTHER arrived in a week's time. In that interlude, she had continued her riding lessons, and although Phineas refused to humiliate himself by going to the stables and keeping an eye on them, he discreetly looked for clues when she returned. Did her eyes shine with excitement? Love? Did Craddock swagger and act with even more insolence? He had written to Carter for more details about Craddock, but he would not receive a quick reply with Carter on leave for another week. And Phineas would put himself in difficulty if he turned the groom off without having a replacement at the ready.

Once the temptation was too great, and Phineas went to the stables at an unexpected time when he knew his wife would be there. He found her rubbing the horse's nose while Craddock stood at her side and watched her. Every one of Phineas's suspicions seemed justified when he saw Craddock's eyes on his wife, even if they were doing nothing suspicious. When Kitty turned and saw Phineas, her eyes and face lit into a smile that allayed some of his fears. No one could look at him that way if they were entirely uninterested. He did not trust, but he also could not abandon his marriage as entirely hopeless.

However, when Phineas turned from the stables and strode back to the house, he clenched his teeth. No matter what, he would not allow himself to be cuckolded.

The day her brother was supposed to arrive, Kitty was more joyful at breakfast than she had been since he returned from Bath. In fact, he had not seen her so natural and at her ease in all the time they were married. There was something about her brother coming that appeared to crack her defenses and give Phineas a glimpse of who she was.

"I think I might be skilled enough to ride with you before long," she said as she sipped coffee. "We shall have to see if Sam is able to ride as well as I hope. I don't believe Erasmus has seen to his training, except for an odd pony lesson at a neighboring stable. I suppose Craddock can test him and see how he is. In any case, he says he has seen my brother ride and that he shows promise, even if he needs lessons."

Phineas shot his head up. "Craddock has seen your brother?" he said with sharp suspicion.

Kitty lifted her head, her eyes squinting in confusion at his tone. Then her brow cleared. "You know, I had quite forgotten to tell you because we have not spoken of it since you were in Bath, but Craddock knows my family. His cousin is one of our neighbors, and although he and I had never met, he has visited and knows my brother and his wife."

Phineas had difficulty controlling his breathing, and her words reached him through a fog. "Did you know of him before you came here?"

He was waiting on tenterhooks to see what she would

respond, what web of lies she might concoct. But her response was very natural. "No, not once. But you can imagine how surprised I was to find that somebody from my street in Bristol was working here."

Phineas's mind was spinning. Was it possible that Craddock had eyes for his wife, and that he sought a position in Phineas's household so he could be near her? Could she be such a good actor as to make it seem as though they had never met? He wasn't sure about that, but he was determined to find out how Craddock had won a place in Phineas's stables and how honorable a man he was. It did not matter if Phineas ended up breaking his wife's heart by tossing the fellow out; he refused to have a snake in his house.

"I have work to do." He stood abruptly. "You may come and find me when your brother arrives." Phineas made for the door and did not turn again to see her expression.

"I will do so." The hesitation in her voice lingered and followed him out of the room, dogging his steps. He had hurt her by his abrupt tone. If only he could be certain of her faithfulness.

What if Craddock was a longtime lover of hers? Dark ideas began to take root in his mind. Maybe that was why she wanted nothing to do with Phineas. What if Samuel were not just her brother? What if she were his…

No. She would've had to have been twelve years old when Samuel was born. How had Phineas become so insane as to entertain such thoughts? That's what love did to a man. Not that he was in love, but perhaps more accurately—one could say that was what desire did to a man. He would have to rid himself of that base feeling. He would focus on the marriage, and make sure that at least the union was kept honorable, even if there were no finer feelings.

He heard the sound of footsteps and the door opening. There was the bustle of an arrival and excited shouts—and

Kitty's warmer tones as she welcomed her brother. He was tempted to go and see, but he had told her to let him know when Samuel arrived. Shortly afterward, there was a light tap on the door, and the footman came to inform him. "Lady Hayworth's young brother is here. She requested that I inform you, my lord."

"Tell her I will come." Phineas waited a few more minutes, pacing back and forth in the study as he determined the appropriate manner to have. He wondered how the influence of her brother would affect his already fragile relationship with his wife. With a solid division into two camps? Her, Samuel, Craddock...?

No! *Aargh*. Phineas rebuked himself again. He was driving himself mad. He paced twice more as Samuel's chatter filled the entryway and resonated off the walls. At last, prey to a mix of trepidation and curiosity, Phineas stepped into the entryway and stopped short at the sight of Kitty's face as her gaze lifted to meet his. She did not look away, and he was struck by the fact that it was the first time she looked happy.

Samuel had his back to Phineas as he examined two swords attached to the wall as decoration. "What are these called?" he asked his sister.

"Those are Cavalier rapier swords," Phineas answered, stepping forward. He was rewarded by a smile as Kitty came to stand at Samuel's side.

"Greet Lord Hayworth," she prompted him.

Samuel bowed. "Good day, my lord." He resembled Kitty much more closely than Erasmus did. His wavy hair was blond with red tints, and his eyes were the same brown, although his eyelashes were fair while hers were dark.

Phineas returned a nod. "Welcome to Giddenhall." He glanced at Kitty, wanting to keep his heart shielded, so he would not be caught by her own rapier thrust should she be playing him false. But he could not—not when there was such a light to her eyes, which she kept trained so steadily on him. He needed to leave before he exposed himself further. "I am sure you will wish to visit everything. I will arrange for your supper to be prepared for six o'clock. I regret that I cannot join you this evening."

He risked a glance at Kitty's face, but she averted her gaze. There were a few seconds of silence before she pasted on a smile and held out her hand to Samuel. "Come. There are many things to see."

CHAPTER FOURTEEN

K itty had her riding lesson, despite the fact that her brother had arrived only the day before. Once the gardener had promised to show Samuel how to improve at archery, nothing would do but for him to go practice today. She had hoped Phineas might spend some time getting to know her brother, but after he had refused to attend last night's dinner, she had little hope for that to occur.

She dressed in her riding habit. Her maid had been brushing off most of the dirt, and she had not been wearing it for long each day. Still, it was beginning to be in great need of a wash. Kitty glanced at the yards of fabric Phineas had brought back for her, sitting on a table in the corner. It was time to do something about those.

She glanced through the window, wondering if she would get a peek of Samuel, who would now be on his way for target practice. Kitty smiled when she caught sight of him, trudging behind the gardener into the woods on the far end of the lawn. After breakfast, the gardener had won Samuel over by re-stringing his bow with a knotted string instead of a continuous loop string. His arrow had gone twice the distance.

Kitty turned her gaze back to the yards of fabric then walked to the door with purpose. She found Mrs. Morley sitting at the kitchen table with a cup of weak tea in front of her. The housekeeper leapt from her seat with a guilty start, then narrowed her eyes as if angry to have been caught.

"Yes, my lady?"

Kitty, hoping to put her at ease, smiled. "Mrs. Morley, I do not mind if you sit at times."

Mrs. Morley clasped her hands in front of her, the muscles in her jaw tight. "What can I do for you?"

Kitty's heart sank. Mrs. Morley had not warmed to her at all, and she was sure her housekeeper despised Kitty even more for having caught her in a moment of weakness. She exhaled. "I would like to know where I might have some habits made up."

Mrs. Morley stared at a spot on the wall beyond Kitty. "I am afraid I cannot recommend anyone local." She met Kitty's gaze with a sullen look. "Not someone skilled enough to make clothing for the wife of a viscount."

Kitty pressed her lips together to keep from uttering an unkind retort. "I see." They stared at one another for a moment, but Kitty did not feel like engaging in a battle of wills over a few yards of cloth. She waved her hand toward the table. "Carry on then."

As she made to leave the kitchen, the housekeeper threw the rest of the tea in the sink and set the cup down with a sharp clink. Kitty set her jaw as she climbed the steps. She would have to speak to Phineas about his housekeeper. It was not until she reached the top of the stairs that her anger deflated. It could not happen any time soon—not when he was just as cold toward her.

When she entered the stable, Craddock was leading the two horses out, both of them saddled. His eyes lit up when he spotted her. "My lady, I've had everything ready for you. I'm looking forward to our ride today."

His intent expression triggered feelings of caution, and Kitty ran her hands along the mare's bristly mane, as she murmured to the horse. "You and I are growing more comfortable together, aren't we?" Craddock's familiarity disconcerted her, and she needed time to think how to respond. At last, she glanced at him before tugging at the girth as he had taught her to do. "Oh? And why is that?"

Craddock's gaze had not left her face, and she felt the weight of it, which made it difficult to breathe normally. She was flattered, but there was something wrong with this coming from a man who was not her husband.

"My conversations with you are the most interesting part of my position here," he said. "You are a most fascinating woman."

Kitty eyed him then looked away. Now was the time to depress such talk, but she did not know how to do it. He had not said anything overtly inappropriate; it was just that he presumed too much. It was the sort of attention she would have been glad to have were she not married—particularly from someone she found attractive, and who possessed an easy temperament. When she and Craddock rode, they spoke of diverse matters, and their thoughts converged on many of them. But this was the sort of complicity she longed to have with Phineas—*her husband*—and nothing would induce her to give it away cheaply to someone else.

She opened her mouth to speak, still unsure of what she would reply, and still feeling the weight of expectation from Craddock, when she was spared the necessity. She heard movement behind her and turned.

"Craddock," her husband called out, striding forward. "I will ride with my wife today. Have my horse saddled."

A flash of anger darted across Craddock's features, but Phineas did not witness it. Without a word, Craddock led his own horse back to the stable, and pulled Phineas's stallion out of the stall, grabbing the tack with one hand from the peg on the wall.

In rough movements, he had Phineas's horse readied, while Phineas himself went to inspect one of the mares that was about to foal. Kitty continued to rub her horse's nose and mane and give other signs of affection to the great beast that would be carrying her, hopefully safely without being spooked. She was grateful for something to do, for she could feel the tension between the two men and did not know how to diffuse it. She wished to let Craddock know she was grateful for his friendship and connection to her former life, but that it would go no further. And she wished to let Phineas know how glad she was to ride with him and to reassure him that he had nothing to fear. His gifts from Bath had shown that there was an underlying affection there, and it gave her hope. However, the unfortunate timing of his arrival had not helped matters. Kitty had some work ahead of her.

Phineas bent down and cupped his hands, helping Kitty into the saddle, while Craddock held the stallion. Then Phineas swung himself up and started forward, waiting for Kitty to follow. Soon the stable was left behind, and the sounds of the horses' hoofbeats on the frozen path broke the silence. They rode for some distance, and unlike the easy conversation Kitty had with Craddock, this silence was weighted, pregnant with unspoken words. Her husband looked ahead without speaking, and Kitty searched for a subject of conversation. In the end, it was Phineas who spoke first.

"For how long have you been in the habit of riding out?" He presented a handsome figure as he turned in his saddle. "I do not know if we dare go as far as the tenants."

Kitty's breath came out in a cloud. "I have ridden as far as two hours, but that taxes my abilities a bit much."

"As long as that," he exclaimed. "You have made more progress than I expected in such a short time. Then we may certainly visit the tenants. I will see to it that we return before you are overcome with fatigue."

Kitty sent a shy smile his way. "Thank you."

"I hope my accompanying you is to your taste, and that you were not hoping for a riding lesson from Craddock." Phineas trained his eyes at some point in the distance instead of at her, and his voice was clipped.

This was Kitty's chance, and she seized it. "Nothing could please me more than to ride with my husband, and I'm sure I could wish for no better instructor than you." She had her eye on Phineas as they rode and was pleased to see a smile on his face before he turned away. His voice lightened when he next spoke.

"I cannot say that I have any expertise teaching someone else to ride, but I can attend to your comfort and safety."

Kitty matched his light tone, hope blooming in her chest for the first time since he'd come home. "I ask for no more than that, Phineas." Since he had returned from Bath, and they had lost the comfortable way between them, it was an effort not to revert to 'my lord'. But she used his name deliberately and was rewarded with another warm glance.

They arrived at the two rows of tenant houses, and some of the women came out and glanced at Kitty curiously. Phineas greeted them and said, "I'd like to introduce my wife, Lady Hayworth. We have taken up residence at Giddenhall, so you are likely to see more of us."

The women dipped curtsies, and Kitty heard murmurs of "milady" from their lips as one of the mothers nudged her son to bow. The women and their daughters were dressed humbly in flowered or plain poplin and the boys in rateen trousers. Their deference was something Kitty had not received from her own servants. Perched high on a horse above them, she could not pretend to herself that their station was so inferior to hers. She wondered if they knew where she'd come from.

Kitty smiled. "What fine children you have. Giddenhall is lucky to have such robust hands to care for the fields."

Phineas spotted one of the men and gestured him over. "Good day, Mills. How do you find your new steward?"

The man stepped to the front of the small crowd. "I've no complaints, milord. He said my house will be next for a new roof, wha' wi' our six children. It'll keep the cold air out."

"I can see the work has started on your neighbour's house. Excellent. You've been in sore need of it." Phineas swept his gaze over the crowd, and Kitty rested her eyes on his face discovering, for the first time, that his features were not just handsome —they were noble. How lucky she was to have married a man who cared about his tenants' well-being. Would the care a man extended to those whose livelihoods depended on him not also extend to his wife? Might they have a chance at happiness? Deep affection—even love?

Phineas addressed the same man, who appeared in the guise of official spokesman for the tenants. "Mills, I cannot have every house seen to before the coldest part of winter sets in, but we'll re-thatch the houses with the very young and the elderly first. If the former steward had done what he was supposed to, we might have done them all."

"Thank 'ee, milord." There was another round of curtsies and bows, and Kitty was starting to feel the cold from sitting still, even though it had not been long.

Phineas glanced at her and looked back at the crowd. "I will return to see how things are faring. And I do believe we will be in residence for Christmas. Either way, there will be Christmas boxes sent this year."

The tenants smiled more broadly, and one called out, "Bless you, milord." The older children turned to whisper to the younger ones about what such a thing meant.

Phineas met Kitty's gaze. "Shall we go?"

She nodded, still smiling at the tenants' reactions. Christmas boxes were something she could attend to. She gave a final glance at the crowd gathered, drinking in their pleased expressions. Maybe some people here would be glad she'd come to Giddenhall.

Nothing could please me more than to ride with my husband, and I'm sure I could wish for no better instructor than you. Phineas turned the words over in his mind after they'd returned the horses to the stables, and he accompanied Kitty indoors. She'd left him not long after, claiming to have a great deal to do, but her parting glance gave him additional cause for hope. Her gaze lingered on his, and she turned away on a smile. Surely, this was not the look of a woman infatuated with another man?

But jealousy did not release its prey easily. When Phineas remembered that she had ridden as much as two hours with Craddock, it was not a great leap to imagine what could be done in those two hours, especially if two people wished to be alone. It appeared he was never to know peace where his wife was concerned.

That evening, Phineas came to Kitty's room to take her to dinner. Samuel was there describing with great animation the tricks the gardener had taught him when aiming for a brace of pheasants. And no, he had not caught anything, but he was sure that the next day would bring him luck. Kitty raised amused eyes to Phineas as they exited the room and still Samuel did not pause in his speech. She closed the door behind them and touched Samuel gently on the shoulder.

"Sam, say 'good evening' to Lord Hayworth."

Samuel cut his speech short and bowed. "I beg your pardon, my lord. It is only that I was so excited about my adventure today." He turned hopeful eyes on Phineas. "Perhaps you would like to hear about it over dinner?"

Phineas hid his amusement over the boy's guileless nature. "I would like that very much. But perhaps you will be so kind as to walk on the other side of your sister, so that I might take her arm to go to dinner."

As Samuel darted to the other side of Kitty, Phineas remembered too late that she had stated her preference not to take his arm indoors. But she had since done so once, and were they not on increasingly good terms?

To his relief, she did not deny his request and slipped her hand easily into his arm. The complicity of their day together had done much to restore the natural feeling between them that had grown before he went to Bath. As Samuel covered the topics of the biscuits Cook gave him and the old armor he'd found in the attic, saving his story of the adventure with the pheasants to regale at dinner, Phineas began to believe it had not been a bad idea to bring her brother here. His wife was relaxed and happy, and that made him happy too.

When there was a pause in Samuel's flow of conversation, Kitty inclined her head to Phineas. "You said you had planned to meet your new steward tomorrow?"

"Yes. Unfortunately, I will not be able to accompany you on your ride, for we have a great deal to discuss and had planned to cover all the grounds of the property." Phineas allowed his wife and her brother to precede him into the dining room as the footmen opened the door and pulled out Kitty's chair.

She took her seat. "It is of no matter. Sam, you will come riding with me tomorrow, will you not?"

Sam shrugged one of his shoulders, flopping himself into a chair. "I would like that, but I haven't a great deal of experience on a horse."

"It is important you learn," Phineas said. "I hear you are to go to Harrow next autumn. Is that so?"

Samuel cast his gaze down, and his shoulders slumped. "I am

supposed to go, but I would rather stay in Bristol with my cousins."

It was not difficult for Phineas to remember his own days at Harrow. He was an only child and had not been accustomed to so much noise and teasing.

"It is always difficult at the beginning to go someplace you don't know. It was hard for me too. But you must look at it as a great adventure and not shirk. You need this education, and I believe you will enjoy yourself immensely." Phineas leaned back as the footman filled their plates. "I'm not sure anyone at Harrow will be as good a shot as you are. Perhaps you will be able to show them what you've learned."

Samuel looked up, his eyes eager. "You believe so? I had thought, rather, that they would all tease me because I don't come from the same society as them."

The door opened and Mrs. Morley entered. "My lord, I apologize for disturbing your dinner. I must inform you that the venison is taking longer than expected because the wood to light the fires was damp and would only smoke. Cook has sent me with cold meat and bread and has promised to send some other dishes while you wait."

"Tell Cook it will be fine, and that the cold meat and bread is most welcome in the meantime. A boy's appetite will not wait."

Samuel grinned, and Kitty gave Phineas a look full of warmth. Mrs. Morley left the dining room after promising to send the footman with the dishes.

Phineas turned his attention back to Samuel. "There will always be bullies, no matter where you go. But you have the strength to fight against them, and you have time to learn the things you'll need to know. For instance, you must be proficient on horseback. I know your brother has only spared you to us for the two weeks until we go to Bath. But we might consider having you return in the winter where you can have daily lessons in riding."

Kitty bestowed luminous eyes on him, and he held her gaze for a moment. Phineas had spoken impulsively, but Samuel reminded him of himself as he left for Harrow. He remembered those feelings all too well, and if he could do anything to help the boy be better established, he would most certainly do so.

Kitty reached over and touched Samuel's hand. "Would you like that? Would you like to come and stay with us again, and for a much longer visit next time?"

Samuel's eyes grew wide. "Would I!" He shoved a large helping of cold beef in his mouth. "I will have ever so much more fun here. I can learn all the places where the animals live. And the gardener said he would show me which ones I was allowed to shoot and which ones I am not."

"Sam, don't speak with your mouth full please." Kitty smiled and picked up her fork, and Phineas caught her gaze again. Kitty treated her younger brother with gentleness and love. She would make a wonderful mother—Phineas would have been pleased to have a mother who was half as warm. Lady Midlington had never given him much comfort in words or deed.

He dwelled an instant longer on the idea of Kitty becoming a mother, and it caused him to cough as his food went down wrong. In order for Kitty to be a mother, she had to be with child. And there was the difficulty.

Phineas cleared his throat. "You will be able to tell the boys in your school that you spent the summer at your brother's house, the Viscount Hayworth. That ought to settle any doubts about what kind of social background you come from."

Samuel looked up in awe. "I hadn't thought of that! We are related now. You are my brother-in-law. I am not so very beneath them, after all."

Phineas shook his head. "Not one bit. You will find many boys at Harrow—some of whom are peers, some of whom are the sons of gentlemen. And you will find others who come from a background of trade such as yourself. You are one of the few who will be able to relate to everybody. That gives you an edge over the other boys."

Kitty smiled at Phineas. "I have been trying to convince him of the same, but I believe you will be more successful, having lived at Harrow yourself." She turned to Samuel. "Do you see? I told you there was nothing to fear."

Beginning with the story of the pheasants, their dinner as three was more lively than their usual conversation with only two. And if they did not have any moments of unspoken communication between them that furthered Phineas's hope for intimacy, what they had was friendship and complicity, and a taste of what it would be like when they had a family. To Phineas, that was nearly as good.

He continued in this cheerful view as he escorted Kitty and her brother to Samuel's room across the hall from Kitty's. She stopped, her hands on Samuel's shoulders and turned a smiling face to his. Without pausing to think, Phineas leaned down and planted a kiss on Kitty's cheek. It was only when he was met with Samuel's inquisitive gaze and Kitty's shocked one that he realized what he had done.

Ahem. Phineas appeared to have a ball lodged in his throat. "I … um … Good night." He turned to go, but not before he caught the corners of Kitty's lips creeping up into a smile.

CHAPTER FIFTEEN

K itty had hoped for a glimpse of Phineas at breakfast, but he had already left to meet the steward, according to the footman. Instead, she settled down to listen to Samuel's conversation. Although she was used to entering into the spirit of all that excited him, she found herself listening with only half an ear and thinking about Phineas. He had touched a chord in her heart the night before the way he listened to Samuel and advised him. It was as if he understood what Samuel was going through. Of course that was impossible since Phineas had been born to the privilege of his set. Undoubtedly he went to school without a fear in his heart other than the natural fear of leaving what was familiar.

Although Kitty had found Phineas attractive upon first sight, his appeal grew the more he'd engaged with Samuel at dinner. She'd barely had to say anything as he listened to Samuel recount his adventures and tell what parts of the garden he had visited. Phineas then offered suggestions of other things her brother might like to do. Occasionally, he would glance at Kitty, his eyes twinkling with shared enjoyment. At times, she thought it might be to see whether their conversation pleased her. Then he would catch her eye and give something close to a wink, sharing in the private amusement of listening to the unedited speech of a boy.

He would make a good father. The thought made Kitty catch her breath. Nothing could recommend a man to her more than that, and yet they were hardly closer to knowing one another than they were before. Apart from that kiss last night. Kitty clamped down on her lips to keep a grin from erupting. What had that been about? She hadn't known he was capable of such a stealthy move. He must have known it had not been unwelcome.

Kitty had sent a footman to warn Craddock earlier that Samuel would be accompanying her. The path that led to the stables was now familiar, and she anticipated the dip in the road that likely filled with mud when it rained. The branches of the oak tree on the lawn were bare, but in the spring they would be filled with light green budding leaves. This was her home now, and she would be here to witness this new life.

After last night, the image of Phineas as a father consumed Kitty. How frustrating that he made no advances to make such a thing possible. He could not have *truly* meant that he expected her to make the first move. How could he think she would do such a thing? Kitty had come to the conclusion that she could only wait to see how all this would unfold. Phineas must eventually have a plan for their union. Since it was clear he was invested in the relationship, he could not let things continue as they were. Did he not understand how impossible it was that she be so forward?

Craddock had received the message, and had Fawn saddled as well as his own horse. A pony that Phineas had acquired before Samuel's arrival, and whose name was Punch, was waiting next to the other horses. Another evidence of her husband's thoughtfulness.

"Samuel!" Craddock held his hand out, and Samuel shook it

gravely. "How are you this morning?" Craddock lifted his eyes to Kitty as he addressed her brother, but Kitty did not wish for the same dynamic that had occurred with her husband last night to mar this morning's musings. She smiled and turned away as Sam answered.

"Very well, I thank you."

"I understand you are not experienced at riding," Craddock went on. "But you know how to get into the saddle, and you can ride a little bit without me holding the bridle, can't you?"

"I can ride some. I'm just not what they would call a bruising rider." Samuel glanced at Kitty. "I can even trot a little. But I am afraid of galloping."

"I know just how you feel on that matter," Kitty said with a smile.

"We will not gallop," Craddock assured him. "All right. Up into the saddle with you while I help your sister—if you are able?"

"If you can bring Punch to a mounting block, I can."

Craddock brought the pony over, and Samuel hopped into the saddle with little difficulty. Phineas had told Kitty it was an Exmoor pony, who would be strong enough to carry Samuel even as he grew. Punch was a caramel brown color and his forelock was so thick it lent him an impish look. He stood very calmly while Samuel adjusted himself in the saddle.

"And now, my lady, I believe it is your turn." Craddock came to Kitty's side and helped her on to the mounting block. She climbed on to the horse and settled comfortably. A pat on her leg made Kitty jump, but when she glared at Craddock, he had already moved away from her. He should not think she would accept such intimacy from the groom—not when even her own husband hadn't touched her leg. Phineas had not even done so the time she had brushed her knee against his at dinner.

"We are ready," she called out in a frigid voice. "Why don't you mount and lead the way."

Craddock grinned, despite the rebuke in her tone, and Kitty was momentarily bereft of further speech. Surely he could not think his familiarity in any way appropriate. Craddock mounted his horse, and the three of them moved forward. "I will take you toward the public road. You've not yet explored this part of the property, and the road is very quiet so you need not fear the horses will be spooked by anything."

Kitty was grateful for her brother's presence. She was going to have to speak to Craddock, but she found it difficult to do so, especially with their mutual connections. What if word made it back to her family that she had become proud in her new situation? Her brother's presence only delayed a conversation that would be inevitable. As they rode, Craddock gave Samuel excellent instruction on how to handle the pony. Despite what Kitty was coming to see as his faults, she had to own that Craddock was a very fine teacher. He not only knew horses well, he knew how to impart his knowledge.

It was probably not enough that she had rebuked Craddock. She would need to speak with Phineas about the groom's impertinence. Such a thing made her uncomfortable. She could be ruining a man's livelihood. Was it possible she was misreading his intentions? Was he simply mistaking the common past they had for reason to take liberties that another servant could not take? A direct warning was an important start before going to her husband. She needed only find a moment when they were alone to do so.

"Careful, my lady. There is a narrow ditch here, and your horse will need to make a very small leap to get over it. Lean into it just slightly, and you will be fine."

Craddock went over first, giving additional instructions to Samuel, who followed him and continued on with a canter, which he reined in. Her brother looked back at Kitty with a pleased flush on his face. Kitty sped her horse up and leaned forward, and made it safely to the other side of the ditch. That was a victory. Her first leap. It hadn't been as hard as she'd imagined, and Fawn had seemed to sail over the ditch effortlessly.

They continued on the path until they came across another rider heading in their direction—a young lady accompanied by a groom. As they drew nearer, Lucretia Dutton came into view, astride a large dapple gray that she rode with ease. Her dark blue riding habit set off her flushed cheeks, and Kitty thought again of the fabrics from Phineas, waiting to be turned into something as fashionable as Lucretia's riding habit.

"How do you do, Miss Dutton?" Kitty called out, impulsively she feared, for it was the first familiar face she had seen.

"Lady Hayworth. It is a pleasure to see you again. I had to beg my mother to let me go riding, because it is such a beautiful day and a little warmer than the days we've had in the past. I do not know how long this will last, but I could not sit inside for another moment."

Miss Dutton's expression held a natural warmth, and Kitty felt that—apart from her connection to her mother—she was someone who could potentially become a friend. "I understand perfectly. It is a beautiful day. Please allow me to introduce my younger brother, Samuel Stokes."

"Good afternoon, Mr. Stokes," Miss Dutton said, turning her eyes to him. Samuel sat up straight at being called by such a formal name. "Are you home from school?"

Samuel shook his head. "I will not go to school until next year. I'm going to Harrow."

"I am sure Harrow will suit you very well," she said. "My cousins went there, although some of their friends went to Eton. There was always a rivalry between the two schools, and I'm sure you will quickly find you have a favorite."

Kitty laughed. "I am very sure he will. And will you be spending the Christmas holidays here?"

"Yes, I am not going anywhere before the London Season,

despite having three married sisters. What is the point of having married sisters if they will not invite you to London and introduce you to Society? It is all very dull." Miss Dutton spoke in a droll voice that made Kitty laugh again.

"Perhaps we may spend time together then," Kitty said. "We will be leaving for Bath in a week, but when we return, I will be pleased to invite you. We plan to remain for the Christmas holidays, as well."

"With great pleasure." Miss Dutton hesitated and added, "We are having a formal dinner party next weekend. If you are free, I would like to send you an invitation."

Kitty's heart leapt at being received by a member of Society, even if it meant meeting Miss Dutton's mother again. "I would like that very much. I will have to ask Lord Hayworth, but I do not believe we have firm plans."

"Excellent. You may expect an invitation to arrive by the end of today." Miss Dutton smiled and lifted her riding crop to wave.

They had just bid farewell, when Craddock began turning his horse. "If we turn here, we can start circling back to the house, so that you are not too tired from your first ride, Samuel. We can increase the time as you grow accustomed to longer rides, although it appears you will only be here for another week before you leave again?" He raised an inquiring eyebrow to Kitty, who did not think a servant needed to know their family's business.

Still, she did not have the heart to snub him, and he would eventually learn of their plans anyway. "Yes. We will be leaving to bring Samuel back to my brother and to visit with Lord Hayworth's parents in Bath."

"I only hope it will be a comfortable visit for you, my lady," Craddock said.

Kitty darted a glance at him and found him watching her. She chewed her lip, wondering how best to handle this familiarity with Craddock. His underlying message was that he doubted she would be accepted among Society there. And although she found the complicity he constantly searched for between them to be bordering on impertinence—and therefore greatly in need of being repressed—she couldn't help but agree. She, too, was unsure of the reception she was likely to have.

SAMUEL HAD BEEN at Giddenhall for over a week, and life with the three of them had begun to take on a comfortable rhythm with Kitty at the foot of the table, Phineas seated close by on her right, and Samuel close by on her left. If Phineas had been worried that Samuel's stay would break up the harmony of his newly established relationship with his wife, he had to own it had done more good than harm. True, there was not the privacy needed for him to court the woman he was married to. Samuel took up too much space in their conversation. When Kitty's hand brushed his as he passed a dish at the dinner table, he could only assume it was innocent rather than a flirtation and therefore could not follow up.

When dinner was over, Samuel accompanied them up the stairs, chattering the whole while. There was no longer that moment of hesitation—that questioning glance as Phineas bid Kitty good night in front of her room. This was both a relief, as it removed the disappointment when nothing came of it, and it was a source of frustration. Because nothing came of it.

Samuel had accompanied Kitty on her riding lessons, which relieved Phineas's mind since she was no longer alone with the groom. However, Phineas offered to replace Kitty and ride with Samuel when he discovered her only habit needed to be washed, and she did not intend to ride. He wondered if she did not like the cloth he had bought for her, and if that was why she had not had her riding habits made up yet.

Phineas found Samuel to be a natural in the saddle. Kitty said that in one lesson he'd advanced more quickly than she had and, indeed, he was already attempting small jumps. "Throw your heart over first," Phineas said, when they came to a short hedgerow.

When Samuel looked at him questioningly, Phineas added, "That means, set your mind about where you want to land and show your determination to go there. Your pony will follow if you do that. But if you show any hesitation on your part, the pony will sense it and will not go."

"He will see that I'm quite determined," Samuel replied. With a glint in his eye that showed his resolve, the boy rode toward the hedgerow and led Punch neatly across. He allowed his pony to go forward a little before reining in. He looked back at Phineas, his eyes shining.

"Nicely done," Phineas said, following him across. "I could not have done it better myself. Shall we head back to the stable? I believe Kitty will want to find out how your lesson went, and you will be able to tell her about your jump. She will surely have finished with Mrs. Morley by now."

Samuel screwed up his lips. "I don't like Mrs. Morley."

Phineas looked at him in surprise. "You don't? Why not?"

"She is not nice to Kitty. She takes her time to answer when Kitty asks for something, and she doesn't get what Kitty requests right away." Samuel brushed his hair out of his eyes. "Our servants at home never treated her like that."

"Ah." Phineas frowned. The thought of one of his servants lacking respect for his wife filled him with anger. That would have to be dealt with. "Thank you for telling me."

Samuel nodded, and they allowed their horses to walk side-by-side toward the stable. The boy looked ahead, and the sun glinting on his red hair was very like Kitty's. Phineas wondered if their own children would have her red hair too.

"Phineas, can I ask you something?"

Phineas had never given Samuel license to use his first name, but the boy must have heard Kitty use it and imitated her without thinking. Phineas did not precisely mind. He was coming to appreciate his new young relative and was even looking forward to having him return after the holidays, when hopefully the connection with his wife might have deepened. He looked at Samuel and nodded. "You may ask me anything you like."

"Do you love my sister?"

The shock of being on the receiving end of such a blunt question sent a flush to Phineas's cheeks that he could not hide. Samuel was looking at him and waiting for an answer. "You know..." Phineas was not sure how to answer in a way that was truthful and would satisfy the boy's curiosity but also help him to see that there were certain aspects of Phineas and Kitty's relationship to which Samuel would not be privy. "Love is not something much talked about among Society."

"I thought as much," Samuel replied, and the easy way he said it caught Phineas by surprise. "But I thought it might be different with you because my sister is not of Society, and she says she loves me all the time. I thought maybe she would say it to you."

If Phineas had felt uncomfortable before, this confession did not help, and it set his mind spinning. So Kitty was someone who was able to say "I love you." He wondered if he would ever be the recipient of such a phrase. No one had ever said it to him before, and he almost thought it did not exist outside of novels.

"I'll tell you what, Sam," he said, returning Samuel's use of his first name with the nickname Kitty used for her brother. "I don't propose to answer your question. This is a subject that is private to your sister and me."

"I beg your pardon." Samuel looked ahead at the far end of the path. "There is Kitty walking toward the stable. We shall meet her there."

An irrational surge of jealousy seized Phineas when he saw her making her way with graceful steps, her head covered with a bonnet so that she did not see or hear them returning. She could only be going to the stable to see Craddock. There could be no other explanation for it. At the nudge from his rider, Phineas's stallion sped up.

"Shall we canter to the stable? It's not as fast as a gallop, and I believe you are capable," Phineas said.

"I am ready," Samuel said, following behind.

Phineas very nearly did ride at a gallop to close the distance. He swung down at the entrance, and led his horse through the wide doorway. He heard Samuel doing the same behind him and was pleased that he had been able to keep up.

"Craddock," he called out, his voice taking on a hard edge that did not hide his jealousy. Craddock was facing his wife, closer than Phineas would permit, but Kitty's relieved expression made him pause. She did not look like she was engaging in a flirtation. "Take our horses."

Kitty stepped forward. "I came to inquire what time the both of you set out because it seemed a very long time for Sam to be riding. Craddock seemed to think it was too long for a boy of his skill so I grew worried."

"I am very well able to handle a horse now," Samuel exclaimed from behind them. He had not led his pony forward but was holding him by the bridle. "You should not have worried. Phineas was with me."

Kitty looked at Phineas, startled, and he was not sure if it was because Samuel had used his Christian name, or if it was because Samuel replied what should have occurred to her without prompting. "You are very right, Sam. It was foolish of me to have worried."

Craddock came forward to take the reins, his expression revealing his displeasure, as if Phineas were the one who was out of line. Phineas did not care what effect it might have on

Kitty's heart to send the groom away, but away Craddock must go. However, Phineas had not yet found a replacement, and he did not embrace the idea of leaving his stable in the hands of mere lads, none of whom showed the necessary skill to keep the stable running smoothly until a new groom might be found. He would bide his time until he heard back from Carter.

On impulse, Phineas lifted a hand to stay Craddock. "I will be giving Lady Hayworth and Samuel riding lessons until we leave for Bath. You may have our horses ready every morning by ten."

"Yes, my lord." Craddock muttered the words through clenched teeth.

CHAPTER SIXTEEN

"Mrs. Morley, I would like to have a word with you."
Phineas entered the room that served as an office for
the housekeeper, down the narrow corridor beyond the
kitchen. When Mrs. Morley saw him, she jumped to her feet in
surprise. "I have received word that you have not been treating
Lady Hayworth with the respect she deserves." He waited for a
response, and as he studied her expression, he thought he
detected a flash of guilt.

"My lord, I apologize if I have given that impression. It is
certainly not my intention to show a lack of respect." Mrs.
Morley smoothed her apron and patted the ring of keys on her
waist. "I do not have an overly friendly disposition. I believe
that is why your wife has chosen to speak out against me."

"It was not my wife who complained of your behavior. I
heard it from another source—"

"Who?" The question left the housekeeper's lips abruptly,
and she seemed to realize she had overstepped her bounds. "I
beg your pardon, my lord. I will make sure Lady Hayworth has
no cause for complaint in the future."

"Very good." Phineas had not looked forward to the interview, but now he was glad he had done it, and that it had gone so well. He exited the small space and returned to his study.

He had little realized that good servants were hard to come by before setting up residence. Phineas had never before had to fill all the positions at Giddenhall because he was so focused on his father's estate. He had relied on Carter to staff the few positions not already held by retainers.

But now with a wife in residence, there was much more at stake. They were here to stay for a good many years, and the tenants needed to be taken care of by a steward who would do the job properly. He had a beautiful wife, and he had no need for an impudent groom, who treated her with familiarity; their capable, but cunning, housekeeper had no right to treat her with disrespect. If anything, Phineas would replace every post in the estate if it meant that his wife would be welcome and protected.

He spotted Kitty heading up the stairs. On impulse, he almost told her about the conversation he had just had with Mrs. Morley but decided against it. He had never let her know that Samuel spoke out against the housekeeper. Better that Kitty see for herself how well-disposed Mrs. Morley was toward her mistress.

"Kitty."

She stopped midway to peer over the bannister and greeted him with a conspiratorial smile. "Phineas, you will never believe this. We have *visitors*," she said in a loud whisper. "It is such a shocking thing to have actual visitors, I little know how to respond." He came up the steps to meet her and was tempted to match her smile with one of his own, but her words brought a crease to his brow. He could not be sure whether she was teasing.

"Did you not have visitors in Bristol? Do you really not know how to receive them?" Even though Phineas thought she might be joking, he was plagued by a sudden fear that this was another example of their difference in upbringing.

Her smile faltered, and she put a hand on her hip as she stepped down to eye level. "No, Phineas. Can you not see I am jesting?" Her voice had lost some of its playfulness. "Of course I know how to receive visitors. It is only that we have had none so far, apart from the detestable Mrs. Dutton and her daughter, Lucretia, who seems to be altogether a different creature. I am just surprised that at last someone has decided to drop by."

Phineas's brow cleared, but he was left with the sinking notion that he had missed an opportunity somehow. "Forgive me. Of course you were jesting."

Kitty turned to go, and Phineas reached for her hand and held it, coaxing her eyes up to his. "Perhaps we will get to the bottom of our lack of visitors before now. Shall I come with you?"

Kitty paused, an arrested look in her eyes. "Would you do so? I would like that very much if you are willing."

"I own to some curiosity. My visits in the past have been so brief, I have not met any of the neighbors. I shall wait for you here then."

"I will not be long. I did not like to have the guests shown into the drawing room with no one to receive them, but I needed a few minutes to retrieve something in my room."

Phineas walked down the few steps to reach the entryway. Muted voices filtered out of the drawing room. It would be the first time he and Kitty appeared in society as man and wife. Phineas rubbed his hand on the carved wooden knob on top of the bannister. The thought pleased him.

In minutes, Kitty joined him in the entryway, carrying a light shawl. "It is a little chilly in the drawing room. I asked the footman to build up the fire." She flashed him a self-conscious smile. "This will reveal to them at once that we are not accustomed to entertaining."

"Never mind that." Phineas held out his arm, and Kitty slipped her hand into it. He had offered his arm deliberately, despite her claim that she would not take his arm indoors, but he had begun to wonder if that were not really so. Perhaps it was only those first days of marriage she'd needed distance from him. At any event, in this instance, he wished to present a unified front.

Inside the drawing room were two ladies of an advanced age. Both women curtsied, and the one with gray curls addressed them. "My lord, my lady. I am Mrs. Abrams, and this is Mrs. Wallace. We would both like to extend our apologies for not coming to visit you earlier. We had not realized you had come to take up residence here. We thought yours a brief stay and did not wish to trouble you."

Phineas gestured for the two women to sit. "It is our pleasure to have you." He turned to his wife. "I believe you have already sent for the tea service?"

"I have." Kitty answered him with an intimate smile that he privately found irresistible. Turning to her guests, she said, "We are pleased to receive you. I am glad there is no more confusion regarding our situation here. We should like to become acquainted with the people in the village, as this is now our home." Kitty spoke with natural grace. How much easier it was to entertain with a wife at his side.

"My lord," Mrs. Abrams said, "I knew your grandmother a very little. She was rather reclusive and was not well known in the village. However, I am the doctor's wife and had been in the habit of visiting her. I assist my husband in delivering medicine to some of the women, for it gives me a chance to visit with them at the same time."

Phineas had barely known his grandmother, having only met her twice. The visits merely served to give him an indication of where his mother's stiff demeanor came from. He could not summon any particular feelings of sorrow when his grandmother had passed away. "You must be of great assistance to your husband in his work."

Mrs. Abrams smiled. "He says he does not know what he would do without me, but it is no hardship to visit neighbors."

Mrs. Wallace was the younger of the two, although she had the beginnings of a matronly look with a broad chest and the hint of a double chin. She turned to Kitty. "Where do you come from? And how long have you been married now?"

"Mere weeks," Kitty answered. "I come from Bristol."

Mrs. Wallace raised an eyebrow. "Such a busy place. And how are you settling into Castle Combe? It is a small village here. Everyone knows each other."

"I like it very well," Kitty replied. "A small village has its own benefits attached to it." Phineas wondered if that was how she felt. It was a beautiful part of the country, but Kitty had not exactly received a warm welcome here.

"Well, as Mrs. Abrams said, we were not aware of your being in residence." There was a slight pause, and she continued. "But I hear you are to attend Mrs. Dutton's dinner party?"

Kitty exchanged a glance with Phineas and nodded. Word traveled fast. "We did receive an invitation and will be there. I am looking forward to meeting more of our neighbors."

The footman brought in the tea service, and Kitty asked the women how they took their tea. When she was done preparing theirs, she prepared one for Phineas and handed it to him. His wife had paid attention. She had made his tea exactly the way he liked it—sweet with no milk.

The visit did not last long, but they made promises to send invitations to future events, and Kitty assured them she would visit as soon as they had returned from their trip to Bath.

When the ladies were shown out, Phineas crossed one leg over the other. "So that was what had happened—why they did not come. The neighbors did not realize we had taken up residence here, and thought we had come for a short stay only."

"*Hmn.*" Kitty glanced at him from the corner of her eye and poured herself a second cup of tea, lifting the cup to her lips.

"You do not think it so?" Phineas could not read her expression.

Kitty made a wry face. "It does not seem a difficult thing to find out. Servants talk. They will know if we are here for some time. After all, wasn't Sterling from the village? She is Bexley's niece. Yet she left her home to work here as my maid and has not returned once. News of that would surely reach the servants in other houses, who are ready to share the gossip with whichever employer thinks to ask."

"True." Phineas had never given the matter much thought. He knew almost instinctively from birth that one did not talk about personal matters in front of the servants. But he had not bent his mind to consider that there might be a network of information passing from the servants of one house to another. Even more reason to have finally shaken off his father's reins and start running his own estate. It was the only way he could learn how to do things on his own.

Over the course of that week, Phineas and Kitty received other visitors, each with similar excuses. And each time, Kitty smiled at her husband with a mischievous glint that included him in their private joke. Each visitor came and inquired after their plans, seemingly unaware of their intentions to remain. Kitty patiently corrected the notion, and they all promised to send invitations for upcoming events. Phineas enjoyed the visits, for it gave him a chance to sit back and watch his wife host with as much grace as one born to the role.

They said goodbye to yet another woman from the village, and Phineas took his courage in his hand and put his arm around Kitty's waist as they saw the woman to the door. He felt her startle under his touch, but he kept his hand firmly in place. Her waist was warm, and he drank in the comfort of her nearness.

When the door closed behind them, Kitty darted her gaze to his, a question in her eyes, and he detected heightened color in her cheeks. When she did not speak, he let go with reluctance and took a step back. "That was the last of the women from the village, I believe."

Kitty clasped her hands in front of her waist, but she did not move farther from him. "How do you know?"

"Mrs. Morley told me there was only one family that had not yet visited, and that we would likely receive their visit soon." He peered more closely at her expression. "What is it?"

She lifted a shoulder. "It is nothing. It is good the house-keeper is keeping you informed on these matters."

Kitty gave the ghost of a smile and moved away at last, and he followed her with his eyes. She sounded disappointed, and he could not figure out why.

THE DUTTON PARTY was held two days before they were to leave for Bath. "Must I stay with Mrs. Morley?" Samuel asked. "I would much rather go with you."

Kitty rested her hand on Samuel's shoulder. "I know you have been given free reign of the house here, and I do love having you. But you were not invited to the dinner party, and children are not generally included in these things. You will see when you get older that dinner parties are not so very exciting."

"I know that," he said, folding his arms and kicking the toe of his shoe against the floor. "It is only that I do not wish to stay home with Mrs. Morley." Kitty hugged her brother but did not try to reason with him. She could find no argument with that.

Kitty chose her second-best gown after the one she wore for her wedding, and it was a dress Phineas had never seen. The color was a rich gold, and the gown had puffed sleeves that pleated at the sides, with a more fitted sleeve underneath that extended the length of her arm. The empire waist had a thick ribbon of the same color, and the dress opened in front to reveal

JENNIE GOUTET

an ivory silk underlay. Sterling twisted Kitty's hair up and arranged the curls to frame her face. And Kitty wore, for the first time, the necklace and earrings Phineas had bought her.

The look on his face was well worth the effort she had made in her appearance. "You look very fine, Kitty." He had come to her room, and when she exited into the corridor, he turned around her, admiring her from all directions. She blossomed under his praise. "I knew those sapphires would become you. The yellow reminded me of the golden leaves from the day we married, and the green reminded me of your wedding dress."

Kitty's mouth opened slightly. He bought the necklace because it reminded him of her wedding dress? Her stomach gave a little *whoosh*, and she felt a warmth run through her. The sensation of being important to someone was entirely foreign to her, and she attempted to appear unaffected.

"Shall we go?"

Why did she need to hide how she felt when they were married? Kitty tried to discern the answer as Phineas helped her on with her cloak and walked with her outdoors, where he assisted her into the carriage. *Fear, I suppose.* Kitty shivered from the frosty air that crept inside. Phineas looked at her more than once in the dark, and she wondered what he was thinking, but he did not say anything.

The Dutton house, lit with blazing candles, was a cheerful refuge coming in from the cold. There were up to twenty couples invited to dine, and Kitty was seated far from her husband, where she had the opportunity to speak with Mr. Dutton. Mr. Abrams, the doctor, was on the other side of her. Mr. Dutton appeared to possess greater sense and a warmer nature than his wife, and it helped her to trust that Lucretia's apparent goodness was genuine. As Kitty ate, she sent glances across the table, watching Phineas speak with the young women placed at either side. He seemed to be at his ease, listening to them and showing interest in their conversation. When he looked up and caught her staring, she turned away, feeling foolish.

The men stayed behind for port, and the women went into the drawing room where Lucretia wasted no time pulling Kitty aside for private conversation. They stood in one of the alcoves, watching the various groups of women gather together around the room. It seemed Lucretia chose the spot because it gave her the best view of the room.

"Tell me," Kitty said when no one was within earshot, "do you know where I might have some riding habits made up? I have the fabrics but need the dresses made." Kitty had decided in advance to approach Lucretia with the question since Mrs. Morley had not been helpful.

"You must try Miss Tour. She is as good as they get in these parts. You can tell her that I sent you—not that you, married to the viscount, would need an introduction from me. However, she has known me since my coming out."

Kitty smiled. "An introduction would be very helpful. Thank you. We are to go to Bath in two days, so I may have two of the riding habits made up while I'm there, but I will be very glad to have the rest made up here."

Lucretia turned to her in surprise. "Do you intend to have so many made up? You must be a notable horsewoman."

Kitty could not help the laugh that bubbled up. "Not in the least. It is only that Lord Hayworth has been encouraging me to ride more and bought perhaps more fabric than I needed. I am only a novice, I assure you."

Lucretia's eyes sparkled. "So you were right in saying it was a love match." Before Kitty could assess how to correct her own lie, Lucretia went on. "I assume you have been receiving a great number of visitors?"

Kitty turned to her, her brows knit. "Why, yes, how did you know?"

"Oh…" Lucretia shrugged with an air of nonchalance, but

her dimples were prominent. "It was just a hunch. No, the truth is, my mother has not been kind where you are concerned. She has deliberately held off the knowledge that you have come to stay, and instead let it be known that you were at Giddenhall in passage. She was spitting mad when I sent you an invitation to tonight's party, I can tell you. But I don't care. Of course, once the invitation had gone out, the rest of the town had to recognize you. That's why I did it—I mean, other than the pleasure of seeing you—to rectify a wrong."

Kitty widened her eyes. "That was kind of you. Why did you go to such trouble for me?"

"Apart from having had enough of my mother's unkindness? Please do not take this amiss, but I am bored. I have known the same people since I was young, and I found you to be perfectly agreeable. I was hoping we might be friends."

"Well, then we shall," Kitty answered with a smile.

They were interrupted by the sounds of the men coming into the drawing room. They had not spent a great deal of time with just the women, and Kitty was glad. Although she did have a new friend, she was not keen to be thrown to the wolves of female society so quickly.

"There you are," Mrs. Dutton said, addressing Phineas. "I was just saying to Mrs. Wallace how happy we are to have new society here. Giddenhall has once again full-time residents." Mrs. Dutton's voice carried across the drawing room. "We are happy to have this dinner party in your honor, and I welcome you and Lady Hayworth. Castle Combe can only be richer for such a union…"—she paused and glanced at Kitty with an enigmatic smile—"especially knowing that yours was a love match."

Kitty had lifted the cup to her lips, but at these words, the saucer fell from her nerveless fingers and bounced harmlessly on the carpet. The soft thunk brought everyone's eyes to her. Phineas met her regard, and she could read the question in his eyes. She did not need a looking glass to know her face was crimson. There was an awkward silence as the crowd of guests seemed to guess that something was amiss.

Phineas switched his gaze to Mrs. Dutton. "Is that so? And who has given you such a romantic picture of our marriage?"

Mrs. Dutton had a glint in her eye when she looked at Kitty. "Why, your wife did."

He looked again at Kitty, holding her gaze for a split second, and she could hear her heart beat loudly over the silence in the room. "Indeed it was, ma'am. As a matter of fact, you might say it was a love match from the very first time I set eyes on her."

Phineas walked to Kitty's side and leaned down to pick up her saucer. After a split second's pause, where he seemed to consider, he took her teacup from her hand and placed it and the saucer on the table behind her. Kitty attempted a smile, but she was trembling from head to foot. Phineas had lied and said he loved her to spare her humiliation. *If only his words had been true.* Her husband reached out and put her hand on his arm, and his warmth calmed her. At least they had a friendship.

He switched his gaze from her. "Mr. Abrams, you had crops grown on your southern meadow, did you not? I believe it had been used for sheep before. What made you make the switch?"

The doctor moved forward to answer Phineas's question, and the conversation in the room slowly picked up. Kitty's tense mortification began to give way as the conversation flourished around her. She dared to glance around the room, and Lucretia lifted her gaze from the woman speaking before her and gave a tiny nod in Kitty's direction.

KITTY DREADED THE TRIP HOME. She was overcome with embarrassment, although she had appreciated Phineas standing up for her and not permitting her to be humiliated in front of everyone. He had even come to stand by her, and that had brought her more comfort than she could have imagined the day she stood beside him in front of the vicar. She allowed the darkness to shroud her face and expression in the carriage. She shivered from cold and, she suspected, from the misery of embarrassment.

"Kitty, if you are cold, you may come and sit next to me, where you will be warmer."

Kitty glanced at him but could not read his expression in the dark. She slid over near him, and his warmth did ease the tremors as the carriage swayed back and forth. She opened her mouth to explain, but closed it again, too mortified to try. After a small distance, Phineas leaned away from her and lifted his arm to put it around her, the weight of it unfamiliar and heavy but not unwelcome. The little tremors stopped, and her muscles began to relax one by one. She and Phineas did not speak.

The hall was silent when they entered, and Phineas handed his cap and gloves to the servant. Kitty shook her head when the footman offered to take hers. "I will keep my cloak on until I'm upstairs. I am still cold."

The silence stretched as they walked up the stairs, and as they made their way to her room, she knew she had to say something. He must be waiting for an explanation not to have spoken a word all that time.

"I beg your pardon for having lied about it being a love match." Kitty stopped in front of her door and turned to face him. "I could not bear Mrs. Dutton's questions that day, and her insinuations that, of course, it was my brother's fortune that tempted you, even though it was no less than the truth. So I said a falsehood, never imagining it would reach your ears."

Phineas peered at her, and although they had not thought to take a candle up with them, the moonlight stretched down the corridor from the window at the very end of it and lit the whites of his eyes. She saw him smile and felt his nearness cloaked under the darkness. "I do not mind in the least," he said. The words came out softly. "Perhaps one day it will be true."

Kitty lifted her head and tried to read Phineas's expression in the dim light, any further words caught in her throat. Phineas leaned down and stopped short of kissing her.

"Kitty, I—"

Kitty could barely breathe as his lips grazed hers. He pulled away a hair's breadth, and she felt his fingertips, warm on her cheeks before he again moved forward, bringing his lips to hers. Her brain finally caught on to what was happening as his kisses grew deeper, and she was about to close her hands around his arms when he pulled away abruptly. Her arms fell to her sides, her breath coming quickly.

They faced one another for a moment. Phineas's eyes were on her, his expression serious. She felt the intimacy of their position—how thin a barrier was keeping them apart. He waited, and she did not know what he wanted her to say, only that she could not say *that*. In the seconds that followed, her chest pounded, reverberating through her and muddling her mind.

At last, Phineas bowed. He turned toward his room, and Kitty was left in the hallway with a gaping breach to her self-sufficiency. In its wake was desolation. Perhaps she should have spoken the words. Maybe it would not have been so brazen after all. She reached for the handle to her room and opened, a dim swath of light from the crackling fire stretching across the room to greet her.

CHAPTER SEVENTEEN

T he day before they left for Bath, Phineas set off riding
with Samuel an hour earlier than their usual lesson time
to allow Kitty to oversee the packing of their trunks. Samuel
had been keen to spend an extra hour in the saddle with
Phineas, knowing he would not have much opportunity to ride
in Bristol. On that subject, Kitty was determined to speak with
Erasmus when she saw him in Bath and win him over to her
point of view by appealing to his love of distinction. If Samuel
did not show to advantage on horseback at Harrow, it would
not look well for the Stokes name, and that was something
Erasmus would care about.

The extra hour had also given Kitty a chance to deal with a
household emergency that had been brought to her attention.
The emergency turned out to be nothing more than a maid's
cheek swelling to twice its size because her tooth needed to be
drawn, and Mrs. Morley not wanting to give her time off to do
it. One of the footmen appeared to have interest in the young
maid and spoke up on her behalf, asking to keep it quiet from
the housekeeper. It was a delicate matter that did not endear

Kitty to Mrs. Morley, for Kitty overrode her decision and ordered that the doctor be sent for immediately.

Kitty wondered if she would continue to have such resistance from the housekeeper. The rest of the servants did not seem to hold her in such small esteem, and she had not yet broached the subject with Phineas. She did not wish for him to know she had difficulty in earning the housekeeper's respect. When that matter had been dealt with, she turned her steps toward the stable, wishing to be ready on time. Her husband promised they would circle back to retrieve her, and Kitty no longer had any fear that Samuel would be too tired from his rides. He showed more courage than she did, and more stamina.

Kitty entered the dim of the stables and heard noises in the back. "Craddock," she called out, walking forward.

He appeared at the sound of her voice, coming out of the stall with his shirt sleeves rolled up despite the cold air. "I've just finished exercising one of the hacks." Craddock stepped toward her with an intimate smile, and she peered beyond him to see if there were other hands nearby.

"I am glad I have not disturbed you in the middle of your task," she said. At the far end, one of the stable hands was mucking out the stall, but only his back was visible. "I came to see if I might have Fawn saddled."

Craddock reached for a peg on the wall that held the bridle. "Certainly. I will attend to it. Perhaps we might go riding together."

Kitty flashed a polite smile that fell quickly. "Lord Hayworth and Samuel will circle back to retrieve me. They should not be much longer."

The groom turned his back on her and went into the stall where Fawn stood across from the small alcove where saddles were kept. The new sidesaddle Phineas had ordered for Kitty was draped over a thick peg, and when Craddock saw her admiring it, he stood at her side, his arms folded. "This saddle is beautifully made. I think you ought to be more comfortable on it, and perhaps your riding will improve even more."

Kitty fingered the saddle, and the stiff leather was gleaming and smooth. When she looked up, his eyes were on her, his gaze intent. She tried to lighten the atmosphere. "I can only hope any hindrance to my progress is due to having an old saddle." She was only jesting to release the tension, but Craddock seemed to take her words at face value.

"You are making excellent progress, my lady." He placed the bridle over the horse's head and glanced at her as he fastened it. "I have missed our lessons. Now that your husband rides with you, we cannot speak of Bristol and our shared community there."

Was her groom flirting? Kitty began to wonder if she were stupid. Sometimes his looks and questions crossed the line, but she could not always tell if she had simply imagined it. After all, why would someone pursue a married woman? It made no sense. On one hand, a groom did not generally say "I missed our rides" as that would imply some complicity or relationship other than mistress-servant. On the other hand, grooms did not generally share acquaintances as she and Craddock did.

His smiles always took on an intimate manner, yet she possessed just enough doubts to wonder if perhaps it was just his way. Perhaps he smiled at everyone like that. She found it nigh impossible to set him in his place, for it would be terribly embarrassing to have made an error in thinking he meant more than he did.

"The important thing for me is to keep riding, so I might become proficient. If Lord Hayworth is able to find the time to teach me, I consider myself fortunate."

Craddock slipped the saddle on the horse's back and tightened the girth straps. He took the reins, and brought Fawn out into the aisle between the stalls that led to the front of the stable. He did all this without answering.

At last he met her gaze over the horse's back, his brow furrowed. "So there is no preference? Your rides with Lord Hayworth or your rides with me? You do not prefer one to the other?" He stopped near the opening of the stable and ducked around the horse's head, still holding the reins. He faced her, lifting a brow in inquiry.

That was the final straw. She could not believe his intentions innocent. "Your discourse has become increasingly familiar," Kitty said evenly, weighing her words. "I would like to remind you that I am married."

"You are married, but you are not happy." Craddock leaned toward her, his voice firm and coaxing. "I can see it. This is *not* where you belong, Kitty, and you know it. There is a genuineness about you that I admire. I've never met a woman like you. It's why I've stayed in this post as long as I have."

"I beg you will not—"

"Allow me to finish." Craddock said quickly, and Kitty went silent. Let him say what he had to say, so she could remove all doubt about where her loyalties lay. In any event, she could not take Fawn on her own, and her husband was not back yet with Samuel. She looked at Craddock impatiently, feeling trapped with him filling the space between her and the exit.

"I never want to regret the rest of my life that I didn't tell you this. And I think you might regret if you don't hear it." Craddock dropped the reins, and Fawn stood patiently in place. "I have developed feelings for you during our time together, and I believe you have feelings for me. I have a plan to breed stallions, and a friend has gone to Scotland to select the stud. I want you to come with me. We will go far—as far as Leith—and no one in Bristol, apart from family, need ever hear from us again. Our family will only wish us happy. They will not reject you for a step that might be considered scandalous in higher Society. After all, we do not move in the same circles."

Kitty's outrage had kept her mute throughout his speech, but she trembled from disgust. "I am astonished you have so wholly misread my character as to think I would commit an adulterous act. That I would run away from the home where I belong. And if that were not enough, you are showing your complete ignorance of my family's values. If you think they would accept me back after I have taken so ruinous a step, you are in grievous error—even were I tempted to follow you."

"You *are* tempted. Your longing gaze shows me you are. And even if your brother does not wish to see you, my family will certainly wish to see me. We are not in a position where we need to worry about what other people think." Craddock held out his hand. "Kitty, I must own the truth. I did not need this position. If I have taken it, it is only because I had seen you on my last visit and was called away before I could present myself. I had decided on you, Kitty. I did not expect your brother to work so quickly to arrange an unhappy marriage for you. That has surely complicated matters, but has not made them irreversible. I will not give you up just because you have been compromised."

Kitty could not listen any longer. "You are mad. Marriage is most certainly irreversible in God's law. Step out of my way—"

Craddock darted to block her path. "Kitty." He lifted a hand to her cheek.

"Kitty?" The small voice came from the entrance of the stable and Craddock whipped away his hand. Samuel stopped short, and his eyes narrowed in Craddock's direction. "We have returned. Are you ready to ride?"

Phineas came in on the heels of Samuel and saw Kitty's close proximity to Craddock, who had now taken a step back. She was certain her face was bright red and knew instantly what conclusions her husband would draw. She had kept silent too long about Craddock's advances. She had been a fool. Phineas would never believe her now.

"I have done all the riding I have time for today, Samuel."

Phineas spoke in a terse voice, which showed Kitty he had seen everything. She wanted to weep in despair—to run and cling to him. "I think it has been enough riding for you as well today. My lady"—Phineas bowed before her—"I trust you will do as you think best."

Phineas turned on his heels and left the stable. Samuel looked up at Kitty in confusion. "A moment ago, he said he was willing to ride. It is too bad he does not want to do so any longer. Are you going to ride without me?"

"No." She kept her eyes on Samuel to avoid Craddock's gaze. "I will keep you company and save my ride for another day. Craddock, have Fawn returned to her stall."

Kitty put her arm around Samuel, and they began walking to the house. She could feel the weight of Craddock's proposition follow her out the door. No one in her acquaintance had ever broken a vow of marriage. Well, there was Mrs. Burns in Bristol, but people had been more shocked that she married at all than they had been at her abandoning the union. Her name was only whispered in the drawing rooms. How could Craddock have thought she would accept it? Or that she held any tender feelings for him? No! He had been a familiar voice and nothing more. If only her own husband had been half as ardent as Craddock had been. Kitty let out a hiss of frustration.

"Do we have to leave for Bath tomorrow?" Samuel asked. "Can I not stay here with you?"

Kitty was pulled out of her problems for a moment, and she hugged him at her side. "It's hard, I know, my dear Sam. But our marriage is so new, and I do not yet know Phineas's parents. I need to go and meet them more informally than what we had at the wedding, and I truly cannot have you there when I do so. But you heard what Phineas said, did you not? Or, rather, I should say Lord Hayworth."

"He lets me call him Phineas, too," Samuel answered. "Or at

least he does not say anything when I do. Yes, he said I could return later after the holidays. But that is a long ways away."

"It will pass quickly." Kitty steered him into the house and stopped to face him. "I promise, Samuel, you will always be my family, and you will always have a place to stay. I just need time to get accustomed to my new life here, do you see?" Samuel paused, biting his lip, then nodded. "Now, why don't you go find the gardener. He told me he wished to see how you've improved with the bow and arrows before you leave."

Samuel brightened at that. "I will fetch them." He started to run off then came back and planted a kiss on Kitty's cheek, to her surprise. He had never done such a thing. At least someone wanted to be around her. As for her husband, she wasn't sure Phineas ever wanted to see her again.

Kitty stood in the quiet entryway, assessing how to proceed. The gleaming dark wood of the bannister and floors, the painted ivory walls with the old frames, the bronze wall sconces —all these were beginning to be home for her. A footman walked by and paused in his steps.

"Do you need something, my lady?"

She lifted her gaze and shook her head. She couldn't very well stand in the corridor like a moonling. Everyone would realize something was wrong. She knew what she had to do.

Kitty gave a timid knock on Phineas's study. This was met with silence. She turned to go, thinking her husband was not inside or perhaps did not wish to see anyone, when she heard the sharp command. "Enter!" She turned the handle at once and stepped through the door, looking up at last to meet her husband's gaze. He sat at his desk, his face lined with unhappiness. Kitty gulped.

"May I speak with you?"

"If you wish." Phineas returned the answer with indifference and straightened the papers on his desk. When she continued to stare at him, he looked up at last. "What is it?"

Kitty's eyes smarted at the sharp sound of his words, so different from the warm complicity in the carriage the night before. But she needed to push through and prove her innocence. She swallowed again, her throat dry. "I would like to request you send off Craddock. That you replace him."

Phineas looked up, a flash of surprise lighting his eyes. He held her gaze intently. "Why?"

Kitty took steps forward. "Because he has become too familiar." She lay her hand on Phineas's desk. "I allowed him liberties in his speech because he is my neighbor's cousin, and I did not wish to put tension in our two families. But he has gone too far."

Phineas shot to his feet and came to the side of the desk where he faced Kitty. "What has he done?"

Kitty pressed her lips together. She still did not want to ruin their family relations, but Craddock had propositioned her after all. This was not something she could keep from her husband. "He has not touched me..." Her words trailed away when she remembered his hand on her knee, his hands on her arms to keep her from leaving, his touching her cheek. "Well, not in such a very bad way."

When Phineas opened his mouth in outrage, she hastened to explain. "I beg you not to do something hasty. I did not allow him to press his advantage. But he did offer me a dishonorable proposition, which I refused at once."

"You refused?" Phineas's words came out harshly, but she saw the hurt and the hope in his eyes. It was the hope that gave her the strength to continue.

"I most certainly refused. Phineas, we are married. I do not take those vows lightly. Although I do not wish to harm my relationship with my neighbor, I see no choice for it but to let him go and replace him with someone"—her brows knit as she attempted to find a suitable word—"older?"

Phineas's tension showed in the cords of his neck and his

clenched jaw, but at Kitty's words a laugh escaped him. A relieved, agonized laugh. "Older?" he said.

She decided to stick to it, and nodded. A nervous laugh escaped her as well. "Older," she repeated.

Phineas looked down at his hand resting on the desk near hers. His shoulders relaxed. "He will be gone by morning."

When Phineas lifted his gaze to Kitty's, it was filled with longing. She thought this must be how he had looked at her when he'd kissed her last night, but she could only imagine it in the dim, moonlit corridor. Now she saw it in broad daylight. She took a tiny step forward, longing to run to him and have him wrap her in an embrace—longing to be comforted with his arms around her—but she did not dare close the distance.

"I did not trust you," Phineas said.

Kitty looked down and lifted a shoulder wordlessly. She'd known it, and it had saddened her, but what could she say? She wasn't sure she deserved his trust when she hadn't cut Craddock's attentions short.

"I am sorry," he said softly.

His gentle words brought her gaze back up to meet his, and the moment grew heavy with meaning and then longing. Kitty parted her lips but could not speak the words he'd claimed he wished to hear from her. He was a good man and was showing himself to be an ideal husband. He even treated Samuel like family. A yearning grew in her own breast for something more than this friendly, civil arrangement of theirs. "Phineas—"

The door swung open abruptly. "Phineas, Kitty! Come and see! I shot an arrow fifteen yards and hit my target!"

Phineas shifted his gaze to Samuel, then looked back at Kitty, a rueful smile hovering on his lips. He gave a small shrug. "That sounds like something I can't miss, Sam." He brushed past her, leaving a scent of sandalwood and warmth.

At the door, Phineas looked back at her. "Coming?"

She nodded and hurried to catch up. Not only was Phineas

kinder than she had had any right to expect from an arranged match—if she were being honest with herself, she would likely not have done much better—but he was extending his heart to her in his own reserved way. Perhaps it would not be long before he declared his love for her the way every woman longed to hear from her husband.

CHAPTER EIGHTEEN

E arly the next morning, Phineas entered the stable. Craddock stood on one side of the aisle, rubbing a saddle with a cloth. He looked up in time to spot Phineas and stood straight, folding his arms.

Phineas came to stand in front of him. "Have you seen that the wheel is aligned on the traveling coach as I requested of you?"

Craddock shifted on his feet and met Phineas's gaze fleetingly. "I have, my lord. The coach is ready to depart for Bath."

"Very good. You may hitch the horses to it and have it brought around to the front of the house by one of the stable hands." Phineas flicked a piece of invisible lint from his sleeve. "You are not to accompany the coach, for I do not want my wife to have to meet you again before you leave."

Craddock's face hardened with suspicion, and he pulled at the cloth between his two hands. "What do you mean ... before *I* leave?"

"I mean you are no longer welcome here. Not after you have made advances on my wife." Phineas had been in control of himself until now—had prepared himself to be perfectly restrained during the conversation—but a burst of anger propelled him a step closer until he was face to face with Craddock.

"And although I have every right to run you through—and do not think I lack the courage or the skill to do it—I will not. It is enough that you have lost. My wife has no interest in you, and you will have to answer to God for what you are. As for the rest, your employment at Giddenhall is done. You may collect your earnings from the steward. If ever I see that you have attempted to contact my wife again, it will be the last thing you do. Do I make myself clear?"

"Perfectly." Craddock spoke the word through gritted teeth, and turned away.

KITTY WAS ALREADY in the entryway, charmingly attired in yet another traveling dress Phineas had never seen. In everything she wore, she demonstrated her superior taste. He noticed a familiar package in her hands as she climbed into the coach behind Samuel. Her maid came next, carrying a small case.

Phineas swung himself into the coach and sat at Kitty's side with Samuel and Sterling facing them. "What is that?" he asked, nodding at the package in her hands.

"These are some of the fabrics I plan to have made into riding habits when I am in Bath. I will have the others made up by a seamstress in Castle Combe to support the work of someone local." Kitty's direct gaze started his heart thumping again. The restraint between them had fled, now that he knew he had been wrong about her interest in Craddock, and the man would not be here to bother them when they returned.

And she was at last planning to have the fabric he bought her put to use. Nothing could be better. "I can take you to the modiste who sold the cloth to me. I am sure she will be very glad to have your business. My friend, Bromley, recommended her to me." Phineas placed his hand on the package Kitty held— a poor second to placing his hand in hers. "I am glad you are going to use them."

"How could I not? The colors suit me so well, and the feel of the cloth is exquisite." Kitty turned to smile at him, and he was momentarily blinded. She looked ahead quickly. "Sam, don't place your feet on Lord Hayworth's seat."

"Sam has permission to call me Phineas," her husband corrected her.

She flashed him another grateful smile before Samuel claimed Phineas's attention. He launched into a whirlwind of what he'd seen on his ride to Giddenhall, asking if they would be traveling back on the same road. Phineas answered his questions whenever Samuel paused for breath, but his mind was on Kitty. *She liked my gifts.* It was too bad he had never been inside her bedroom to see whether she had had the painting hung and where she put it.

They arrived in Bath without much difficulty, and Phineas directed the driver to the house Erasmus had rented for the wedding. He had received a letter stating that Erasmus would be renting the same house for Kitty's arrival, and that they could bring Samuel there. The coach pulled up in front of the door, and the footman went to ring the bell. Phineas ordered the driver to take the maid to his parents' townhouse and then come back for them.

"Sam!" Edward came running out to greet his cousin, with Helen following behind. Kitty climbed out of the carriage and lay her hand on Phineas's arm. "Are we intending to stay for a bit or do we go directly to your parents' house?"

"What would you like to do?" Phineas placed his other hand over hers as the groom stepped down to stand at the lead horse's head.

"I would like to see the children if possible," Kitty answered. "Perhaps we might go in just for tea?"

Phineas nodded and modified his instructions to the driver to have the coach brought to the mews after having deposited Sterling. Inside, they were relieved of their outerwear, and Mrs. Stokes came forward with a smile that did not appear to Phineas to hold any warmth.

"Kitty, my lord—Erasmus will be right with you. He has only to finish a letter. We have been expecting you, and I had the tea service readied. The maid will bring it up as soon as the water is hot. Please come to the drawing room."

Phineas followed Kitty into the drawing room, where Samuel was demonstrating his archery victory to a rapt younger cousin in the corner of the room. Kitty faced her sister-in-law. "Mary, will you bring William to see me?"

Mary signaled for the footman to notify Nurse, then turned to Kitty. "Yes, he has grown since you last saw him I believe. He is quite a handsome boy by now and looks very like Edward." Mary took a chair near Kitty and cast an indulgent glance at her oldest son.

"He was always a darling," Kitty said. William was soon brought in and immediately reached out for Kitty, who sat and tucked him into her arms. She mouthed sweet nothings to the baby, who beamed at her in return, then bent down to kiss his neck, making William laugh. It was a beautiful moment, if a bit tortuous to watch. This woman was destined to be a mother, and if her children looked anything like her, they would be beautiful. Still, so little progress had been made in that direction.

Kitty glanced at him, and Phineas averted his gaze, fearing his desire was written on his face. He ardently wanted this woman to bear his children. She so clearly wanted to be a mother as well—but did she want that with him?

Erasmus entered the room. "Hayworth." He walked forward and reached out his hand, and Phineas shook it.

Kitty darted her eyes to her brother, and Phineas wondered whether it was because Stokes had dropped the 'my lord' or because he hadn't bothered to greet her. To tell the truth, the intimacy of his name on Stokes's lips irritated Phineas, but he hid it. This was his wife's brother, and it was part of the bargain.

Taking a seat, Erasmus asked about their journey and the improvements at Giddenhall but directed all his questions to Phineas. Kitty kept her attention on William and did not seem to notice the slight. At last, Erasmus paused and glanced at his wife. "Why do you not both join us for dinner this week, now that you are here? What evening would be suitable for you?"

Kitty directed pleading eyes to Phineas. He could see that she was pleased by the invitation. As for himself, he had little desire to dine with Stokes, but he supposed he owed it to his wife since they were staying with his family.

"I believe Wednesday next would suit," Phineas replied. "I will have much to attend to once we arrive, but my family cannot claim our attention every day."

A smile lit Kitty's face as Erasmus announced, "We will have dinner on Wednesday, then. Well, Samuel." At last, Erasmus noticed his younger brother. "How did you find your stay at Giddenhall?"

Samuel abandoned his conversation with Edward at once and came over, eyes shining. "I learned how to shoot my arrow farther than ever, and I learned to ride."

"That puts me in mind of something, Erasmus." Kitty swiveled in her seat, her hands still caressing the baby's head. "You must see to Samuel's riding lessons if he is going to find his place at Harrow. I know you would not wish him to be behind in such matters. Lord Hayworth went to Harrow, and he can tell you." She turned to Phineas. "Is that not so? That he must have riding lessons?"

Phineas did not wish to tell another man how to rear his own family, but he could not be insensible to Kitty's plea on Samuel's behalf. "It is true. Without them, he will be at a disadvantage compared to the other boys. However, if the idea does not displease you, we thought to invite Samuel again early in the winter for another stay." Samuel was following the conversation closely, and he turned eager eyes on Erasmus.

Stokes rubbed his chin and nodded. "Of course, of course. Whatever you think is best for the boy. I hope he was not too much trouble for you?"

"None at all." The conversation passed on to other topics, and they took tea while Kitty focused on keeping the cup far out of William's reach. When finished, Phineas called to have the carriage brought back around before riding the short distance to his parent's house.

"I fear you may have to put up with another round of tea with my parents," he said in the carriage, glad to have her alone again. He wondered where his mother would put them in their house. There was a larger bedroom on the west side of the house that would be perfect.

"Not to worry," she said, her mind appearing to be untroubled by such thoughts as he was entertaining. "Although I'm not sure I can drink very much more before I float away."

Phineas laughed at the sally, but he was nervous. He hoped his parents would be on their best behavior and treat Kitty with the warmth and respect she deserved as his wife.

Seamus showed them into the drawing room, and Phineas's parents joined them shortly afterwards.

"Well, Katherine…" Phineas's mother pinched her lips as though it was hard enough for her to say Kitty's proper name. The nickname was nigh impossible. "I hope you are pleased with your marriage so far—and your life at Giddenhall."

Kitty curtsied to Lord and Lady Midlington. "I am very pleased," she replied. There was respect in her tone, but no obsequiousness, and Phineas was glad. She would finish by earning his parents' respect; there was no question.

"And what changes have you begun to make to your estate?" his father asked Phineas, settling into the armchair across from theirs. He had done little more than nod at Kitty.

Phineas launched into the repairs made on the tenants' houses, while his mother and Kitty listened to their conversation. This was not exactly how he'd hoped their first real meeting would go. He hoped his wife and mother would discover shared interests and have their own conversation.

When the subject of repairs was spent, Phineas's mother sat up straighter. "We have decided to host a ball in a week. This will introduce Katherine to Society and show everyone that we are pleased with the match. It is something we should have done from the beginning, but the betrothal was performed in such a rushed manner." Lady Midlington's eyes darted to Kitty's belly, and Phineas was startled. The realization of what his mother had implied filled him with shock and disgust. She went on smoothly. "If you have no objections, that is."

Phineas was unsure if Kitty had seen the glance and all that it meant. She answered in an even tone. "I've no objections at all, my lady. I will be very happy to meet your acquaintances."

Phineas's mother primmed her mouth. "Mind you, it is not so much for you to make their acquaintance as it is for us to show them there is nothing wrong with your marriage. Nothing could be worse than scandal attached to our name." At those words, Kitty's expression fell.

It was the worst timing and Phineas felt it acutely, but it could not be avoided. "I beg your pardon—Mother, Father." He glanced at his wife, sympathy in his expression. "Kitty, I have arranged to meet Carter to bring him up to date on the affairs of the estate. I did not intend to stay so long at Stokes's house, and I see now I have fallen behind. Mother, I know you will make Kitty feel welcome while I attend to this visit. I am sure Kitty would like to rest after her journey."

Phineas stood and took a step toward Kitty with an impulse to kiss her on the cheek. He could not bring himself to do it, however. Not with his parents watching, and not with the memory of his mother's meaning-filled glance at her midsection. He opened his mouth to speak but could not think of anything that would make the situation better, so Phineas gave a brief nod instead and left.

The silence that ensued as he shut the door behind him was not reassuring. He stood in the corridor listening, thinking that perhaps he should send word to Carter that he would not come after all. It would only delay matters, and they had weeks of work to catch up on, but he could not bear for his wife to suffer any awkwardness so soon upon arrival.

After a long moment, he heard his mother speaking, then his father. He heard Kitty's voice as well. The conversation had picked up again in his absence. This would give them a chance to know one another more freely. A sense of relief coursed through him, and he picked up his hat and gloves that were lying on the side table as the footman opened the door.

HAD it really been necessary for Phineas to arrange to meet his man of business on the day they arrived? By doing so, he had left her completely unprotected, and Kitty's breath quickened in her irritation. She refused to be nervous before her in-laws, although she did not feel their welcome. Lord Midlington got to his feet immediately and muttered about having some important affairs to see to. She stood and curtsied, then sat again and turned to Lady Midlington, hopeful of finding some common ground.

"I am glad we were able to come to Bath. It gives me a chance to discover where Phineas spent his childhood."

"Well, you should know that Phineas grew up on Midlington Estate. He is the son of an earl, although I understand if the significance is difficult for you to appreciate, having had no experience with grand estates."

Kitty's tea was practically untouched, and although she had taken it again in her hands, she now set it down on the table before her. "It is true. I have never lived on an estate until Giddenhall, but I do have some understanding of how estates are run from my time spent there."

Lady Midlington began lining up the spoons on the tray before her. "Yes, but you have spent mere weeks. Not a lifetime like my son has. Giddenhall is nothing like Midlington. It is much smaller, and neither Lord Midlington nor I can under-stand why he chose to go there rather than continue working on the estate he will one day inherit."

Kitty clutched her hands in her lap. Apparently her body had not received the information that she was not to be nervous. "I'm sorry, but I thought Giddenhall was your mother's. Are you not glad that your son is bringing the estate into order? I had understood it was much in need of repair."

Lady Midlington knocked the teaspoons askew and sat back in her chair. "Yes, and it has been brought to order with *your* settlement. I know that. Truth be told, I have no particular affection for the place. I did not grow up there. I grew up on my father's estate, and my mother retired there when my father died, but by then I was married." Lady Midlington got to her feet. "I imagine you are very tired. Come, I will show you to your room."

It was not a suggestion. Kitty followed her to the door, feeling like an unwanted puppy. She did not understand how those glimpses of humor and affection she sometimes saw in Phineas came to be with two parents who were so cold.

Lady Midlington led the way up the staircase. The town-house had three floors and was much larger than the one Kitty's brother had rented on Laura Place. On the second floor, Lady Midlington gestured toward a room on the back of the corridor.

"That is Phineas's room. I did not arrange for you to stay there since it is too small for two people, and I know he is accustomed to that room and to his privacy. He will not wish to leave it. Besides, the largest guest room is in need of refurbishing. I have put you in a room upstairs."

"Whatever arrangements you've made will suit me, my lady." Kitty did not attempt to make further conversation as she followed her mother-in-law up another set of the stairs. Lady Midlington opened the door to a room that was of a decent size and tastefully decorated. A rush of relief went through Kitty that she wasn't being sent to stay in the servants' quarters. She had begun to fear that was where she would end up.

"I hope you will be comfortable here." Lady Midlington kept her hand on the doorknob of Kitty's room. Her expression was tight, and it sounded as if the polite words were forced out of her.

Kitty would not give Lady Midlington the satisfaction of thinking she regretted being placed so far from her husband. She faced her mother-in-law in the doorway. "I also like my privacy. This room is perfect."

CHAPTER NINETEEN

Phineas was shown directly into Carter's office, who had been waiting for him. "My lord, it is good to see you. I hope married life suits you well."

Phineas noticed the careworn lines around Carter's eyes that were not there before and asked, "How are your parents?"

An expression of pain flitted across Carter's face. "I am afraid my father has left this world. My mother is doing as well as can be expected. I thank you for your patience and understanding that has allowed me to attend to my family during this difficult time."

"I am sorry to hear about your father. And I could do no less —you have been such a help to me. If there's anything else I can do?" Phineas let his voice trail away into a question.

Carter shook his head. "No, in life, these things must come. Let us instead talk about your affairs. How are you finding the servants I hired for you?"

Phineas settled into his seat. "Well, I did not wish to bother you with such trivial matters when you had greater ones at hand, but I cannot claim to have been fortunate in my servants. The steward you had hired a year ago did not do what was required for the tenants' houses—which I discovered upon arriving after the wedding. I was obliged to come to Bath and use my father's man of business to find a new steward. And Craddock—you know the overqualified groom you had hired, who applied for the position, as if brought by fate?" Carter nodded, and Phineas went on. "He appears to have had designs on my wife."

Carter shot his head up, and he lay both hands on the desk. "What?"

"I dismissed Craddock. I am also not sure about the house-keeper, Mrs. Morley, although she was not your hire. I have given her a warning. I believe she will now treat my wife with the respect due."

Carter's face was ashen at the number of servants who failed to suit their posts. "I have let you down, my lord. I will under-stand if you wish to have your affairs handled elsewhere."

Phineas chuckled softly. "No, nothing so drastic as that. After all, in one area you have done very well." Carter met Phineas's gaze with a look of inquiry. "Yes, you have chosen my wife well. I am most pleased with her."

Carter leaned back in his chair and allowed his shoulders to relax. "That is a relief. When you wouldn't even look at a minia-ture of her, I could not help but fear you might not find her to your liking."

Phineas shot Carter a wry look. "You knew very well that Lady Hayworth is a remarkably handsome woman, and she has a sweet temper. All in all you did your research, and I am most obliged. There is one more post to fulfill, however. I came to see you about the valet."

"I have found one, my lord. I was only waiting for you to arrive in Bath to send him to your father's house. I hope that he should meet with your approval."

"Very good. It puts an end to the servants borrowed from my father. This will give me a clean break from the management my father has exerted over my life. You have done well." With a mischievous smile, Phineas added, "You need have no fear for your position."

"You relieve my mind, my lord." Carter grinned.

They spent the next few hours going over the most pressing details of Phineas's affairs, and at the end of it, Carter stacked the papers on his desk and Phineas stood. "Are you married, Carter?" It had never occurred to Phineas to ask, although Carter knew nearly everything there was to know about him. He suspected Carter did very well for himself. Phineas knew he lived in fashionable quarters and had studied at Oxford. He supposed it was the personal talk of Carter's parents and Phineas's own marriage that moved them a degree forward in intimacy.

Carter looked up in surprise, and although he was older by a year or two than Phineas, he gave something close to a blush. "No, my lord. Was there a reason...?"

"Oh, no." *Heavens no.* What had ever possessed him to start asking personal questions of his man of business? "I had just wondered."

Carter shrugged and fingered the leather envelope he was holding in his hand. "My father left me something in the way of investments, and I suppose I should begin thinking of it now."

"May I suggest something?" Carter looked up with interest and nodded, and a smile hovered on Phineas's face. "Have your man of business find you a wife."

Carter laughed, as Phineas made his way to the door. "You promised to come to Giddenhall again, and it might be useful to come if you have time before Christmas. I want you to meet the new steward, since you will need to communicate with him on matters."

"I have nothing pressing to attend to before Christmas," Carter answered.

They bid farewell, and Phineas headed back to his parents'

house. Once inside, he peered into the drawing room where his mother sat, lost in thought.

"Mother?" He took two steps into the room, wondering how Kitty had fared with his parents while he was gone. It was foolish to suppose she would still be sitting with his mother having a cozy chat. "Where is Kitty?"

His mother broke out of her reverie to look at him. "Did all go well with Carter? Has he taken up Giddenhall affairs once again?"

"He has. Where is Kitty now?" Phineas sat across from his mother.

"Katherine is in her room. She said she needed to rest before dinner." *Her room.* So they would not be sharing a bedroom. "She is a rather timid thing for a viscountess. I hope she will be suited to her role after her training."

"She is not so very timid." As far as Phineas was concerned, she had no problem telling him exactly what she thought. "What room is she in? I thought you would put us in the west-facing room that is large enough for two." He fiddled with his shirt sleeves to avoid looking at his mother. The truth was, it would have been a sweet torture to be in the same room as his wife if she refused to release him from his oath, but he was certain it would have brought them over the final hurdle to being married in the proper sense.

"She did not seem to wish for that. I put her in the second largest room after yours."

The one on an entirely different floor. A sharp pang of disappointment hit Phineas in the chest. He molded his features into austerity rather than reveal to his mother how much that hurt. *She did not seem to wish for that?* "Did she come right out and say she wished for her own room?"

"In so many words." A gust of air caused the bare branches of a nearby tree to scratch at the window, and his mother peered through the glass. "She said she preferred to have her own room, as she was accustomed to her privacy."

"I see." Phineas leaned on his chin, attempting to digest the news. Perhaps he had not made the headway into his marriage he'd thought.

STERLING ALERTED Kitty to the fact that the family was meeting for dinner. She'd grown accustomed to seeing Phineas on the other side of her door when it was time to go down, and the shift disconcerted her. It was as though Kitty were adrift and unanchored without her husband there.

Phineas was waiting for her in the drawing room, however, and he looked anxious when he spotted Kitty, wasting no time in approaching her. "Are you comfortably settled then? Is the room to your liking? I am sorry that my affairs kept me until now."

She glanced at her mother-in-law, remembering the words about how much her son liked his privacy. There was only one answer to make. "The room suits me perfectly. I am very happy with it."

She could not read his cryptic expression. Phineas took Kitty on his arm and followed his parents into the dining room. What was in that expression he wore? It seemed as though his face fell. She supposed if he liked his privacy that much, he was not about to change it for her. Kitty could not help but wonder how important it was to Phineas to maintain his own room. Would he still do so if they were married in the proper sense?

When they were seated, Lord Midlington put his fingers on the table as the footman attempted to serve him without spilling anything. "Did you get everything established with Carter? Will you have time to visit Parkson as well? There are some outstanding issues on Midlington that you were responsible for

—and still other issues I think you should continue to keep an eye on since you will one day inherit it."

Phineas allowed the footman to place a venison steak and garden peas on his plate before answering. "My visit with Carter was successful, and he is caught up on all matters for Giddenhall. My valet arrived, and I've seen to it that he was settled in the servant's quarters."

Lord Midlington frowned under bushy eyebrows. "You could have continued to use the valet I provided for you all these years."

"You know very well I needed to hire one of my own. Your valet was not willing to leave Bath, even for the short stay after my wedding, and I need one that can follow me to Giddenhall."

"*Hmph.*" Lord Midlington grunted and began cutting his meat.

"We've decided that the dinner ball to celebrate your marriage will occur next Thursday," Lady Midlington said. "Bath is thin of parties these days, so I do not think anyone will mind the last minute notice. Is there anyone you would like us to invite, apart from our usual set?"

Phineas looked up, his fork poised mid-air. "Yes, as a matter of fact." He turned to Kitty, startling her. She had grown accustomed to passing unnoticed in his family. "I have sent word to Robert Bromley that we were in town and have already received a note in return inviting us for tea tomorrow. Does that suit you?"

The idea of leaving the house for a social outing lifted Kitty's spirits. "I would like that very much," she replied.

Phineas nodded and turned back to his mother. "I would like to have Mr. and Mrs. Robert Bromley invited."

His mother narrowed her eyes. "Who are the Bromleys?"

"Phineas spoke of him when he was in school, if you'll remember," Lord Midlington said, lifting his gaze briefly to his wife's. "I've met Bromley's father. He is suitable enough to invite to our ball."

The names of the other guests flowed past Kitty, leaving her out of her depth. She'd known it would be difficult to integrate into a society that was not her own. Not that she'd ever felt that way in Phineas's presence. It was only his parents ... and his servants, she thought wryly, who made her aware of her station.

"You may give their direction to me," Lady Midlington said. "I will have an invitation sent tomorrow."

CHAPTER TWENTY

The next day, Kitty went with Phineas to visit the Bromleys on Great Pulteney Street. She had asked him if they might stop at the modiste first and was pleased to see his eyes brighten at her request. He could not have doubted that she would put those beautiful fabrics to good use, surely?

Kitty peeked at Phineas through the crack in the curtains as she was being measured, while he sat in the waiting room. He never did anything so indecent as to come into where she was being fitted, although technically as her husband it would not be considered as such. She did, however, see his gaze continually shift in her direction before quickly looking away again. At one point, Mrs. Laurent asked if Phineas would not like to come and see how the cloth draped across his wife, but he demurred. Kitty was relieved. She would not like his first glimpse of her in *déshabille* to occur in front of an audience.

When they arrived at the Bromley's residence, the butler showed Phineas and Kitty into the drawing room where the couple was sitting. The Bromleys stood as soon as they entered the room, and Mrs. Bromley came forward first and greeted Kitty with a curtsy. "Lady Hayworth, it is a pleasure to meet you

—and you, my lord. I was thankful when Robert informed me he had run into an old schoolmate. There are not many friends in Bath who are our age, and even fewer that Robert would wish to spend any time with. How long are you staying?"

Phineas smiled. "Only two weeks. A pleasure to meet you as well, Mrs. Bromley. I hadn't thought Robert would be able to tempt anyone to the altar, but I can see he is fortunate, indeed."

Mr. Bromley shot Phineas a look heavy with irony. "I might say the same for you." Kitty suppressed a bubble of mirth.

"Oh, mine is merely an arranged marriage," Phineas replied with a sigh of resignation. "One of convenience."

The blunt nature of his words surprised Kitty and sent a bolt of pain through her. Was he always to introduce her that way? She darted a glance at her husband, who appeared to be waiting for her regard because he gave an exaggerated wink. Kitty's shoulders sank with relief. This was the first time Phineas had teased her, and she hadn't known he was capable of it.

Phineas turned from her, a smile still on his lips. "By the bye, I believe you will be receiving an invitation to a select ball my parents are holding next week. My parents wish to present Kitty to Society. And speaking of introductions, might we all address each other by our Christian names? Robert and I go far enough back, and I hope the informality extends to our wives."

"Hear, hear," Bromley said with a smile.

"Oh yes. It suits me perfectly for my friends to call me Teresa," she replied. "I am not one to stand on ceremony, as Robert will tell you. And as to the invitation, we have just now received one, as a matter of fact. Of course we will be there."

When they'd sat and Teresa had ordered tea, she turned to Kitty. "How do you find married life?"

Kitty did not know how to answer, and one glance at Phineas told her the question struck him as just as awkward. "I like it very well," Kitty replied, turning her gaze back to Teresa. "I suppose I was fortunate in the choice of a husband, although you now know our marriage was merely the product of a tire-some contract." She said the last bit with a droll look that made everyone laugh, and she saw a twinkle in Phineas's eyes.

The soaring in Kitty's heart continued along with the conversation. Not even when she'd lived in Bristol did she find such friendly discourse as this. It had never struck her before how very few friends she had, even where she had grown up. Yet here, and in one day, she'd found people who appeared to possess enough depth of feeling and sensibility to become true friends, but who were light-hearted enough to opt for playful banter. And as Phineas's wife, she was being brought into the relationship as though she'd known them both for years.

"Will you be coming to Bath often?" Robert asked Phineas. "I am surprised we have not run into each other before, although I suppose it has not been that long since we took up residence here."

Phineas consulted Kitty with a glance before answering. "It will depend. I suppose we will come a few times a year. I really must bring Giddenhall into a good state of affairs. I also believe Kitty will need time to adjust to her new role there." The work-ings of an idea lit his face. "If you are not overly busy, you must come and visit us, as well. We are not very far."

"That sounds delightful," Teresa said. "I, for one, am pleased to have you in Bath, even if it's just for a short stay. Robert has been positively moping." Robert rolled his eyes, but his glance at his wife was indulgent. "And we need little by way of excuse to visit friends in the country."

"Even if my father keeps me busy this week, we are sure to meet again the night of the ball," Phineas said.

Kitty added, "If you can spare the time, Teresa, I would not mind coming for a morning visit." She bit her lip in sudden real-ization. Phineas, in conversation with Robert, was not listening and could not guide her as to whether she could receive guests at his parents' house. "Of course, I cannot return the invitation and invite you."

"Never mind that," Teresa said. "I will be glad to have you visit. No need to send back an invitation."

When they left the Bromleys', Kitty breathed a sigh of relief. This was the first relationship where she felt as though she'd been placed on equal footing. "I quite like your friends," she said as they turned toward his parents' house. "Which family does Teresa come from?"

"From a very old family—the Balfours. She is the daughter of an earl."

Kitty placed her hand in the arm Phineas held out. His nearness was so comforting, she had to consciously refrain from clutching his arm. "So she is Lady Teresa then. Her parents did not object to the match? Mr. Bromley is a gentleman, but not a peer."

Phineas covered her hand on his arm with his own as they walked. "Her parents merely wanted her to be happy. They did not object at all." His words seemed to lend meaning that extended beyond the Bromleys, and she looked up and found him watching her. Their steps slowed, and Kitty's heart began to beat in her chest. Would he kiss her again?

He pulled his gaze away and began moving forward again. Of course he would not kiss her in the middle of the street. What had she been imagining? Kitty sighed quietly, thinking about his last words. Teresa's parents just wanted her to be happy. She could not but wish that his parents had been the same. Still, the Bromleys' relationship gave her hope that there was something better in store for her and Phineas.

On Wednesday night, the door to Erasmus's house in Laura Place opened, and the sounds of more chatter than Kitty had

HIS DISINCLINED BRIDE

been expecting for a mere family dinner reached her ears. She exchanged glances with Phineas and saw in his face the same look of wariness.

The butler bowed before them. "I will show you to the drawing room where everyone is gathered."

Kitty furrowed her brows. "I had not understood this was going to be a dinner party. I had rather thought it would be a family dinner."

She wasn't precisely expecting an explanation to her murmured comment, but the butler had been with the Stokes family for years, and he took the liberty of answering her. "My lady, Mr. Stokes has invited a few of his business associates and their wives."

When she looked back at Phineas, he raised an eyebrow and gave her a half-smile. He was about as pleased with the development as she could expect him to be.

When they entered the drawing room, the conversation stopped, and all eyes turned toward Phineas. No one paid any attention to Kitty. Erasmus walked forward and stuck out his hand.

"Hayworth, I would like to introduce you to my business associates." He put his hand on Phineas's shoulder, and Kitty saw her husband tense as if he wanted to throw off Erasmus's hand. "This is Mr. Menkes, Mr. Browning, Mr. Thrup, and Mr. Fudge. And this"—with a sweep of his arm, Erasmus gestured at Phineas—"is Lord Hayworth, my brother-in-law."

The gentlemen greeted Phineas while their wives remained behind, their expressions akin to awestruck. It was no great surprise that Erasmus had not considered the wives worthy of introduction. Kitty cornered Mary. "I thought I might see the children tonight. Is Samuel adjusting to his time back?"

"The children are with the nurse." Mary answered Kitty with more warmth than she usually showed, but Kitty was not deceived. It was for the sake of their guests. "We could not have

197

them to an adult dinner party, but rest assured, Samuel is well. I believe he is happy to be back with his cousins."

Phineas bowed before the women without an introduction, but it did not appear to Kitty as though Erasmus had noticed he'd been remiss. They were soon shown into the dining room, where an elaborate spread was laid out on the table. Phineas was seated across the table from Kitty and was sitting at Mary's right. She knew this would be one of those events where Erasmus wanted to demonstrate his wealth by not settling for a simple dinner with a couple removes but having actual courses that would last well into the night. She hid an internal groan as she contemplated the evening stretching out ahead of them.

"Hayworth." Erasmus's voice boomed out across the table, letting everyone know he was on informal terms with Phineas. "How are the repairs to your estate proceeding? I should hope the marriage settlement has been helpful."

Kitty froze in her seat and peered at Phineas from under her lashes. She had never seen him so tense. He set his wine glass down carefully in the expectant silence. "I am not accustomed to discussing my affairs in public as much as you appear to be. Giddenhall is in good order."

"Of course, of course. That is the way of the peerage, is it not? One doesn't publicly talk about such things. However, money puts things on equal ground. It is something we all need and cannot do without." Erasmus laughed heartily, and the other men followed.

Kitty knew from having lived with Erasmus her whole life that he was notable in the shipping business. The men followed his lead, and tried to stay in his good graces. But this ... She wanted to die from shame at his crude discussion of money. Although she rarely allowed herself to look at her brother with a critical eye, she could not help but do so now. How had she ever thought Phineas's world and hers could collide?

Erasmus seemed to have been dipping heavily into the

brandy before his guests arrived. He did this occasionally, especially when he was nervous. His face was flushed, and his manner jovial as he continued his boisterous one-sided jesting.

"Well then, I shall not ask you any direct questions, Hayworth. I should not like to put you to the blush, *eh?*" Another laugh followed. "But Kitty—" She looked up, startled, as all eyes turned to her. "Maybe it's time to think about giving Hayworth an heir, don't you think? After all, that was yet another reason this was such an advantageous match. My business affairs don't just benefit me, even if I know how to make a shrewd bargain. I don't cheat my partners, do I, Mr. Thrup? You should know, right?"

Mr. Thrup gave Erasmus a pained smile and nodded, and Kitty had almost thought Erasmus was done torturing her before his guests. She would need some time to recover from the humiliation of being exposed in front of these gentlemen, and especially in front of Phineas. But Erasmus was not finished. "I know you've had many offers, even some secret ones I'm not aware of, isn't that so? But none of them were ever good enough for you. None but the best would answer for you, now, would it?"

Kitty lifted her eyes in horror at the scene of embarrassment unfolding before her. How could she put this spectacle to a stop before her brother exposed them all to public disgrace? She shot a fleeting look at Phineas, whose stern eyes were fixed on the centrepiece. "Erasmus," she answered in a tight voice, "as little as Lord Hayworth wishes to discuss his business matters, I little wish to discuss my personal matters."

"But it was a good match, you have to admit." Erasmus lifted his fat finger and wagged it at her. "You were ready to split me in two for attempting to put the two of you together, and now you can see it has all been to good account." Erasmus looked around the room. "When I follow a good business instinct, I am never wrong, am I now?"

His business associates nodded, generous in their assent, and their wives smiled vaguely. Kitty knew it was all just for show, and she was sure they did not respect her brother as much as he thought they did. She didn't think the misery of her wedding could be topped, but she was being proven wrong. And this was only the first course.

When, after midnight, they finally escaped from the dinner and began walking to his parents' townhouse, Kitty looked up at the bright starlit night, her breath coming out in a cloud. "Phineas." It was hard to get the words out, and she was grateful for the cover of darkness. "I am so terribly sorry for my brother."

"There is no need to apologize." Phineas did not turn toward her, and his voice was curt. Kitty's heart sank. He must be wondering what in heaven's name had ever possessed him to marry her. She thought he would not speak further, but the words came out in an explosion.

"Of all the impudent, toad-eating—" Quickening his steps, Phineas dropped her hand, lifted off his hat and ran his free hand through his hair. "I have never spent a more disagreeable evening."

Kitty hurried to keep up. She knew she ought to be indignant, but she truly could not blame him. Erasmus had been unpardonable. Phineas seemed to recollect himself, and he slowed his steps, allowing her to catch up. He held out his arm for her again, and she placed her hand in it.

"I do not know how to respond," she said, clasping her hand around his arm. "I am mortified."

Phineas slowed his steps even further, and she felt him adjust his arm, sliding it around her cloak to clasp her around the waist. They were now walking much more closely, and he bent his head to hers. "Say no more. *You* are not your brother. You are infinitely"—his eyes glinted—"more attractive."

Kitty laughed, and it eased some of the embarrassment that threatened to fill her eyes with tears. "I should hope so."

"Thank the heavens," he murmured, and she chuckled again. After a moment's hesitation and another intimate look, he pulled his arm from around her waist and offered it up for her hand again. It was more appropriate should they chance upon other people, but she missed the closeness.

"Thank you for Sam," she said. "Thank you for allowing him to come and for entering into his interests." She smiled up at him and Phineas returned it, holding her gaze until a group of people spilling out of a house pulled his attention away from her.

"Sam will always be welcome at Giddenhall," he replied.

Despite an evening that Kitty would likely remember with particular humiliation, the day had not been completely lost. She had discovered just how gracious her husband was and had received his reassurance that her younger brother was welcome in their home. It was also the second time she thought her husband might kiss her on a public street. And what was more —she had hoped for it.

CHAPTER TWENTY-ONE

P hineas had been glad to peel off his clothes the night before, hand them to his valet, and climb into bed. The evening at Stokes's house had been unpleasant in the extreme. He could not understand how Kitty could come from such a background and still possess an air of refinement. He had had to put up with simpering and flattering and familiarity until he almost couldn't stomach it. Thank the heavens they did not live in Bristol where Erasmus Stokes had his residence. With any luck, they would not need to meet above once a year at most. And Phineas would make sure their future dinners would be on his terms.

Despite the bad taste the evening at Stokes had left in Phineas's mouth, the walk home had made up for it. He had been able to put his arm around Kitty, and she had not pulled away. They had even laughed together. Why, any casual bystander might look upon their affectionate marriage with envy.

Phineas frowned and rubbed the stubble on his chin. If they were so compatible, however, how did she end up sleeping in a separate room on an entirely different floor? Was that his mother's doing or had she expressed a wish for her own room? He could not ask his mother about such a delicate topic, nor could he be sure of receiving a straight answer. Phineas threw off the covers. There were times he feared he was no closer to achieving intimacy in his marriage than he had been the day they wed.

The sun shone brightly through the windows, although Phineas could tell from the cold in his room that the sun was deceiving. It was fast coming on winter. Sounds of his new valet moving about in the adjoining room reached his ears. Harris was quiet and efficient, just what Phineas preferred in a servant, and he soon entered to ready Phineas for the full day ahead of him. It was to be their ball tonight, and Phineas wanted to ensure that nothing prevented Kitty's enjoyment.

He went upstairs to the room where she was staying and stood outside her door for a moment, listening to the sounds within. A smile played on his lips as he wondered what gown she would be wearing tonight and whether it would bring out the colors in her hair, her eyes or her skin—like the dark rose-colored gown she'd had on yesterday. The fresh vision of her each day never ceased to force Phineas's breath out of his chest, and he had trouble believing he was married to such an extraordinary beauty.

He knocked, and Kitty opened immediately, dressed to go walking, with her pelisse slung over one arm and a soft-crowned poke bonnet on her head. She raised her face to his, a smile lifting the corner of her lips. Today's dress brought out her noisette eyes.

"Where are you off to?" Phineas had been hoping to spend time with her. It was only now that Phineas saw Kitty ready to step out that he regretted not being invited into her room. Why hadn't he thought of that before? There would be nothing untoward about such a thing. They were married after all.

"Teresa has invited me to walk to the Pump Room. I am to

write my name in Mr. King's subscription book." Kitty's eyes glimmered with amusement. "She is also going to introduce me to the members of Society there."

Phineas leaned against the door jamb, studying the way her smile reached her eyes. "And increase your acquaintances among the septuagenarians?"

"Something like that," she admitted with a grin. "She has warned me that the greater part of her acquaintances in Bath have reached a certain age. To tell the truth, I'm grateful she wishes to spend time with me at all, for I should like to know her better."

Kitty closed the door behind her and began to put on her pelisse. Phineas leapt to assist her into it, and when she secured it in front of her, he resisted the strong impulse to pull her into an embrace. He was jealous of a cloak!

"And if we are to return to Bath," she went on, "it would be good for me to learn how to go about. I have never been here, apart from a visit I was too young to remember as a child."

"And our wedding," Phineas added, one eyebrow raised.

"And that," Kitty replied, her eyes twinkling. "How could I have forgotten?"

"Let me walk with you to the Pump Room," he said. "I shall leave you to your meeting with Teresa. But I have nothing to do just now, and I should like your company." This was not precisely true. He had promised his father he would use his time in Bath to go over the accounts with Parkson to learn where economies might be made. Walking with his wife held more appeal for him.

"I should like that very much," she said. They walked down the corridor to the stairwell. "Did you sleep well?"

They descended the stairs, and moved by a sudden urge, Phineas leaned in, his mouth next to her ear. "I should have liked to have been placed in a room together." He caught her arm as she missed a step, and they arrived at the next floor. He wondered why she'd stumbled ... *Was it because of what I said?* They reached the floor where his bedroom was located and rounded the corridor for the final staircase down. "But I slept as well as I could."

Kitty's face was heightened in color. She raised her eyebrows and peered at him from the side. He continued, "But I should be the one asking you how you slept. After all, I am not the one unfamiliar with my room."

Kitty knit her brows. "It was very comfortable." She opened her mouth to speak again, but his mother met them at the foot of the stairs. "Katherine, our dinner will be as early as six so that we are ready to open the ball at eight. I hope you have everything you need for your toilette?"

Kitty pulled on her leather gloves. "Of course, my lady. I will be ready. Do you require assistance?"

"No, I am perfectly capable of making all the preparations." His mother walked toward the kitchens, then turned back. "Where are you going?"

Phineas answered. "We are going to the Pump Room. She is to meet Teresa Bromley there."

"Oh, very well. Just be sure to be back in time. After all, tonight's *soirée* is for you, and I should like to see that you are presentable before we introduce you."

Kitty nodded, but Phineas noticed her expression had shut down. He did not like to see his mother's quelling influence over his wife. He had hoped for a more harmonious relationship between the two of them. Could his mother not see that his wife was quality whether or not she had the bloodline to show it? They escaped into the cold air.

The clouds were heavy outdoors, and the wind brisk enough to pull the few remaining leaves from the trees. Phineas held out his arm for Kitty, and they walked like that in comfortable silence. He wondered if that was what a happy married life was like. One's arm felt empty without someone's hand on it.

Kitty's silence went on too long for Phineas's liking, and he turned to her as they walked downhill. "What were you going to say before my mother interrupted us?"

Kitty hesitated, darting a glance at him and nearly tripping as her half-boot caught in a cobblestone. He caught her forward motion and slowed their pace.

"It is only that your mother said you wished to be in your usual room and that you desired privacy. And just now you said you'd hoped to be put in a room together." She did not turn to look at him, and the broad rim of her bonnet hid her face.

"I believe my mother arranged for us to stay in the rooms that suited her own notions and did not consider what we might desire." Phineas stared ahead at the buildings at the bottom of the street and took in a lungful of cold air. "She also told me you preferred your own room and needed privacy, so of course I could not insist we take the larger room together."

They had not long to walk until they reached the Pump Room. Kitty curled her fingers around his arm, her eyes straight ahead and the bonnet hiding her expression. He could only guess that the subject raised feelings of delicacy by the way her voice went quiet. "How could I respond any other way after she let it be known that you are a man who values his privacy? I had to say that I was the same."

"Would you have liked to stay in the same room?" Phineas felt her steps falter. Did the thought cause her to shy away? Or was it as welcome an idea for her as it was for him?

"It is rather sudden to take such a step, I suppose—and to do so at your parents' house?" Kitty's voice was so hesitant, Phineas took a long step so he could peer around the rim to her bonnet. Her face was aflame, and she averted her eyes until he released her from his gaze. She so clearly could not look at him, it felt almost wrong to insist. "After all," she added, "we have not taken such a step in our own home."

"And do you realize what has kept such a thing from

happening?" He pulled Kitty to a stop because they were near the entrance, and although his heart was beating fast, he had to find out where she stood on the matter.

"You spoke of … spoke of invitations and such, but…"

"Do you think you are starting to warm up to the idea?" Phineas asked, eagerly, now facing her.

"The idea?" Her eyes darted from him to the people around them, revealing her terror at the direction the conversation was taking.

He knew he should bring the discussion to a stop. It wasn't fair to put this on her when they were not even in their own home. But having come thus far, he could not stop now. "Kitty," he murmured low in her ear. "You know you need only say the word."

Kitty looked at him, her jaw stiff. "I cannot do what you ask of me. I was not raised to be bold in that way." In a few words she had dashed Phineas's hopes to the ground.

He gulped. "What do you think it would take for you to be able to say those words?" *Please don't say more time*, he silently pleaded.

Two women, barely out of the schoolroom, if looks could be trusted, walked by Phineas and Kitty, staring at each of them curiously. Kitty darted a glance at them then hid her face from Phineas by staring at the ground. He waited, his breath coming in shallow bursts.

At last, she clasped her hands and spoke to the ground. He almost did not catch what she said. "I should like to hear tender words from you, Phineas. I would like to know how you feel about me, that you …"

Phineas reared back to stare at her. Her words had died away, but he thought he understood what she expected of him. She wanted to hear that he loved her. Her serious eyes were now fixed on him. That was not a request he had expected to encounter when he'd had his marriage arranged. Why did she insist on *words* when he showed her every day in action? He took a deep breath and looked up, still conscious of the weight of her stare.

"I don't think I can say those words just now," he muttered, taking a step closer to allow a middle-aged couple to access the entrance of the Pump Room.

She dropped her eyes. "Then I believe we are at an impasse."

Phineas paused for another moment to contain his frustration. How could she be so *stubborn*? The words she asked of him were much more difficult than the ones he asked of her. She needed to be patient with him. Phineas gave a long exhale. His next reflection was disagreeable as it pointed the accusing finger at his own actions. It was wholly unfair to press her for change when they were in a home not their own. He took her elbow and led her in silence to the entrance of the Pump Room.

A footman opened the dark red wooden doors, and they stepped inside. He felt his wife's furtive glances and softened. It had not been his wisest move to broach the subject of their intimate marital relationship on the city streets of Bath. Phineas leaned down to whisper. "We will let the matter rest."

Kitty turned to him, her expression relieved, and she opened her mouth to speak—

"Oh, Phineas, you are here, too." Teresa Bromley was standing near the entrance and she had spied them both. "I am introducing your wife to a few friends and putting her into Mr. King's book. She said you have not yet had time to see to it, so I hope you will allow me to be of service."

Phineas bowed before Teresa. "I am much obliged to you for that. It's what I should have done a couple of days ago, but I was caught up with my father's affairs. Is Bromley here?"

"No. He only comes to the Pump Room when I drag him—and with much moaning." Teresa laughed. "But we will see you both at your family's house tonight."

Phineas bid them farewell, noting that Kitty's face had

almost returned to its normal color. She offered him a tentative smile before turning back to Teresa, which reassured him somewhat. She would not hold it against him for pressuring her.

One thing still troubled him. Outside, a gust of wind had him huddling into his tail coat. The clouds had gathered in the short time they had been inside, and it seemed almost cold enough for snow. He turned reluctant steps toward Parkson's office to go over the finances of Midlington estate, as he had promised his father. He really did not have the mind for it.

His thoughts turned instead to the conversation he had had with Kitty. True, he should not have pressed her under such circumstances. It was too soon—even though they had been married weeks, and it was not soon enough for his liking. But if he was truly going to be honorable and give her back the power she lost when she was bartered in marriage, he needed not to pressure her before she was ready. However, why had she not trusted him enough to tell him that his mother had placed her in a small room, far from him, against her wishes? He could have addressed the situation, although not—he supposed—without a bit of awkwardness, as doing so equaled forcing her hand to give him that blasted invitation he was waiting for.

And why had she not trusted Phineas earlier to tell him about Craddock, now that he thought of it? He would have got rid of the groom without a second's hesitation had he known the man had made advances. She did not trust Phineas. Yet he showed her day after day that he trusted her by waiting. When would she finally honor him with her trust?

CHAPTER TWENTY-TWO

The instant Phineas completed his work with Parkson, he wasted no time in returning home. He did not have much of it before he would need to be ready for the dinner that preceded the ball. In his room, Harris was brushing out the creases of his coat.

"My lord, please have a glance at what I've laid out for you for this evening and let me know if you approve of it. I will assist you in dressing as soon as you are ready."

Phineas glanced at the white breeches, paired with the dark gray coat. Harris had selected a white cravat with an onyx pin that would be perfect. He would no longer have to worry about pulling himself together in such a clumsy manner with hastily tied cravats and loose-fitting coats. Perhaps this would be an additional temptation to his wife. "It will do very well," he said.

When he was properly attired, he went to join his mother downstairs, who was directing servants to place the remaining candles in the chandeliers. They wouldn't begin lighting them in the small ballroom until just before the guests began to arrive.

His mother pursed her lips as she went over the guest list a final time. "We have one last-minute addition that we have to fit around the table. I had not realized that the Earl of Hawkins and his wife were in town. We are not greatly acquainted, but I had to send them an invitation, and they have sent their acceptance. They will have to take precedence over some of the other guests. It's a shame we have to put your wife in such a prominent place at the table, but I suppose we must do so since the object of the ball is to present her."

Lady Midlington's voice carried, and Phineas saw a maid glance her way with keen eyes. She would likely regale the story to the other servants downstairs. Phineas could not believe his ears. He crossed the room to speak to his mother in a low voice, so that at least the servants wouldn't have a family brawl to dissect over their supper.

"Mother, I am astonished you would say such a thing, and I hope you don't do so in Kitty's hearing. She is my *wife*, and she deserves the place of honor. I never want you to say such a thing of her again."

"You are overly sensitive," his mother said, although she had the grace to look conscious of her error. "Facts are facts, and she does not rank as highly as some of our other guests. For goodness sake, we have a duke's daughter, who is married to a baron and must place her lower than Katherine. It should not be." She frowned at him before running her fingers over the list. "But you must see that I am making a great deal of effort to present her."

"If only I could be assured that the effort was not more for you to avoid being exposed to gossip than it was for her, I would be gratified."

His mother did not deign to answer this. Phineas decided to leave her to the last-minute preparations since the guests were very shortly to arrive.

Kitty stood at the foot of the stairs. Her dress was white with a pale green embroidered overlay, and gold drops dangled from her ears, echoing the auburn strands of her hair mixed in with the red. Phineas walked up to her and laid his hand on the bannister as he studied her. Her face was pinched.

"What is it?"

She shook her head. "It is of no matter. The guests are to arrive any moment, are they not? Your mother requested we be in place so I might receive them."

Phineas did not trust she was telling him everything. There was a troubled look on her face, and he hoped she had not heard what his mother had said. However, the sound of the first guests arriving forced him to put off a conversation. "Let us go then." Phineas brought Kitty to take her place in line next to his parents, who had gathered in the entryway.

The guests arrived in a steady stream, and Phineas made sure to introduce each one to Kitty with a bit of whispered information so she could place them if they met again. Robert and Teresa Bromley appeared, and it was the first time he saw a genuine smile on Kitty's face. As the Bromleys moved down the receiving line, Phineas introduced Robert to his father, who explained how he'd met Bromley Senior.

It did not take long for the final guests to straggle in since the select ball would open with a dinner that could not be put off. The duke's daughter his mother had been speaking of arrived with her baron husband, and Phineas did not think she would mind at all being seated in a less prominent position. The same could not be said for the Hawkins, who appeared to expect every attention paid to them—never mind that they did not outrank the Midlingtons.

The last guests to arrive were Lord and Lady Leighton, followed by their daughter, Lady Jane. Phineas suppressed a groan. He should have guessed they would be invited because it would be rude not to include them, but he wished it had been possible to do so anyway. He'd always felt the pressure to court her—not only from the Leightons, but from Lady Jane, herself. There was nothing in her to inspire him. Her coloring was pale and her hair flat and insipid. It was certainly not her thin frame he longed to pull into a mad embrace. His wife smiled as the Leightons came in, innocent of any history or expectations between the two families.

"May I introduce Lord and Lady Leighton, and their daughter, Lady Jane," Phineas said. Kitty curtsied.

"So this is your wife, eh? We had not heard of any engagement before you tied the knot. It must have been quite a secret —or a rushed affair, hm?" Lord Leighton leered at Kitty in a way that caused her to look up to Phineas doubtfully. He wanted to thrash Lord Leighton. Thank heavens Phineas had escaped from being joined to this family.

"Not a rushed affair. More of a secret," Phineas responded with a bland smile. "Lady Jane." He bowed before her and she glanced at Kitty, then at him, before offering a quick, reproachful smile. She followed her parents into the drawing room.

Phineas was spared from having to explain who they were, as the guests were quickly escorted into the dining room where the footmen pulled out chairs for them. Soon the sounds of dishes clinking and soft conversation filled the room. At the close of the second course, Lord Midlington got to his feet and lifted a glass in Phineas and Kitty's direction. "As you all know, this ball is to introduce our new daughter into Society. Please join me in welcoming Lady Hayworth."

All the men stood and raised their glasses, and Phineas glanced at Kitty who inclined her head in acknowledgment. Every man in the room had to see what a prize he had. Only the most callous of them could accuse him of having married beneath him. She was a diamond of the first water.

The gentlemen sat, and conversation resumed. Kitty's face was still tinged pink. Apparently she was not someone who enjoyed attention, which was just fine for him. He preferred their quiet dinners at Giddenhall to all this fuss. He leaned in. "You are doing just fine."

She returned an enigmatic look and took a small sip of water. "You are kind."

Phineas turned back to his plate, sensing that somehow his comment had been misinterpreted. Her reaction was cordial, but not overly warm. He wished he could get her alone and find out what was behind her reserved demeanor. Perhaps his mother had been difficult, or the duress of meeting so many people at once was causing her to close up. It was frustrating being married to a woman who did not give up her reflections willingly.

At the close of the dinner, a separate smaller room was set up for those men who wished to drink port. Phineas was obliged to go, but he stayed as little as he dared before reclaiming his position at Kitty's side. The pinched look was back on her face. He leaned in to whisper to her, "You can dance, can you not?"

Her look lightened. She glanced at him, her eyes showing half-humor, half-exasperation. "Of course I can dance, Phineas."

"Of course you can," he repeated. "We will lead the guests in dancing. I forgot to tell you about that, but I hope it will be of no matter."

She shook her head wordlessly, following him to their place at the head of the line as the musicians completed the music that accompanied the crowds milling in. At last, Phineas would be able to take her in his arms and would not need to let go until the set was finished.

CHAPTER TWENTY-THREE

K itty lay her hand in Phineas's outstretched hand as he led her to the top of the ballroom. Other couples took their place next to them, forming a line. Kitty looked for the only couple she could claim as acquaintances, but the Bromleys were on the far end. They would not cross paths in this dance.

Lady Jane, whom Phineas had introduced to her as the guests poured in—whose father had made veiled comments about the nature of their marriage—took her place next to Kitty. Strains of the violins and cello began, and Kitty met Phineas in the middle of the line, clasping his hand and turning around him. Though Phineas was one who should naturally have cause for confidence, given his title, there was an endearing gaucheness to her husband. In truth, it was what she liked best about him. It had led her to assume his dancing would follow suit, but Phineas moved with a grace she had not expected from him.

The dance brought Kitty around Lady Jane, and she caught her eye and smiled. It was not returned. Instead, Lady Jane averted her face in an obvious snub. Phineas had not seen the exchange, but the conscious look on the gentleman squiring

Lady Jane showed he had seen it. Kitty could not understand what she had done to deserve the cut. This was supposed to be a ball in her honor, and all she wished for was to run back to the anonymity and comfort of Giddenhall, with Phineas and Samuel to share her company.

Kitty followed the steps numbly, barely feeling the touch of Phineas's hand as they completed the dance. She'd have to have a word with her husband and find out who this Lady Jane was and why she was determined to set Kitty in her place. She had certainly done nothing to deserve it, but she felt the sting of every barb in a way Mrs. Dutton had not succeeded.

Phineas escorted Kitty to the sidelines and stood next to her as new couples formed for a set. "I imagine there will be many who will want to claim your hand. I am glad to be the first. May I get you something to drink?"

How could he leave? Did he not see she was in distress? She could not let him do it. Kitty lay her hand on Phineas's arm and pulled him to a place that was more secluded. There was only the empty corridor behind them, leading to the family's private quarters. "Who is Lady Jane? You introduced me to her, and her father made a cryptic observation about our marriage. She just gave me the cut direct during the dance. Is it because I am not of the *ton*?"

Phineas's brows snapped together, but he had no chance to respond because Lady Midlington, coming up from behind them, had overheard the question and answered it. "Lady Jane was supposed to be Phineas's intended." She paused at Kitty's side, watching the couples weaving through the line on the dance floor in front of them. "Everyone thought she would be, too, but he chose you instead. I believe Lady Jane is not inclined toward friendship for that reason."

Phineas shot his mother a quelling look. "Lady Jane received no hint from me that such a match would take place. It existed only in the desires of our parents."

"But you know very well that the match would have suited our families best. We have been friends for many years, and we come from the same circles." Lady Midlington glanced at Kitty, and her gaze softened a fraction. "Of course, what is done is done. Phineas is married to you now, and we must get over our disappointment. But it is not surprising that we should require some time to do so, and that Lady Jane should feel it as well."

"Mother," Phineas said quietly. "This is not a discussion for the ballroom. In fact, I wish it were not being discussed at all."

A slight buzzing filled Kitty's ears, as she reeled from the litany of insults. It was as though Lord and Lady Midlington expected that she should apologize for having dashed all their hopes for Phineas's future. But what had Kitty to do with the affair? It had all been arranged between her brother and Phineas. In fact, from what she could gather, Phineas's man of business had approached Erasmus first. *She* had nothing to apologize for.

Kitty straightened. "As you say, my lady, what is done is done. I am very sorry to have contributed to your disappointment, but it was not of my doing. However, I should like to be treated with respect as your son's wife. It will serve him no good to settle for less." She glanced at Phineas, who had a crease between his brows as he studied her—as if he could not understand why she was upset. Yet he had done nothing more than to dismiss Lady Jane's expectations as false and tell his mother to save the conversation for a more opportune moment.

"You are right," Lady Midlington said. "It will not do for our daughter-in-law to be cut by anyone of the *ton*. I will have a word with some of the ladies here and say how pleased I am with the match. That ought to set tongues wagging to good purpose." Phineas's mother fixed her lips in a firm line and marched off.

Phineas gave Kitty a tentative smile. "She will see to it that you don't receive any such treatment from another member of Society."

"*Hm.*" Kitty kept her expression closed.

"What is it?"

Phineas had turned to look at her, and she lifted her face to his, a flash of anger causing her cheeks to go hot. But this wasn't the place to say anything. She shook her head. "Nothing."

Phineas had been considerate as he introduced the guests, and it had been nice to dance with him. She'd had to admit, as they performed the figures, that he was nothing short of dashing in his tailored coat and crisply tied cravat. But he did not seem to comprehend her distress. Surely he could not imagine his *mother* as an ally.

Kitty was solicited several times to dance before begging a pause to take refreshment on the sidelines. Robert Bromley had partnered her once. He had been attentive and gracious, while also making her laugh. While many of the guests were so distinguished Kitty felt the chasm between them, Robert was different. It was a credit to Phineas that he had chosen him for a friend.

A few furtive glances came Kitty's way from various people attending the ball. It appeared that none of them were willing to offend the Midlingtons by expressing disapproval, but that an equal number of them found something to gossip over in Phineas's choice of a wife. Although she knew he was not the first peer to marry solely for money, it was hard to recall that fact when she was viewed as an oddity. It was as if she had reeled him in for what she would gain by the match, when in fact it had been the other way around. Kitty sipped her ratafia, taking refuge in the small crowd on the sidelines.

"How does it feel to have managed to snatch one of Bath's few eligible bachelors?" Lady Jane appeared at her side. Although she was richly attired in a red silk dress, her skeletal white shoulders and spare bosom made it seem as though she lived off other people's downfall rather than food as normal people did.

Kitty inhaled quietly and tried to rein in her temper. "I am sure it appears to you as though I am crying victory for having married a viscount—as if I'd set out to catch him. But I assure you it was no such thing. He approached my brother about the match."

Lady Jane turned, her eyes wide with interest. "Oh, is that so? I thought Hayworth said it was a love match. Or, at least that's what he hinted at when he spoke of keeping things a secret—why he did not offer for ... anyone more closely acquainted." She snapped her fan open and waved it, though the cold from the outdoors had kept the crowded room from growing too warm. "So, in fact, he sought the match from your brother?"

Kitty blinked slowly. She did not turn to Lady Jane for fear her embarrassment and confusion would be all too evident. He *had* said that in the receiving line, and she had forgotten. Once again, Kitty would have to lie about the true nature of their relationship. "We were acquainted, and our affections had grown. However, it would not be right to seek my hand in marriage without speaking to my brother first."

"*Hm.*" Lady Jane did not look convinced and continued to wave her fan back and forth in sharp movements. "You hardly look like a couple that began as a love match. Has it begun to sour already?" Her mouth took on a pout. "I imagine it must be difficult to maintain a peaceful union when based on such differing social statuses."

Another voice joined in the conversation, and Kitty went limp with relief when she saw it belonged to Teresa Bromley. "In such matches, most of the affection is carried on behind the scenes." Teresa returned Lady Jane's smile with a bland one of her own. "As you know, Jane, I married beneath me according to Society. However, no one can deny our affection for one another. It is just that we do not display it publicly like people who have no manners." Teresa leaned in. "You must acquit Lady Hayworth of falsifying the facts just because it does not appear to *you* that she and Lord Hayworth are in love. They, too, prefer to keep their private matters from public consumption."

"What Lady Teresa said is quite true," Kitty said, emboldened. "Of course, she and I are on friendlier terms, and she has been witness to the warmth in my marriage that is otherwise hidden from public eye."

Teresa held out her arm for Kitty. "Lady Jane, I do hope you will excuse us. Lady Midlington is looking for Kitty."

She allowed Teresa to lead her to a section of the room that held less people, and Kitty flashed her a grateful smile. "I cannot thank you enough for rescuing me back there. I did not know how to deflect her unnecessary attention."

"Jane and I went to school together. She is not well-liked. I cannot be surprised that Phineas did not fall for her, but it is clear he is smitten with you." Teresa squeezed Kitty's arm tighter and gave her a conspiratorial smile.

"Since we are becoming better acquainted, I must confide in you that looks are deceptive. He has not spoken of love." Kitty stopped with a shy smile unable to say more.

"Men generally find it hard to do so, I believe." Teresa glanced at Kitty. "How did your match come about?"

"Oh, it was nothing out of the ordinary, I suppose. I believe my husband..." Kitty could not finish the thought—could not admit that her husband had sought the alliance purely from a mercenary ambition. To do so would throw him to the wolves and trample her own reputation as well.

She began again. "Erasmus, my brother, was looking for ways to connect his..." This was impossible. She could never get the words out. How could she speak in such base terms about a marriage that had begun as a contract, but which had begun to grow into something else?

Teresa saved her from replying. "It was a match arranged by two gentlemen for monetary purposes, which has fortunately begun to grow in affection."

Kitty relaxed her shoulders and nodded. Teresa had understood the matter at a glance.

"Well, that is the way of many matches," Teresa said in a matter-of-fact voice, "and there's no reason that the marriage cannot prosper despite the beginning."

At two in the morning, people began to take their leave. Kitty had done her best to smile and talk to everyone, although the reserve some people maintained gave expression to their thoughts regarding the match. She could not help but wonder what they expected to achieve by alienating Lord Hayworth's wife. They could not think she would put up with such treatment in silence? As soon as the thought sprang to her mind, her conscience smote her. *Well, that's just what you've been doing.*

At last, only Lord Midlington was left with Phineas and Kitty near the refreshment tables, while Lady Midlington directed the servants to scrape the melted wax from the floors and pick up the fallen napkins and bits of sandwiches that had been served at midnight to boost the flagging energy of the crowds.

"Well, that is now out of the way. I faced Lord and Lady Leighton and put this whole sordid affair behind us." Lord Midlington glowered at Phineas. "I daresay they shall come around to the idea, but it was not a very nice trick you turned on me. It made for very awkward conversation when I had to go tell Lord Leighton about the match. I suppose now they can see for themselves you have tied the knot and will stop hinting at breach of contract."

Phineas did not react to his father's words, and Kitty stared at him, compelling him with her eyes to say something. His father had called her welcoming ball "sordid" and went on about how disappointed he was in having to explain their marriage to a peer. But Phineas appeared lost in thought and did not glance her way.

Lord Midlington sighed, the night's events seeming to loosen his tongue. "Whether they believed our story about a love match is another thing. Then again, I would not wish you to hang upon one another in a vulgar display."

Lord Midlington walked toward the exit, glancing back at Kitty. "But we've done the thing. That ought to settle the gossipmongers. Everyone can see for themselves that we have not only welcomed you as a daughter but have held a ball in your honor. We've done this kindness for you, Katherine. I suppose you will never know what it cost us to settle for something other than what we'd considered ideal, but we can only look forward."

Phineas had remained silent, his face impossible to read. Could he not see that his father was insulting her? She was not their ideal. She ought to be grateful the earl and his wife noticed her at all. Kitty silently urged him to meet her gaze. She longed to know what he made of his father's offensive and bizarre discourse.

Lord Midlington walked over to the table that still had two untouched glasses of wine. He picked one up and drank it. "Once you've given my son an heir, all will be forgotten." At last, Phineas looked at Kitty and smiled.

A smile? Kitty swallowed and averted her eyes. She could not trust herself to respond with anything like grace.

With such a dull audience, Phineas's father exhaled, as if disappointed. "I have some affairs to see to before I retire. Good night."

Lady Midlington began to follow her husband out the door but stopped just short of the exit. "I will declare tonight's ball a success, however. As much as I would have liked to have hosted one under different circumstances, you behaved well, Katherine. There was nothing to be ashamed of."

There was no answering that. It was not worth it for Kitty to antagonize her mother-in-law, although she thought her husband could do so very well without losing his status. He remained obstinately silent, his arms folded, and his gaze appearing to see right through his mother. When the door shut behind Lady Midlington, Phineas seemed to snap to life. He gestured to the door, and they exited, climbing the stairs in silence.

Kitty was too exhausted to make conversation, and too discouraged after the afternoon she'd spent with her mother-in-law, followed by the evening spent among the wolves of Society. Phineas had only exacerbated her feelings by questioning whether she was capable of dancing and condescending enough to tell her she hadn't embarrassed him at dinner. *You're doing just fine*. A growing sense of irritation filled her breast. They stopped in front of her door.

"My parents are coming around to the idea of our marriage." Phineas had finally broken his silence, but they were not the words Kitty expected. An apology would have been an excellent beginning.

"I am not so sure," she said carefully. "Your mother was bemoaning having to give me a prominent place at the table when the daughter of a duke would be dining with us."

Phineas widened his eyes. "You overheard that conversation?" When Kitty nodded, he blew out through pursed lips. "That explains your troubled look. I wish you had said something then. But you must not have heard what I replied to my mother. I did defend you, Kitty."

"But that is just the problem. I am a wife who needs to be defended—because I'm not good enough for Lord and Lady Midlington's son. And what is particularly goading is that I was more successfully defended by Teresa Bromley tonight, whom I have just met, than I was by my own husband."

Phineas faced her squarely and put both his hands on her arms. "No, no—you don't need defending. You were a vision tonight. Everyone thought it. And I was heartened by my father's words. I had been starting to fear that there was no chance of my parents accepting you. But you heard him—as soon as you give me an heir, my parents will be reconciled to the idea of you joining our family."

Kitty looked at him with wide eyes, her jaw slack. "Do you think those words were conciliatory? I thought they were rude."

Phineas studied her more closely. "Rude? Both my parents said how glad they were that the party was a success."

"So it could settle the gossipmongers."

Phineas knit his brows. "And they said you behaved beautifully—which was the *truth!*—and that no one could have anything negative to say about you."

Kitty glared at him and put a hand on her hip. "Because they assumed that since I am not born of the gentry, I could not possibly know how to conduct myself. And some of your own remarks have shown me you think the same."

"I don't think it." Phineas shook his head, as if unable to wrap his mind around her accusations. "But … but my parents said once they had a grandchild to dote on, nothing more would be spoken of your background. It shows there is hope for you all to rub along well."

"Yes." Kitty bestowed upon him an artificial smile. "Their acceptance is conditional upon the fact that I give you an heir."

"But you do plan to give me an heir, so what is there to worry about?" Phineas's voice had gone up a notch.

Kitty's jaw grew rigid with indignation, and it took her a minute before she could get the words out. "If you cannot figure that out…" She opened the door behind her and turned to face him, eyes glaring, "I can assure you, there will *be* no heir." She shut the door behind her with a loud *clack.*

CHAPTER TWENTY-FOUR

T*hat* had not gone well. Phineas's steps were heavy as he made his way to his room. For the entire ball, he had looked at Kitty with pride. What an exquisite creature she was— far more elegant than any other woman present; there really could be no comparison. He could think of nothing but her.

After having successfully opened the ball with Kitty, her hands light in his as she turned graceful steps around him, he had imagined that his wife was as charmed by the ball as he was —that the romantic atmosphere would take effect and sprout the desire in her to deepen their relationship. As it was, he knew himself to be the envy of every man present.

He had completely missed the barbs—had barely heard what his parents were saying when the party came to a close—as he dwelled on the idea of taking their romantic night to a satisfying conclusion. Now, as he examined her reproaches, his parents' words did not seem so generous as they had appeared in the moment. In fact, every compliment was laced with a cut. And he had not protected her.

He knew his parents—knew they were far from perfect. He even knew he had much to regret over their lack of love for one another. Whatever had come between them when they were young in their marriage had destroyed any hope of affection, and he had been a victim of their indifference. However, they *had* made an attempt to approve of Kitty and had even thrown a ball in her honor. It was only after he'd received a piece of her outrage that Phineas was forced to admit that neither the ball, nor his parents—and no, not even he—had given her the respect that was her due as his wife.

He turned the doorknob to his familiar, empty room. The valet had laid a fire for him before retiring, as requested. Phineas pulled the pin out of his cravat, which had begun to strangle him, and untied it. He paced back and forth in his room, as the memory of the day his parents' marriage had changed—a memory he'd suppressed because it threatened to sink him into gloom every time he remembered it—filled his mind. Except that now there was nothing he could do to stop it.

He had escaped from his nurse that morning and had run to the library, eager to share his catch from the trout pond. He wanted to show his father his biggest fish yet, sure that it would bring him the smile of approval that was a prize for kings, given how rare it came.

Phineas had not been entirely sure his mother would approve of his bringing a dead fish inside the home, but that fear was the easier one to grapple with. The hardest and most subtle was whether the fish would be big enough to impress his father. Voices inside the library stopped him in his tracks.

"I wish you will have your say and be done with it."

He had peeked through the crack in the door and seen his father, wearing the same expression as when he scolded Phineas, his arms folded on his chest.

"You would rather I not say anything at all. You would rather I turn a blind eye to your affairs." His mother was sitting somewhere out of sight.

"Yes, to be perfectly honest. My affairs are none of your concern. Most women know better than to bring them up."

"Perhaps most women would not, but we were a love match, Edward. We married for love. I did not expect you to seek affection in the arms of another woman." His mother's sob had reached his ears, and even as a man, Phineas could still remember the tendrils of dread that had crept up his spine. Why was his mother crying? Something must be terribly wrong.

"Have done with your tears, if you will. I was blinded by your beauty, but such a thing can not last long. You have given me one son, and he is a paltry example of a boy. You have given me no other heir for the past six years."

"You are spilling your seed into your lightskirts. How do you expect me to give you another child?"

His parents' voices had raised in volume, and when Phineas heard his father walk toward the door, he ducked behind a tall vase. His father had come only to slam the door, but he could still hear their muffled voices.

"You should be grateful. You've married well and are the envy of many women. A countess, living in a fine mansion. You did not bring anything into this marriage other than your beauty. Console yourself with your son now."

"Phineas?" His young heart had shrieked in alarm at the disgust he heard in his mother's voice. "You say he is a poor example of a son? *You* did not have to spend countless nights comforting him from nightmares or coddling him back to good health. You were not even here. He has given me nothing but trouble. Less freedom, less sleep, a painful birth that does not bear speaking of ... I never wanted children. I only bore one for you, and I was prepared to give you more."

"Well, as he is my only heir, apply yourself, if you will, to coddling him less. If ever I saw a less appealing scrap of a boy ... I will have to hire a tutor who can turn him into more of a young man before I send him off to school." Phineas's heart had beaten loudly in his ears.

"Oh, he is now fully in your hands. As you imply, a mother's role is done by now. It is the father who shapes him, unless the father is too busy squandering the son's inheritance on mistresses."

Phineas heard the sounds of his mother coming to her feet. He feared she would walk toward the staircase, where she would discover that he'd heard everything. He had no time to hide, but sank back further behind the vase, holding the dead fish to his chest.

His mother opened the door. "Whatever you do, don't expect me to come to your bed. I don't plan to share it with other women."

With that, she slammed the door behind her and walked the opposite way to the drawing room where she exited into the gardens. Phineas stood a moment longer, not daring to breathe. When he heard the sounds of servants climbing up from the kitchen, he dropped the fish in the vase and ran up the stairs. His innocence had died that day, along with his heart's assurance.

Now, Phineas sat and dropped his face into his hands. He had tried so hard to win his wife over. He followed Bromley's advice and had bought her gifts. He had given her full power over the intimacy of their relations to make up for the power that was stolen from her when she'd had her future arranged without her consent. He'd sat with Kitty, and talked to her; he admired her…

You haven't given her the tender words she asked for. You haven't told her you love her.

The accusation shot through his conscience, and Phineas leapt to his feet. Of course he couldn't tell her he loved her. Who did such a thing, unless it came as a whispered, strangled confession deep in the night when she was asleep and could not hear? He resumed his pacing and glanced at the bronze shaving bowl, having a sudden urge to hurl it through the window pane. But that would be costly to replace and embarrassing to explain. Plus, it might land on the head of some poor unfortunate below. Instead, he grabbed the tall post of his bed and shook it hard, then threw himself down on the tick mattress, not bothering to take off his shoes. His marriage was just as doomed as his parents' was—except they, at least, had gotten a child out of it.

A knock on his door interrupted the silence, and Phineas pulled himself up to his elbows then darted out of bed. In a few strides, he had opened the door and was staring down at his wife, who was holding a candle, dressed in her night shift with a dark blue dressing gown tied loosely over the front. Her head was bare, and her long hair was tied in a thick red braid. Phineas gulped.

They stared at each other for a moment, and Kitty's gaze dropped down to his bare neck and open shirt. A blush lit her face, and she directed her gaze to his chin where it remained. "I would like a wedding breakfast." She inhaled quickly. "Or perhaps *not* a wedding breakfast where we would again be the center of attention. But a meal in our own home, where we can celebrate our marriage and invite the people we like."

Phineas's mind tried to absorb her request, as much as her sudden appearance. A wedding breakfast was actually a good idea, now that she mentioned it. His wife should have had one in the first place. But she wished it to be intimate enough that she was not made to feel all eyes were on her. How would he accomplish such a thing? Who would they invite?

And ... why had she come back after he had failed to protect her? He did not deserve such a thing.

Kitty took one glance at his face and creased brow then looked down the corridor and back at him. "I would like the breakfast to be at Giddenhall with friends only in attendance. And I want to replace Mrs. Morley. She is a dreadful housekeeper, and I do not wish to be looked down upon in my own home."

"It shall be done," Phineas said softly. Was this an olive branch? Were olive branches sometimes offered in marriage?

"I would like to have you teach me to ride, and to become an excellent rider—and to accompany you on your social visits, and even on hunts ... that is, do you hunt?"

Phineas nodded. "I do," he said, hope again inflating his lungs. He stood upright and leaned against the door jamb. A smile played about on his face. *She had come to him!* "Any other requests I might fulfil, my lady? You have only to ask." An awareness that his words held an unintended double meaning stole Phineas's breath. Would she ask?

Kitty sniffed and looked at her hands before glancing up at Phineas. Her eyes were shiny, and he could not be sure whether it wasn't from tears.

"I should like to become a mother."

The words slammed into Phineas's chest and he tensed. As if on its own, his hand reached for the door and opened it wider. Kitty's eyes grew round when she saw the gesture, and she took a step back.

"Soon." Her voice came out in a squeak. She backed up toward the staircase, her eyes still on him, and a tiny smile lighting her face. Phineas saw the amusement—and the apology —in her eyes. She was going to be the death of him.

In two strides he was in front of her, and he caught her hand in his. He held it, caressing her fingers until the spark of appre-hension disappeared from her brows. He took her other hand and pulled her closer. She came willingly. Skimming his hands up her arms, he grazed them over her shoulder and up her neck until he was cradling her face. Her eyes went wide, but she did not move. He leaned down and kissed her, pulling her toward him and giving himself into his longing for one brief moment. She kissed him back, and he felt no resistance.

But Phineas had given his word. He broke away and took a step back, and then another until he was again in front of his room. Her eyes fluttered open.

"Soon," he repeated, firmly.

She walked the rest of the way to the staircase, her gait unsteady, and Phineas could not resist calling out again, loud enough that she would hear, but not enough to disturb the servants. "Lady Hayworth." She turned back slowly, her small dimpled smile still in place.

"I have decided that it will be judicious to return to Gidden-hall tomorrow. Will you honor me with your presence on the journey?" Phineas had his hand on the door and was leaning out into the corridor for one last glimpse of his beautiful, playful, torturously elusive wife, whose visit had removed the painful weight from his chest. His breath expanded and lifted like one of those hot air balloons he had once seen demonstrated at Oxford.

"With pleasure, my lord." Kitty dipped into a small curtsy and began climbing the steps.

Phineas closed the door behind him, unable to understand how he could go from such a point of bitter despair—a marriage failed before it had got off the ground—to one of such hope. He would not think about what might have happened if her last request had been the invitation he had thought it at first. As it was, sleep would not come easily tonight.

But he had been given a taste of love and a taste of hope. Kitty had forgiven him before he had even gathered the courage to ask for it. Then she had kissed him back. Perhaps the inclinations of his bride would not be so very long in changing.

THE NEXT DAY, breakfast was served late, and Phineas discovered both his parents at the table. "Good morning, Mother. Father."

"Good morning, Phineas. I trust you slept well." His mother stirred cream into her coffee and set the spoon down on the saucer. His father remained silent.

Phineas filled his plate on the sideboard, barely glancing at what he had taken. His mind was filled with the determination to set things straight with his parents and not to waste the rare opportunity of finding both parents in the same room. He brought his plate to a seat where he could see them both and poured a cup of coffee while he tried to sort out how to begin. At last he looked up.

"I should like to discuss something with both of you, and I find it convenient to do so now while you are both here." *And Kitty is not*, he added silently in his mind.

"Over breakfast?" His father's ironic glare would not deter Phineas.

"Why not? I have decided to return to Giddenhall today, but before we leave, I wish to speak to you about Kitty."

"What have you to say about her unless it is to thank us?" His father's cutlery was poised above his plate. "We gave a ball in her honor, although she is not from our circle. Other families might have rejected her outright."

"It would have been a—" Phineas cut himself short. He had been about to say *a foolish thing to do*, but that would not reconcile himself to his parents. "It would have been unnecessary. She came with money, she has good breeding—and handing the inheritance over to Bartholomew simply because you did not appreciate your son's choice of a wife would have been going to the extreme, in my opinion. It is not as if you could give him the earldom, too." Phineas sipped his hot, bitter coffee to bolster himself for the rest.

"We have been very good about this quirk of yours to marry

beneath you. I do not know what more you want of us." His father cut his sausage and rammed a piece in his mouth while his mother pulled her cup of coffee closer without drinking it, her expression unreadable.

"I merely wish to notify you that I will not accept any disparaging words about my wife spoken in my hearing, or hers. If you wish to pour out your disappointment into your friends' ears, there is nothing I can do to stop you." He sent his mother a pointed look. "I do not want to hear disappointment expressed over the fact that my wife must take precedence over a duke's daughter, who is married to a baron. My wife is a viscountess, and one day she will be a countess."

Phineas frowned, fearing he had gone too far. "Not that I wish for that to occur any time soon." He now turned his regard to his father who, surprisingly, had not cut him off with a quick retort.

"And yes, she will bear me a fine heir, but I do not wish to hear that she will become acceptable to you only when that happens. If either Kitty or I hear more of these kinds of things, you will not meet the heir, or any of the other children born to us, because we will not come to visit you. In that case, Midlington Estate will have to run itself, Father, between you and your steward—with the knowledge that it will eventually fall into my hands to be reaped or ruined."

The door opened, and Kitty stepped into the room, her eyes wary when the stiff posture of the room's occupants was born upon her. She dipped a curtsy and wordlessly reached for a plate on the sideboard. She looked to Phineas as though she were ready to take flight.

"Good morning," Phineas said, and he smiled at her when she met his gaze. It seemed to reassure her, because she returned it, along with a soft greeting.

"There will be freshly cooked eggs coming in a moment." Phineas's mother sipped her coffee. "If you should care to wait."

Kitty risked a glance at Lady Midlington, then at Phineas. "Thank you, my lady. I will."

She sat, and poured a cup of tea from a pot that had been steeping on the table. Phineas noticed that her hands trembled a bit, but she managed to pour the tea without spilling any. His wife could not know this, but his mother's seemingly benign comment was a peace offering. She would not apologize, but she would not be hostile.

Lord Midlington stood. Of course his father would not take his words to heart—Phineas had not expected such an easy victory—but his father would soon learn how seriously Phineas had meant them. If he wished to have a relationship with his son and his grandchildren, he must accept his son's wife.

"I must see to today's correspondence," Lord Midlington said. "I understand you are to leave. You are sure you both will not stay for Christmas?"

Phineas swallowed carefully, fearing he would choke on the bite of bread that was in his mouth. Had he heard his father correctly when he'd specified them *both*?

He felt Kitty's glance and turned to her. His surprise was reflected in her eyes. "We had agreed our first Christmas would be held at Giddenhall, did we not?" She nodded, and he returned his gaze to his father. "To tell the truth, we must be off. There is much to be done there with the Christmas boxes and feast for the tenants. However, we will be delighted to return to Bath for Twelfth Night if that would suit you."

His mother pursed her lips and studied the blue fluted pattern on her saucer. "We ought to have the guest room redone by then. You must simply send word when you will arrive."

"We will." Phineas could hardly believe that his parents had been so easily won over. Had it only been wanting that he stand up for what was important in order for them to come around? Perhaps they were not so very obstinate as he had always thought. Time would tell, but this was a first step.

CHAPTER TWENTY-FIVE

K itty had Sterling pack her few gowns from their stay. Her maid would be leaving first with Phineas's new valet in one of the earl's borrowed coaches, which meant that Kitty would have a quiet ride with her husband. The thought filled her with contentment.

At the start of their marriage, Kitty could not have imagined arriving at a place in life where her husband equated comfort. The best she'd hoped for had been an uneasy truce. How it would have astonished her to know that her marriage now was not only something she'd grown accustomed to, but also something that felt like home.

They bid Lord and Lady Midlington farewell after breakfast and stepped into the coach to make a few morning visits before they headed back to their estate. Their first stop was at Mary and Erasmus's house, where they were shown into the drawing room.

"Come in. I am glad to see that you have returned for a visit. I was beginning to think you never would." Mary removed the embroidery so Kitty could sit down. "Although, we had intended to invite you for another dinner party. Erasmus is home this morning, so you are in luck. He will have to leave this afternoon to oversee the shipments going out, but just now he is working from home in his library. I have told the footman to notify him that you are here."

Phineas sat next to Kitty. "We cannot stay long. We have other calls to make before we are on our way to Giddenhall."

"Oh, are you off already?" Mary's lips formed a pout. "What a shame. I know Erasmus was planning on introducing you to more of his associates. It will be a great misfortune if you leave now."

Kitty was accustomed to being conciliatory with her sister-in-law, but this could not stand. "Mary, my husband is not Erasmus's business associate. He is his brother-in-law. We come for social visits only, not to smooth the way for Erasmus to gain an edge in his business dealings."

Mary had the grace to blush. "I did not intend to imply anything by what I said," she said defensively. "It is only that we thought Lord Hayworth would like to meet men of influence."

Kitty exchanged a swift glance with Phineas. "My husband already knows many men of influence. He has no need to meet more." The door opened, and Erasmus walked in.

"Excellent. You are here." Erasmus came forward to shake Phineas's hand, ignoring Kitty completely. "We had intended to invite you to dinner—"

"Erasmus, never mind. They are on their way to Castle Combe and will not be able to join us for any more social engagements." Mary attempted to catch Erasmus's attention with a pointed look, but he did not appear to notice it.

"It is most inconvenient that you should leave just now. It is not for the social engagements that I wished to invite you, but for something of far greater importance. I am working on a deal with some men of influence who particularly wish to meet you. If you leave just now, it puts my deal at risk."

Kitty saw her husband tense, and although she wished to

leap to his defense again, she knew he would prefer to have his own say. To her surprise, Phineas put his arm around her on the settee and rested it on her shoulder. Mary's eyes widened at the display of affection.

"I am afraid I will not be able to assist you in this affair, and you will remember that our arrangement did not include any such thing. You wished to have your sister wed to a title, and I wished to have a settlement that would allow me to develop my estate." He glanced at Kitty. "I admit I gained much more than I bargained for, but I still hold to no business dealings. There were none mentioned in the contract." He gave Kitty's shoulder a little squeeze.

Erasmus turned red around his shirt points. "I did not intend for you to do anything in particular for those men. I only meant to remind you that my relationship to you would smooth the way in this deal. I know how to conduct my own business affairs."

"I know you are quite capable of running a business. As Carter said, no one who doubles his father's fortune in a few short years could be lacking in business sense." Kitty admired the grace with which Phineas complimented her brother, and it seemed to mollify him somewhat. "I only wish to express that the benefit you reap from our relationship is one of title and connections rather than service. You may address me as Hayworth and speak about our relationship. You can spread it about that Samuel is coming back to visit…"

"About the visits, I do believe that is a very fine idea." Erasmus pursed his lips. "I have a mind for Samuel to join me later on in the business, and it will be good if he gets on well with the boys at Harrow. The right connections, and all that. When might you be able to take him?"

"We will be returning to Bath for Twelfth Night. Perhaps we might make a similar arrangement to meet here, and we will bring him with us when we leave for Giddenhall," Phineas said. "If that suits you."

The servant brought the platter of tea, and Mary stood to take the tea leaves from their locked cabinet. "I should like some distance between Samuel and his cousins. The notion suits me very well."

"Never mind about Sam and our children, Mary," Erasmus said, curtly. He turned back to Phineas. "I care most that Samuel is able to mix well with his peers at school. I believe he can achieve such a thing by staying with you."

Phineas brought his arm from Kitty's shoulder and folded his hands. "Then we understand each other very well. I will acknowledge my family relationship to you, and you will not importune me by arranging for any more business dinners. Our meetings will be family visits, with an occasional dinner party that has some other purpose than to conduct business. We will take a higher hand in raising Samuel, because I know that Kitty wishes for it." He added as an afterthought, "And I do like the boy, myself."

"We have a deal then." Erasmus nodded, a tad eagerly, Kitty thought. She would have to make sure her brother knew his place in their future visits—and that Samuel did not become a commodity that Erasmus used to achieve his own ends.

Mary asked how Phineas drank his tea, then prepared a cup to everyone's liking. Kitty took hers and asked, "May I see the children? We do not have a great deal of time, because we have two other places to go before we leave Bath."

"Three places to go," Phineas corrected. She turned her gaze back to Mary, who nodded and signaled for the servant standing by the wall to go fetch the children.

"Kitty! Phineas!" Samuel ran into the room and threw himself into Kitty's arms, while Erasmus looked in astonishment at Phineas.

"He calls you by your Christian name."

Phineas grinned and shook Samuel's hand. "It started in innocence, and I did not have the heart to change it." He turned to Samuel, who had gone back to sit next to Kitty. "How would you like to come back to Giddenhall with us after the Twelfth Night festivities?"

"Oh, would I!" Samuel leaned against Kitty, and she turned her eyes to Phineas, brimming with the gratitude she felt for him.

The door opened and Edward and Helen ran in, followed by the nurse carrying William. There was the same hubbub of excitement as everyone rushed into Kitty's arms, and she exclaimed over each one of them. William reached out his chubby arms to her, and she took him on her lap with a caress.

"I may just have to buy a permanent place in Bath," Erasmus said.

It was a balm to Kitty's soul to listen to her niece and nephews' chatter, as Samuel stood quietly at her side—as if the change that would come over him when he went to school had already begun to take place. She was unable to bring the visit to a close, and even though she knew Phineas was impatient to be off, he showed an extraordinary amount of patience, she thought, before they finally bid her family farewell. Kitty followed Phineas out to the coach, which had been brought back around, and he helped her in and tucked a blanket around her legs.

"I believe the affair with your brother was settled nicely," Phineas said.

"Yes," Kitty said. "And Sam was *aux anges* about coming to visit us. I can't thank you enough. That was one of the hardest things to reconcile myself to about being married. It is going to do him a world of good to stay with us."

"I quite like the idea of Sam's frequent visits. He will bring me back to my days at Harrow, which were happy ones, and he will fill Giddenhall with life."

She nodded, a smile hovering on her lips. "And you were able to put your foot down with my brother. He is without shame. Everything is about business to him. It matters not if he might disgrace himself or anyone else in the bargain."

Phineas leaned to the side so he could face her more comfortably. "I don't believe that for him he is disgracing himself. He is so absorbed by growing his business, he cannot be hurt by any reproach that he has gone too far. But I am glad I put my foot down for our future peace. It would become increasingly difficult to spend time with your family if I had to endure more of that last dinner."

Kitty laughed. "Yes, that was rather unfortunate."

A silence settled as the carriage moved over the cobblestones. Kitty decided to continue in their vein of truth telling. "I did not like being reminded of the terms upon which we married." She lifted her eyes to him. "Even though I knew they were perfectly true, it's such a dispassionate way of discussing how we were married. There were no warmer feelings involved. Do you think we shall ever overcome it?"

They'd not had far to travel, and the carriage soon came to a stop. Phineas frowned and looked at the door that the footman was about to open. This was a chance for him to say some of the things Kitty had been longing to hear, and she held her breath, waiting for him to talk about the other reasons for being married—the merits she brought to the match just from who she was. She sincerely hoped he perceived them.

The door opened, and the footman waited for Phineas to step out. He paused for a second and met her gaze before leaning over to murmur, "No, our marriage will not always be spoken of in such a manner."

Phineas stepped out and went into the building. He had told Kitty it was not necessary for her to come in as well, for he was just discussing replacing Mrs. Morley with his man of business. Kitty waited, knowing she had to be content with the promise he had made, although it did not fill her heart with peace. She wanted more. She wanted to know that their marriage could grow into a love match. She patted the soft folds of her cloak and examined the brown fabric against her tan kid gloves. It wouldn't do to hope too much.

As promised, Phineas was not long. Their next stop was to retrieve the finished riding habits from Mrs. Laurent, and Phineas sent the footman to fetch them for Kitty since an icy rain had begun to fall. When the parcel was delivered, the coach moved forward again. "Only one more stop before we leave for Giddenhall," he said.

Kitty scrunched her eyes. "Where is that?"

Phineas turned to her in mock surprise. "Why—to visit Robert and Teresa Bromley, of course. You cannot think we will leave without seeing them?"

"Oh yes," she exclaimed. "I would so like to visit them one last time. I wish we lived closer, so we might increase our acquaintance."

The carriage traveled a short distance farther and stopped in front of the Bromley residence. They were admitted at once, and Teresa came into the hallway to greet them. "Oh, are you dressed for travel?"

"Yes." Kitty clasped Teresa's hands that were held out for her. "We are headed back to Giddenhall today. We have much to prepare for Christmas. And as glad as I am to go back, I do wish I'd been given more time to get to know you."

"That can be arranged," Teresa said, warmly. "Come into the drawing room. Phineas, you are often in the habit of visiting Bath are you not? You need only bring your wife each time."

"Yes, it is true. My father involves me a great deal in the affairs of his estate. We will most certainly be back." Phineas hesitated and turned to Robert. "You had something you wished to show me in the study, did you not? Perhaps we might have a glance at it now before we leave Bath." A brief look of confusion passed over Robert's face before he said, "Oh, yes. I had forgotten. Please, follow me."

The two left the room, and Teresa invited Kitty to sit down. "Why are you returning so soon? Oh—you mentioned Christmas boxes and festivities. Of course you must go. Would you like some tea first?"

Kitty shook her head. "We had tea at my brother's house before we left."

Teresa sat forward. "Who is your brother? Does he live in Bath?"

"No, he lives in Bristol. He is Erasmus Stokes." Kitty was about to say that the name would not likely be familiar when Teresa gave a small gasp.

"Is he related to the Stokes shipping company?"

Kitty's eyes widened in surprise. "Yes, you have heard of it?"

"I suppose most have," Teresa said, "considering it is such a large shipping company. But my brother traveled with one of his ships coming home from India one year when he had been weakened by the climate. The captain of his ship took very good care of my brother, so I feel particularly indebted to Mr. Stokes —although, of course, I've never met your brother personally."

Kitty felt a glow of satisfaction that her brother could have indirectly rendered service to Teresa. "I am glad to hear how well the captain took care of your brother. And although I should not say this of my own relations, I fear it would not be wise to introduce you to Erasmus in case he should think you are fair game for increasing his distinguished acquaintances." Teresa laughed, and Kitty could only follow suit. She shook her head. "He has an unfortunate habit of boasting about what he has acquired, and I'm afraid that includes people."

Teresa chuckled softly. "I could probably manage him, to be perfectly honest. But I suppose we will not attempt to connect our circles further."

Kitty sighed and laid one hand over the other on her lap. She listened to the distant noise of their husbands talking in the study.

"Don't tell me you are melancholy so early in your marriage," Teresa teased.

"Not melancholy, no." Kitty met Teresa's gaze. "But if I am being truthful, I do wish Phineas and I had more of a love match than we do. I'm constantly reminded of the differences in our social status."

Teresa studied Kitty, her head to the side, as if reflecting on the words she would say before she spoke them. "I cannot claim to know Phineas very well. But I do think he is capable of being a man who loves his wife. He has only to realize it for himself, and when he has, I believe he will show it."

Kitty gave a tiny shrug. "Yes, I suppose so. It is only that, having stayed with his parents, I have come to realize how very like them he is. He is not an expressive man." She looked up at Teresa with a self-conscious smile. "This is probably another example of how different I am from the peerage. How much a husband and wife love each other is not spoken of in Society."

"It is not. But I have always prided myself on not being *too* much like Society," Teresa said. "And I am happy to say from personal experience that love matches are possible. I don't see why it should be any different with Phineas."

The men entered the room. "Teresa, darling, do you know of a reliable housekeeper that would be keen to work at Gidden-hall? Hayworth is in need of one just now."

Teresa thought for a minute, then her eyes lit up. "Yes, as a matter of fact, I do. Remember Mrs. Ambley who worked for the Dowager Kentworth?"

"The one who died last year," Robert confirmed.

"The very one. The new Lady Kentworth was pleased to bring her own housekeeper with her, so Mrs. Ambley has been in need of a new position." Teresa turned to Kitty. "My own housekeeper spoke of her last week. They are acquainted, and I promised I would help if I learned of a position."

"Write to her at once," Robert said. "Save our poor Kitty from a poorly-run estate where Phineas puts his foot through the threadbare sheets, the cobwebs grow to gigantic proportions in the drawing rooms, and dinner is brought to the table cold."

"Heavens," Kitty murmured, grinning. "Save us, indeed."

Phineas came to stand by Kitty's chair. "Are you ready to leave?"

She looked up at him in surprise. "So soon? But you have not sat with us. I thought we were here for a social visit."

Phineas paused with a conscious look then chose a seat across from her. "And so we were. I have allowed my haste to return to Giddenhall to get the better of me. Yes, let us sit for a while. Threadbare sheets and cobweb curtains can wait. After all, the servants know enough to have dinner ready for us." He threw his legs out and folded his hands on his stomach.

"A dinner, of course, that will be cold." Kitty turned back to Teresa, her eyes filled with mirth.

CHAPTER TWENTY-SIX

The ride back to Giddenhall was smooth, and there was none of the tension that had accompanied their wedding journey. At the same time, there was no lingering regard that might lead Phineas to think Kitty would welcome his embrace once the carriage doors were shut. To refrain from giving in to the temptation, he leaned back in his seat and folded his arms. "I hope you are getting accustomed to Giddenhall, and that it pleases you."

Kitty faced him with a ready smile. "I like it very much. It is starting to feel like home."

"I will have an interview with Mrs. Morley once we arrive. I hope Mrs. Ambley will be able to make her way to Giddenhall without delay. I believe we will do very well without a house-keeper for a few days, but I should not like to be without one for too long."

Kitty shrugged. "I am not overly concerned. I know how to direct servants so that things are done. True, a large estate needs more people to oversee it, but I believe we will fare well enough without it."

Phineas rested his hand on Kitty's arm. "Yes, I am sure of it.

You know, I had spoken to Mrs. Morley before I left, instructing her to treat you with more respect."

She turned to him, the surprise evident in her eyes. "Did you though? I did not see any change in her behavior." Kitty sighed. "We should give her a character reference. I don't like the idea that someone should suffer at my hand needlessly."

"Well, one reaps what one sows," Phineas said. "I do not like having a housekeeper who thinks herself above her mistress. However, I shall do my best to please you and handle the matter in a satisfactory way. I will dismiss her, but kindly."

Kitty gave a dimpled smile. "That is good of you."

Their conversation touched on mundane topics, and a sense of friendship settled about them that Phineas both appreciated and hated. On one hand, he was happy to know his relationship with his wife would not take on the distance his parents' marriage had—long silences and barely tolerating one another's presence. On the other hand, one glance at his wife, and the longing for her consumed him until he had to look away. He was no further to broaching the topic of intimacy than he'd been when they left. Perhaps one of their quiet dinners would solve the problem.

Perhaps there he could inch his hand closer to hers, brush his knee against hers...

When they arrived at the estate, Mrs. Morley stood in the entryway to greet them. "Good afternoon, my lord." She curtsied. Then, as an afterthought, she added, "and my lady." She did not curtsy a second time. Phineas exchanged a glance with Kitty and turned to the housekeeper.

"Have a maid bring tea to our rooms, and after I have cleaned up from our trip, I would like a word with you in the study."

Mrs. Morley's look turned apprehensive, and she curtsied again. "As you wish, my lord."

She turned to go, and Phineas and Kitty climbed the steps

together, much in the way they had done before they left for Bath. The servants who crossed their path dipped a curtsy and murmured a welcome back.

Phineas walked Kitty to her room and opened the door for her. He put a hand on her back. "This time, if the footman does not bring you your trunk, come knock on my door."

Kitty laughed. "Except this time it will not be quite so urgent because I have a stash of gowns in my wardrobe."

"Come and knock on my door anyway," he replied with mock austerity before leaving to go to his room.

Phineas could hear bustling in the room next door and paused to listen, a smile playing on his lips. To have her in an adjoining room brought him a pleasant sort of ache. It had been odd and unsettling in Bath to have her stay in a room on an entirely different floor. She was his wife after all.

After he had his tea, Phineas went to the study and rang the bell to summon Mrs. Morley. She presented herself at once. "My lord, I suppose you will wish to have an accounting of everything that has occurred while you were away—"

"That will not be necessary, Mrs. Morley. In any case, that matter is usually addressed with the mistress of the house. And that is precisely the problem I have here. Lady Hayworth has told me that there has been no change in your behavior toward her, even after you and I spoke."

Mrs. Morley frowned. "I mean no disrespect, my lord, but perhaps Lady Hayworth has chosen to see my words and actions in a different light than what they were intended."

Phineas shook his head. "I will not allow you to cast aspersions on my wife, who is your social superior. If she says she has not felt respect from you, it means you have not shown it. I saw for myself that you did not deign to curtsy before her when we arrived." He glanced at the pen on his desk, the nub of which needed sharpening. "I am relieving you of your position here, Mrs. Morley. You will be sent off with a character, but you will be sent off all the same. I cannot have any servants who are not completely loyal to both me and Lady Hayworth. It is not one or the other. I would like your keys." Phineas held out his hand.

The housekeeper glared at him for a moment then unhooked the keys from her waist and handed them over. She marched across the room, turning back at the door. "I do not know how you will manage without me, my lord. I hope you do not regret this day. I have served Giddenhall for six years."

"And that is why I am giving you a character reference—that, and my wife begged me for leniency on your behalf. As far as I am concerned, a servant who does not know how to show respect to her mistress is not a servant worth having." Phineas pulled a sheet of paper from the narrow desk drawer. "As I've said, Lady Hayworth believes you should be given another chance. And in terms of how well Giddenhall will run without you, I am certain Lady Hayworth will manage just fine." Phineas watched with satisfaction as the housekeeper exited then turned to the stack of mail the butler had left on his desk.

Dinner was served late, and it was not run with quite the usual efficiency. The scullery maid was kneeling by the hearth as Phineas and Kitty entered the dining room, and she had only just lit the fire. "Excuse me, milord and milady. Mrs. Morley did not give me the instructions to light the fire in this room. Bexley called for me to see to it just moments ago."

Kitty leaned over the table to light the candle. "It is of no matter. A new housekeeper will arrive soon enough, and we will make do in the meantime. Tomorrow morning, I shall conduct a meeting downstairs with all the servants, and I will give instructions for what needs to be done, and at what time."

The maid bobbed a curtsy. "Yes, milady. I will inform the others."

Phineas held out Kitty's chair, and the footman brought the simple repast then left the room at Phineas's bidding. Kitty tucked her head down, hiding a shy smile. "I hope your interview with Mrs. Morley was not too disagreeable."

"Not in the least," Phineas said, cheerfully, spearing a potato wedge on his plate. "I did not spare her another thought once she had left."

"Phineas," she scolded mildly in a way he quite liked. She picked up her fork, and they worked their way through their dinner with only occasional remarks to break the companionable silence. When the sweets were set on the table, Kitty said, "Perhaps you might tell me a bit more about the Christmas boxes, and what sorts of things we shall do to prepare for Christmas at the estate."

"We have a Yuletide log stashed away somewhere, I believe. In general, one of the stable lads should cut a new one every year, and we should have the one from last year. But I need to check on that, for I was with my parents at Midlington. As for what we should be putting in the Christmas boxes … To tell you the truth, I should have asked my mother. She would have known."

"Or I—Teresa—who would have known as well." Kitty bit her lip, her eyes teasing. "Mrs. Morley would have been of great use in the matter. Have we made a mistake?"

"No mistake," Phineas said. "We are keeping servants who are respectful to their mistress, stewards who are not lazy—"

"And grooms who do not make indecent proposals," Kitty finished for him.

Although they were alone, Phineas leaned over and murmured close to her ear, "The only indecent proposals you receive should be coming from your husband."

He felt the warmth of Kitty's flush as soon as he said it and resisted the urge to press his lips on her cheek. She looked straight ahead as she murmured a reply. "Then I suppose it would not be an indecent proposal, but rather, a *decent* one."

"If we are speaking of proposals—"

"Oh, had we not exhausted that subject?" Kitty observed innocently.

"If we are speaking of proposals," Phineas continued as though she had not interrupted, "Surely one should soon be forthcoming?" A twinge of frustration made his voice lose its playful edge as he captured her gaze and held it. "I believe my gestures have given you full proof of my feelings."

Kitty kept her steady gaze on him, and there was a beat of silence before she answered. "Surely my gestures have confirmed for you mine."

Phineas reached for her hand on the table, attempting a smile. "But you know, my dear, it is not the gestures I need. It is your words. I made an oath."

She raised an eyebrow. "I believe I have told you that very same thing. It is your *words* I need."

"But I gave you those words at your brother's house." At Kitty's look of confusion, Phineas explained. "I said that I had received much more than I'd bargained for with you as my wife."

Kitty stared at him, unmoving, her expression nonplussed. "This ... these were the words you thought to woo me with?"

Phineas leaned back in his chair, a finger of alarm tapping at his awareness. What more tenderness did she want than for him to declare his regard for her in such a public way? He could only nod in answer.

Kitty stood, and Phineas shot to his feet, as well. "I believe I am tired after our day's travel," she said, turning to the door.

"What is it, Kitty?" Phineas followed, then leapt ahead to open the door. He fell silent as they walked past a footman, who left his post to clear the dishes in the dining room. No words were spoken as they went up the stairs and to the door to her room.

The silence between them was weighted, and Phineas scrambled to think how he might coax Kitty to answer. Fortunately, since he hadn't the faintest idea of where to begin, he did not have to pull the words out of her.

"I hope for deeper emotions in our marriage than"—Kitty grimaced—"a satisfactory bargain. And as for those words you wish to hear from me … they seem to get stuck in my throat. I think I'm afraid that you will never bring yourself to say the tender words I wish to hear. And if you don't say them first—"

Phineas's heart sank. He knew what it was to get words stuck in one's throat. What if he gave her his heart, and committed himself to words of love, only to one day overhear her exclaim what a paltry excuse of a man he was?

"—I fear I will always be left wondering." Kitty placed a hand on his arm and turned to go into her room.

"Wait!" The word was wrenched out of Phineas, though his pulse was beating in his throat from fear. He did not know if he could get the words out, but he could not let Kitty go on thinking he did not have deeper feelings for her.

She turned back expectantly, and he saw a gleam of hope come to her eyes. They sparkled in the light from the candle on the small table in the corridor as she moved back to where he stood.

"Do not imagine that because I am not a man of easy words … I do not harbor any feelings for you. In fact"—Phineas brought his hand up to caress her cheek, his courage faltering at the last minute—"I esteem you." He leaned down and kissed her gently on her lips.

Kitty's lips were soft and full, and tempting. When Phineas pulled away, her eyes were slightly unfocused, as though he had broken through her defences. But he had sworn an oath—and in all fairness, he had not given her what she wanted. "Good night, Kitty."

CHAPTER TWENTY-SEVEN

The next morning, Kitty's heart beat quickly at the thought of seeing Phineas again. The expectations on both sides had deepened, and it felt like the stakes had too. But when he stepped out of his room at the sound of her door closing, Phineas gave her a benign smile and asked how she had slept. As to that, Kitty had slept fitfully after that kiss, but it had not weakened her desire to hear words of love from Phineas. She put her hand in his arm as they walked downstairs, grateful that they could share this closeness at least.

After breakfast, he proposed they go riding together. This began a new habit of Kitty attending daily rides with her husband and accompanying him as he visited the estate. Each day, she delighted in wearing a new riding habit with the matching hat he'd bought her, just to see his reaction. His eyes lit with pleasure each time, and he found a new way to compliment her appearance.

Kitty was growing much more adept on horseback and could now jump into the saddle on her own, using a mounting block. Despite that, she allowed Phineas to assist her. She believed he liked holding her hand to help her up as much as she liked having it held.

The days were busy as they prepared the Christmas boxes for the servants and tenants, including ham, jellies that Mrs. Morley had had the foresight to set aside, some old clothing, sweets for the children, shortbreads that the cook had made up, and a coin or two. Cook had guided them on what to include, begging her pardon for being forward, as she was to have a box as well. The servants and tenants would all receive them the day after Christmas.

Each night, Phineas would accompany Kitty to her room after dinner where, "I esteem you" turned into "I admire you," which turned into "I delight in you." And each time his phrase was followed by a kiss that made her long to invite him in, if it weren't for some missish impulse—which she could not explain to herself—that held her back.

"It is time to gather the decorations for Christmas," Phineas announced on their fourth day after returning from Bath. They went on horseback, accompanied by the stable hand, who drove one of the wagons put on sleds to get over the few inches of snow that had fallen the night before. They filled the wagon with evergreen that would be used to decorate every window and door. Then they spent the rest of the day filling the corners of their house with touches of the outdoors and ribbons and felts Kitty had found stashed away behind the table linens. They laughed when a bough of evergreen fell off the bannister, landing on the helmet of the suit of armour underneath, causing it to appear as though he had plaits.

That night after dinner, Phineas placed his hands on her shoulders and gazed into her eyes. Her heart beat painfully.

"I cherish you." Phineas kissed her again, more deeply than he had the other nights until Kitty's heart sputtered like the candle on the small table in the corridor. He pulled away, and she swallowed over what felt like a lump of nerves.

Phineas turned, as he had done each night, and walked to his room. She opened her mouth to speak but did not know how to frame her request. The door to his room closed before she could think how.

The next day, Kitty woke up late, and her arms and legs were sore from all the decorating. She had insisted on helping Phineas and the servants create the evergreen paradise that now filled Giddenhall. The scent of greenery had trailed them, making Kitty nostalgic for something she had never had. Christmas was celebrated to a small degree in Erasmus's house, but it was mainly for the sake of the children.

She rang for Sterling, who came carrying hot water. "Lord Hayworth sent me to wake you, my lady. He said to dress quickly for there are visitors here."

Kitty had crossed to the dressing table, and she started out of her chair in alarm. "Visitors? And I have not even had my breakfast yet. Do you know who they are?"

"No, my lady." Sterling poured the hot water into the basin and came forward to help Kitty remove her night shift. "He did no' say. But he said to wear the fine gown."

"What fine gown?" Kitty asked, leaning forward to scrub her face before rinsing it.

Sterling handed her the towel. "I dunno, my lady. Maybe he thought you would know."

The nicest dress Kitty owned was the one she'd worn for her wedding. And maybe it was whimsical on her part, but there was something about having the house decorated for Christmas with all the greenery that inspired her to reach for that one. It would set off perfectly the green embroidery that was woven through the ivory bodice. Kitty smiled as a fanciful thought struck her. She would become part of the idyllic Christmas setting.

"This one," she said, pulling it out and handing it to her maid.

"Yes, my lady." Sterling shook the dress and stretched it across the bed. "As soon as we have you in the gown, I will dress your hair."

Kitty put on her wedding dress, and Sterling pulled her hair into a series of pretty coils that looked stylish despite how quickly they were done. Kitty then put on the necklace that Phineas had bought her and pinched her cheeks to make them glow.

"Well, I believe this is as good as it's going to get, given the short period of time. How do I look?" It was a strange thing for Kitty to ask her maid, as they had not yet developed a warmer relationship than brisk efficiency on the part of the maid and occasional requests on the part of the mistress.

Sterling put her hands on her hips and cocked her head. "You are a vision, my lady—if I may say so."

Kitty flashed her a smile and hurried down the hallway. She almost expected Phineas to exit his room and join her, as he sometimes did when he heard her leave her room for breakfast. But he did not come. As she descended the stairs, she heard voices coming from the breakfast room.

Why would Phineas have shown guests into the breakfast room instead of the drawing room? It was most unusual, and Kitty did not feel prepared to meet anyone without having something in her stomach. She should have asked Sterling to bring her a tray to her room, even though it would only have delayed her further. But it was past time for that.

Kitty opened the door to the breakfast room, and four faces turned toward her. She looked from one to the other in astonishment.

Phineas stood and came to her side. "I knew you would understand which dress I meant," he murmured.

Kitty dragged her gaze away from the guests and whispered, "Sterling said to wear my nicest gown, and although I have others nearly as fine, I chose this one on a whim."

"No, I think it was instinct." Phineas took Kitty by the hand and faced the crowd, saying in a louder voice, "You are dressed in your wedding gown, my lady, which is only natural when one attends one's wedding breakfast."

Teresa Bromley, seated on the far end of the table and wearing a broad smile, stood. "Robert, shall we not get to our feet?" She gave him a pointed look, and he lumbered to his feet and bowed to Kitty.

The other person in the room, besides the Bromleys and her husband, was Lucretia Dutton, who also stood and said with a teasing smile, "Best wishes for your happy day, my lady."

Robert gestured to the coffee cups on the table. "Lord Hayworth must have decided it was too early to toast with wine, so I believe we will be toasting with coffee. Although"—he tipped the cup to show it was empty—"for a toast, it is preferable to have liquid in the vessel."

"The wine is on its way," Phineas said with a chuckle. "But feel free to toast with the coffee cups. The coffee is on its way as well."

"To the newly married couple," Robert called out.

Teresa and Lucretia lifted their empty coffee cups, laughing. "To the newly married couple."

Kitty smiled and shook her head, touched by such a show of affection, as Phineas put his arm around her. He twisted to meet her gaze. "This was the wedding breakfast you never had, even though you might get a tiny bit more attention than you asked for."

Teresa sat again. "I am afraid it cannot be avoided when you have friends crowding around to wish you well."

Kitty turned a bemused expression on her husband. "How did you arrange it all? We don't even have a housekeeper. How did you manage to invite the Bromleys? They had no time to prepare."

"So many questions." Phineas kissed the tip of her nose. "Oh, it was a simple matter of speaking to Robert when we stopped at their house on the way to Giddenhall. I let the Bromleys know when we would be hosting the wedding breakfast to make sure they would be able to attend, since they had the farthest to travel. Then I sent a servant over with an invitation to Miss Dutton's house, and we were fortunate to be able to secure her presence, as well.

Kitty darted a glance around the rest of the room. "And no one else is coming? No ... family?"

Phineas's look was careful, tinged with apprehension. "No family. I thought you wanted something simple."

Kitty breathed a sigh of relief. "Good. As much as I hope for our family relationships to grow in peace over the years, this is ... perfect. It is just how I would want my wedding breakfast to be."

Phineas gestured to the table. "Then, might I suggest you have a seat?" Two footmen began to bring out plates, piled high with hot rolls, pots of jelly, and fresh slabs of butter. Instead of setting them on the sideboard, they brought the plates directly to the table, as though it were a dinner. Afterward, they brought out eggs and ham, coffee and tea, and a pot of chocolate. And the final addition—the wedding cake, dense with dried fruit— was set with ceremony in the middle of the table as Bexley surveyed the procedure from the side of the room. Phineas poured coffee into Kitty's cup, and with a few sips of coffee and a bite of her roll, she began to feel revived.

There was a knock on the door, and Bexley left to answer it, returning shortly to poke his head in the doorway. "There is a Mr. Carter to see you, my lord,"

Phineas got to his feet. "Bring him here."

Carter entered and bowed before the guests assembled. "Good morning, my lord. My lady." He then glanced at the other guests, his eyes lingering on Miss Dutton and his speech momentarily suspended. Kitty glanced from one to the other and bit back a smile. Lucretia was certainly at her most ravishing this morning with a blue gown that matched the color of her eyes.

Phineas indicated the other guests. "Carter, may I present you to our guests? These are the Bromleys—Mr. Robert Bromley and his wife, Lady Teresa. And this is Miss Dutton."

"The honour is mine," Carter said to Robert and Teresa. His eyes back on Lucretia, he added, "Enchanted." She had risen to her feet and curtsied, and Kitty glimpsed a touch of pink on her cheeks. There was another pause, then Carter seemed to come to himself. "Well, I must be going. I'm happy to be able to carry such an important part of your wedding breakfast, but I must not detain you from your celebrations."

"I would like you to stay." Phineas came to Carter's side, his gaze encompassing those assembled. "I asked Mr. Carter to bring the wine, but it was really just a pretext to get him here. It is not often that one wishes to invite one's man of business to a wedding breakfast, but I would not have a wife—or at least not *this* wife—were it not for him." Turning to Carter, he added, "You've been instrumental in bringing this wedding about, and you deserve to be part of the wedding celebrations."

Carter hesitated, but after another glance at Lucretia, he demurred. There was only one chair left at the small table and it was next to her, so he took his seat, and they exchanged shy glances.

Cheerful conversation abounded while they ate, and Kitty eyed the growing friendliness between Mr. Carter and Lucretia with satisfaction. Lucretia did not appear to have much of a chance to meet eligible bachelors, considering her one London Season had not met with success, and her sisters had made no push to invite her back. Perhaps something might grow from this?

Although Phineas met Kitty's smiles with ones of his own, he grew quiet over the meal. He appeared nervous, though she could not understand what he had to be nervous about. He had done an excellent job in bringing everyone together for their celebration.

Toward the end of the breakfast, Phineas got to his feet and ordered the footman to pour wine in everyone's glasses. When that was done, he lifted his. "It was a bit early to bring out the wine before now," he began, "but as we take the wedding cake, I wish to make a toast to my wife and to our friends—new and old. I must confess I had a very different view of marriage going into it than I do now. My objective was just to make a prudent match."

Phineas reached down for Kitty's hand, and she set hers in his. He met her gaze, his glass raised. "What I did not expect was that I would be given a wife with more beauty and more *quality* than I could ever have dreamed of."

He cleared his throat, and a patch of color lit his cheeks. "Lady Hayworth, you are worthy of a wedding breakfast at the Royal Pavilion, attended by everyone of consequence. Instead, you are given a wedding breakfast in a small estate in the middle of the countryside, attended by everyone of worth. And somehow I do not think you mind. On the contrary, the only thing you ask for is an affectionate husband and a happy home. I promise to do my best to make this a happy home. And I can assure you of my undying affection."

Sounds of "Hear, hear!" filled the room, and robust applause broke out for such a small gathering. Phineas tipped his glass and Kitty raised hers, and their eyes met as they drank.

After they'd all eaten some of the cake, and the conversation died down, Bromley glanced at his wife and stood. "Well, I suppose we must be getting back."

"You're going all the way to Bath?" Kitty asked. "You traveled early this morning just for our wedding breakfast?" Her eyes widened at such devotion on their part.

"Yes, we could not miss it," Teresa said. "But I think it's time for the newlyweds to enjoy the rest of their married life together."

Kitty raised an eyebrow. "We are not all that newly married, you know." Teresa merely grinned.

Carter gave Lucretia a sidelong glance. "And I suppose I shall be getting back as well. Miss Dutton, if you are not far, I shall be happy to accompany you to your home."

She smiled and stood. "I should like that very much. It is not far." He held out his arm, and after bidding Kitty and Phineas goodbye, they left.

It was just the two of them.

CHAPTER TWENTY-EIGHT

"What would you like to do now, my lady?"

The happiness that expanded inside Kitty somehow swept away some of her shyness. "I would like to invite you—"

Phineas's head came up, his eyes wide. The eager look coaxed a bubble of laughter from Kitty. She sent him a teasing look. "I would like to invite you to go for a ride, Lord Hayworth."

"A ride." Phineas's shoulders slumped comically. "A ride … Very well, Lady Hayworth"—he took a deep breath and gave a sweeping bow—"a ride it is."

Kitty went to change into her last of the new riding habits and hurried down to the front entrance where Phineas was waiting.

"Very fetching hat, my lady," he said, a gleam in his eyes that spoke to his admiration.

"Someone with exquisite taste chose it for me," Kitty answered. She welcomed his regard as she brushed past him to the stairs leading outside.

In the stables, the newly hired groom, who possessed a

decidedly paternal air, had their mounts saddled, and soon Kitty and Phineas were leading their horses down the path. Light flakes fell from the gray, cloudless sky. Phineas gestured to the meadow on the right, covered with a thin blanket of snow. "Let us go this way. We will see the tenants in three days' time for the Christmas boxes, and there's a part of the property on the east side I would like to show you."

Kitty followed him over the meadow, veering off in a direction they had not yet taken. Her horse picked over the ground carefully. Phineas looked behind him and reined in so she could keep up. "Do not mind the hill. Fawn can handle it, and so can you."

"I begin to believe I can," she replied. "Where are you taking me? This is off the path."

"It is. It can be slippery with mud as well, although it will be too cold for that today. It requires just a bit more skill in riding because of the incline, which is why I held off until now."

Despite the hill, Kitty was gloriously at ease in the saddle, and she breathed in the frosty air, surveying the line of Scots pine trees as they neared the top. "This is magnificent."

"I am pleased you think so." She could hear the grin in Phineas's voice and knew just what expression he held before she turned her regard to him. The grin was arrested on his face when she turned. "You look enchanting with a bit of color in your cheeks."

She faced forward again, raising her eyes to the heavens. "I do not need any more color in my cheeks, or anywhere else for that matter. I am much too chromatic as it is." She smiled, glancing again at Phineas. "This hair of mine, which Mary likes to say is the root of my temper—never mind that Erasmus's temper is much worse—is my bane."

"No," Phineas countered, resolute. "I wouldn't change a thing. You are magnificent."

At his words, a swell of warmth ran through Kitty, even as

they cleared the top of the hill. Her lips still turned upwards, she peered down the slope, her gaze now caught on the charming structure nestled in the lone oak tree among the pines.

PHINEAS HELD HIS BREATH. It wasn't so very earth-shattering, showing Kitty a tree-house he had discovered right after he had inherited the property. He had never been invited to Giddenhall as a boy, so the house should mean very little to him. However, he found the steps to be charming that led from the downward incline to the large tree holding the house. In a fit of whimsy, he'd had the treehouse refurbished, although he could ill spare the expense at the time. He could already imagine showing it to his child for the first time, as soon as he or she was old enough to climb stairs.

"It's lovely." There was delight in Kitty's voice. "Sam didn't speak of it. I am surprised."

"Sam didn't see it. I asked the gardener to wait until his next visit to show it to him, so I could show it to you first."

"Where did it come from? Did your mother have any brothers?"

Phineas shook his head. "It must pre-date my grandmother. I cannot think of any other explanation, as she would not have authorized such a fanciful thing."

"It *is* fanciful. Wonderfully fanciful. I can picture..." Kitty looked up to the top of the tree, which was not much higher than where they were at the summit of the hill.

"What is it?" Phineas prodded.

"I can picture our children playing here." She darted a glance at him but did not remove her gaze at once. Phineas thought his heart had reached its point of fullness and could not hold any more when she looked forward again. "And I love these little steps. Much safer than a ladder. You will take them here? Our children?"

"Of course," he said. The tree house was made of polished cut wood, and it possessed a thatch roof and even a terrace that curled around the house. He was entirely pleased with it. "I would like nothing better."

They stayed seated on horseback at the summit rather than go over the ridge, as the trees were thicker on the other side. Despite the view, the chill soon had them turning their mounts toward home. And by the time they left the horses with the groom in the stable, the snow had begun falling in thicker flakes.

"*Brr.*" Kitty clapped her hands together. "I'm chilled through. I must change out of my habit into something warm and dry."

"I will do the same." Phineas put his arm around Kitty, guiding her over the parts of the path he feared might have ice. "And then what shall we do?" He tried to keep his question innocent, but a corner of his mouth crept up into a grin.

"Oh…" Kitty's tone was light and playful. "Perhaps, I shall invite you"—her mouth puckered out with the last word as she darted a glance at him—"to take tea with me, husband."

He laughed. The teasing was an unexpected gift his wife had bestowed upon him. He could not have imagined such a thing possible when he'd pictured having a wife, and it made his light frustration at their slow progress easier to bear. "So, it is 'husband' now? I like it. Very well, wife. We will take tea."

Phineas and Kitty agreed to meet in the library, where the muted wood tones and small pane-glass windows created a perfectly cozy setting for tea between husband and wife. The fire crackled, and the railings near the bookshelves were draped with greenery. Pine boughs scented the air.

"Come and sit with me in this chair." He gestured to a small settee with armrests that held two people if they were willing to sit very close. Kitty sank down next to him, and he felt the warmth of her thigh next to his.

"Phineas," she said with a sigh. "I am so pleased with our wedding breakfast. Thank you for remembering my request and for fulfilling it in such a magnificent way."

The footman brought the hot water, and Kitty reached for the canister of tea that she had brought with her from the drawing room cabinet. The footman left after setting down the tea tray. "And thank you for showing me the tree-house that will one day be in use again, I have no doubt."

"With Samuel making full use of it in the meantime." This earned Phineas a grateful smile. Kitty mixed in the tea leaves and stirred the tea, allowing it to steep. He watched her dainty hands preparing his cup the way he liked it, and he put his hand around her shoulders, careful not to jar her in her ministrations.

He leaned in and whispered into her ear. "I love you."

Kitty wore no bonnet, and her hair was pulled away from her alluring face. His only sign that she had heard him was a slight lift of her cheeks and a mild trembling of her hand as she stirred his tea. She handed him the cup, and they drank in silence, but he could see the pleasure his words had given her in the way her eyes smiled at him above her cup. One sip of the hot beverage. Two sips ... three.

She set her cup down and tapped her finger on her chin as if struck by a thought. "*Hm.*"

Phineas felt a slight tremor run through her, and although she was smiling, he felt something between them shift. He set his saucer down next to hers and waited.

Kitty kept her face trained forward, but he could see her catch her lip between her teeth and a tiny crease form between her brows. "Now that we have had tea, we shall have to think of something else to do."

Phineas cleared his throat. "Very true." He could not remove his gaze from her face as he waited for her next words. He could not breathe.

"I suppose it will be dinner soon enough, and I should like to choose my dress." She risked a shy glance at him, her face lit with that color she found so detestable, but of which he could not get enough. "To be very sure that my dress has met with your approval, I believe I will invite you to help me choose it—if …" Her expression took on a slightly panicked look. "If you should wish it."

Phineas took her hand carefully in his and turned in his seat. "I find myself…" He stopped and leaned forward to kiss her softly on the lips, then pulled back a hair's breadth to murmur, "for the first time in my twenty-eight years…" He leaned forward again, capturing her lips with more insistence, his restraint cracking as she met his kisses eagerly "…*Most* interested in what gown my lady will wear to dinner."

Kitty's face was very near his, but he could still see her smile. She leaned in and kissed him back, before whispering, "Then, I believe, we should waste no time in choosing one."

EPILOGUE

Phineas stopped at the row of tenant houses, where the roof on the last house had been completed. He knew Carter had come into town again, and he found him speaking with the steward over the transfer of funds to begin draining the east meadow to make it more profitable. There was enough room on the south lawn for their flock of sheep, and the east meadow could be turned into crops by implementing a new drainage system.

"Carter, you are back again, are you?" Phineas came forward and shook his hand, a habit they had only recently begun since Carter's courtship of Miss Dutton threw them more frequently into company. Lucretia and Kitty had become fast friends, and Mrs. Dutton had all but washed her hands of her daughter, whom she declared "an ungrateful minx who was all too like her father" before turning her attention to the more promising future of her married daughters and their increasing families.

"Does Miss Dutton know you are in Castle Combe?" he asked when the steward stepped away to intercept the men carrying a load of building materials.

"I stopped to see her first before coming here." Carter looked down at his shoes, then over the meadow, striving for nonchalance.

"And has her father accepted your suit?" Phineas met his gaze, pleased to be on the other side of the duress of having to secure a wife, whether by arrangement or begging.

Carter looked up in surprise. "How did you—"

"I didn't." Phineas laughed and clapped Carter on the shoulder. "But I suspected, and you just confirmed it. Kitty thought Lucretia was in high hopes of just such a happy resolution."

"Ah, so the women talked about it?" Carter did not look put out by the knowledge.

"The women always talk about it," Phineas confirmed, glad for once to lean on his own wisdom gleaned from marriage. "I wish you happy."

Carter, a discreet man, attempted to mask his joy but was unsuccessful. They soon split ways. Phineas was in a hurry to get to the house, because he only had a few hours with Kitty before Sam arrived from his first term at Harrow. She had secured permission from Erasmus for their brother to come directly to Giddenhall and stay for Christmas before sending him to Erasmus's house for Twelfth Night.

Phineas entered the hall and spotted a footman. "Have you seen my wife?" The footman shook his head, and Phineas took the stairs. He thought he knew where she might be—where she spent most of her time these days. He opened the door softly and spotted the vision of his wife sitting on the window seat, as the low winter sun illuminated her face. She turned, her hand on her belly.

"I knew I would find you in the nursery," Phineas said, softly. He walked over and kissed his wife's swollen middle before taking her face in his hands and kissing her lips.

"Where else?" she asked, looking up at him. He pulled her to her feet.

"You looked melancholy." Phineas scrunched his brows in concern. "Your pains have not begun?"

"No, dearest. Not melancholy—and no pains. I was just attempting to remember where I had placed the worsted wool, for I had thought to make a rug for the treehouse. Would that not be charming?" Kitty placed her hands on his chest and smiled up at him. "And Baby would not dare make an entrance before we've celebrated Christmas."

Phineas caught her hand and kissed it. "Carter has spoken to Mr. Dutton, you know."

"I know." Kitty laughed when she saw Phineas's surprised expression. "Lucretia left here not fifteen minutes before you arrived. They will make a happy couple, I believe."

"And I had something to do with it." Phineas said with a knowing grin.

"Oh…" Kitty poked his chest with her finger, laughing. "Only a very little bit. Not nearly as much as he had to do with your marriage."

"Mine? I won my own wife fair and square." Phineas thought the better of his wife being on her feet, and he sat and pulled Kitty on to his lap.

"You did, *hm*?" Kitty smiled primly. "You would not even be aware of my existence were it not for Carter."

"And you would not have a love match were it not for me," Phineas insisted, a mischievous glint in his eyes. "For it to be a love match, a wife needs to be loved."

"And a husband, as well," Kitty answered pertly, kissing his nose.

"You are not *quite* so disinclined to be Lady Hayworth as you once were," Phineas teased, certain of her response, yet wanting to hear it. Her answer, therefore, caught him by surprise.

"Oh, I suppose not *as* disinclined as I once was, although it is not so very important to me after all." Kitty shrugged a shoulder, biting the corner of her lip to keep it from creeping up.

"Not so very imp— Kitty." Phineas turned her on his lap to look at her more squarely, and Kitty was hard-pressed to hold in her giggles.

"I care very little about being Lady Hayworth, to own the truth," Kitty insisted. She met his gaze and held it, and her smile softened. "But I am quite inclined to be Phineas's wife."

And since his wife was perfectly positioned for Phineas to demonstrate how equally inclined he was to be Kitty's husband, he tucked her legs up on the window seat, pulling her toward him in his arms. And he showed her.

SEASONS OF CHANGE BOOKS

The Road Through Rushbury by Martha Keyes

A Forgiving Heart by Kasey Stockton

The Last Eligible Bachelor by Ashtyn Newbold

A Well-Trained Lady by Jess Heileman

The Cottage by Coniston by Deborah M. Hathaway

A Haunting at Havenwood by Sally Britton

Join the Sweet Regency Romance Fans Facebook group to connect with the authors in this series and learn more about what's coming next.

ABOUT THE AUTHOR

Jennie Goutet is an American-born Anglophile who lives with her French husband and their three children in a small town outside of Paris. Her imagination resides in Regency England, where her best-selling proper Regency romances are set. She is also author of the award-winning memoir *Stars Upside Down*, two contemporary romances, and a smattering of other published works. A Christian, a cook, and an inveterate klutz, Jennie writes (with increasing infrequency) about faith, food, and life—even the clumsy moments—on her blog, aladyin-france.com. If you really want to learn more about Jennie and her books, sign up for her newsletter on her author website: jenniegoutet.com.

* Photo Credit : Caroline Aoustin

Printed in Great Britain
by Amazon

61419904R00160